THUNDERBIRD

A BEN PECOS MYSTERY

Susan Slater

INTRIGUE PRESS

Philadelphia

ISBN 1-890768-41-3

First Printing, February 2002

This book is a work of fiction. Names, characters, places and incidents are either the product of the author's imagination or are used fictitiously. Any resemblance to actual events or locales or persons, living or dead, is entirely coincidental. Although the author and publisher have made every effort to ensure the accuracy and completeness of information contained in this book, we assume no responsibility for errors, inaccuracies, omissions, or any inconsistency herein. Any slights of people, places or organizations are unintentional.

Library of Congress Cataloging-in-Publication Data available from the Publisher upon request. 215-753-1270

Risking the possibility that I may never make another friend, I admit to drawing upon those I know for inspiration—thanks Kurt for owning a D-type Jag, and Cathy for sharing those fabulous Fabio stories. T-Bird is richer for your contributions.

But thanks must also go to my agent, Susan Gleason, who over the years has supported me with her enthusiasm and undying belief that I can tell a good story. And to Connie Shelton who first invested in that belief and George Phocas who made dreams come true. Thanks to you all.

Other books by Susan Slater:

The Pumpkin Seed Massacre
Yellow Lies

ONE

Moonlight coaxed the wrinkles out of the asphalt around the high school and bleached the color from a stand of nearby poplar. Tommy Spottedhorse leaned against a white Bronco with tribal insignia and waited for Brenda Begay to get out of night class. He'd asked her out for coffee and she'd said, "Maybe". Not too encouraging but something. So he said he'd drop by and help her make up her mind. Was he pushing too hard? He couldn't tell. All he knew was he wanted this woman to give him a chance.

He ducked down to check his image in the side mirror and ran his palms along the bristly sides of a new burr haircut. Slick black strands stood straight up in front giving length to an angular, but rounded face. Summer sun had burned his skin a rich red-brown that contrasted sharply with his pale khaki shirt and slacks. He adjusted his badge and grinned. Overall, not bad if he did say so himself. He sucked in his stomach and stood sideways.

"Don't hurt yourself."

"Brenda." Her name swooshed out with exhaled breath.

She had managed to walk up behind him and now stood two feet away. She was small boned and short enough to have to look up at him, and he couldn't help but notice how her jeans hugged her body. She wore a blue chambray western shirt with the collar turned up, and etched silver loops hung from her earlobes. Long thick black hair, caught at the neck by a ribbon, cascaded down her back. Beautiful, Tommy thought to himself, just plain beautiful. And he'd throw in smart, too. She should almost have her degree by now.

"I thought there was an offer of coffee, but if Narcissus is busy. . . ." Her laugh was quick and genuine. There was a word in his language for a woman with a laugh like bells. He'd have to remember to ask his sister.

"Well?" She was leaning toward him, dark eyes sparkling in an oval face.

"Yes, well, uh, coffee . . ." The words didn't seem to want to form a pattern. Again, that tinkling laugh. She was already opening the door on the far side of the Bronco before he moved. Quickly he climbed behind the wheel. But then the two-way squawked and he reached for the receiver.

"Need some backup this side of Smith Lake, you free?"

"Yeah." His voice must have given him away. He looked at Brenda and she mouthed, "Rain check". He listened to the details of a possible hit and run involving a van full of vacationers and a half-ton full of chickens. Then assuring the dispatcher he'd be there in under 15 minutes, he turned to Brenda.

"I think this is one of those Murphy things." He shrugged. She was already slipping out of the front seat.

"Listen, it's okay. Here's my number at school. Call me tomorrow. I need a date for our fall festival. A hundred and fifty elementary students and their parents—think you could handle that? We have a cake-walk."

"Hey, cake-walks are my specialty. If it's angel food with orange icing, it's got my name on it." Stupid, but she laughed.

He watched as she climbed behind the steering wheel of Elmo the Rabbit Chaser, then turned toward him to wave. He remembered that truck from his high school days when he ran around with her brother—if he'd just been smart enough to have made a move then. Hindsight, nothing he'd ever majored in. He turned the key, pumped the accelerator and peeled backwards before laying rubber up the incline that put him on the highway.

10:25 p.m., SEPTEMBER 14

Brenda couldn't stop smiling. Men could be so vain. But she liked Tommy—wanted him to like her. Still, there were complications, maybe insurmountable ones.

"Damn."

She slammed on the brakes and clutched the steering wheel until the bald tires bit into the pavement, and the pickup sashayed to a stop. That was close. The furry flag of a tail carried parallel to its body had barely moved as the coyote trotted across the highway. She watched as the thick plume disappeared into the brush. She could swear that he knew she would stop. And it had been a male; she was sure of that, too. Who could miss the jaunty nonchalance? That hit-me-if-you-dare attitude? What stupid bad luck. The animal had crossed her path and now, ten-thirty at night, she'd have to double back and take a two-rut dirt road some forty-five miles out of her way.

Unless she wanted to brave the consequences. Her

Anglo friends would laugh, but didn't they have their black cats and ladders and cracks in the sidewalk? And it wasn't so much that she was afraid; it was her mother who would know because something would happen—maybe the baby would get a sore throat—and silently, not in words but in looks, her mother would upbraid her. And she'd be right. It never failed. Ignore a taboo and the Ancients got the last laugh.

Luckily the coyote had been moving right to left, traveling south. Had it been the other way around, had he been heading in the northern direction of evil spirits and darkness, she would have had to retrace her steps and cancel her journey. No way. She had to get home; there was work tomorrow. And besides, the coyote crossing her path was mostly an omen—dangerous only if she ignored him altogether. She was showing him deference and putting herself out—surely that would be enough. Sometimes the Ancients just had to cut a person a little slack.

She looked at the tangle of books and papers that had flown off the seat when she stopped. Child Development 410 taught by Dr. Ben Pecos, psychologist from Crownpoint—the last class she needed before graduation. She felt a blip of excitement. With a B.S. in elementary education from the University of New Mexico, Gallup Branch, her life was finally about to begin. Living in a trailer behind her mother's hogan, sacrificing, always thinking of Mariah first—

Thoughts of the baby's father drifted across her memory, and she pulled down those invisible shades that kept her from dwelling on something she couldn't have. Yet, he was coming for a visit. His squadron would be moving to New Mexico for maneuvers in a couple months. He'd been vague about the mission, something about testing aircraft. He'd be stationed at Hollomon Air Force Base near Alamogordo, a good five hours drive southeast of Gallup. But he seemed close just being in the same state. Frankfurt had been half a world away. Mariah was two and this would be only the second time he'd seen her. But he sent money. A lot of men wouldn't even do that. Yet, if she had any sense she'd go out with Tommy Spottedhorse and give their friendship a chance to turn into something.

Brenda pushed the gearshift into reverse and stepped on the gas pedal. The truck, now old and more than a little tired, whined its discontent at being forced to back up. The windows were down and the breeze felt good. There had never been air-conditioning, but she'd put in a radio powerful enough to pick up Albuquerque, even out here. And she'd splurged on a CD player, too, with speakers in the doors. The guy who put it in suggested that her sound system might be worth more than the truck. He said it tactfully and added that he'd be glad to transfer the system to a new automobile when the time came, no extra charge. She thanked him. She hoped the transfer wouldn't have to happen for awhile. She'd grown up seeing the truck's tan hulk parked in front of the house. Parting wouldn't be easy.

She jolted to a stop, turned, then accelerated slowly watching for the dirt road that left Highway 666 and angled to the east. She hummed along with Reba McIntyre, tapping her fingers on the steering wheel. The September night was mild without a hint of fall. What breeze there was ruffled her hair, pulling wisps across her forehead.

Abruptly, the radio faded, fizzling like a sparkler before going mute. She fiddled with the knobs. Its lights glowed reassuringly above the push-button dials. That was strange.

It was on, but she couldn't bring in a station. Then from nothing, a faint static rippled and skipped over the airwaves; its jarring staccato a far cry from the Country music she'd been listening to. She stopped once again on the edge of the highway before she would nose the truck down a short incline to join the barely discernible tracks that led home. It had to be the antenna. Maybe it had jiggled loose.

She pulled the emergency brake, tugged the gearshift into neutral and jumped out. But that wasn't it. The antenna was fine, firmly fixed to the fender and extended to its limit. Odd. The truck might be twenty years old but a radio less than two months old wouldn't just quit working. Brenda frowned. It was bad enough that she was committed to driving an extra two hours out of her way, but it didn't seem fair to have to do it in silence.

"*Merde.*"

The word slipped out. Her mother hated her to curse. She hardly spoke English, but she recognized those words. It was better if the word went unrecognized; so, "shit" in French it was, had been since she'd learned the word at boarding school. She didn't know when she'd find the time, but she'd have to take the truck into Albuquerque and have the radio fixed.

She climbed back behind the steering wheel, the wooden bead seat cover snagging her jeans. She popped the emergency brake and eased the truck into gear. Hopefully, she could nurse the truck along another year and have a good-paying job before she had to junk it and buy a new one.

"Ow."

Her head grazed the roof of the cab as the truck slipped sideways and bounced heavily across a rut cut deep by last year's runoff. The road itself was just the sandy bottom of an arroyo some thirty feet across with a three-foot rim. The once-a-year riverbed was usually smooth, only occasionally littered with boulders or other debris stranded by high water. She would need to pay attention; she hadn't come this way in awhile.

But it was the scenic route. That brought a chuckle. With the full moon sparkling across the packed sand, and the air carrying the scent of piñon and juniper, things could be worse. She started to hum, then stopped to watch a jackrabbit try to outrun her. Which wasn't difficult to do. Top out she could only go about twenty-five miles an hour on the infrequent straightaways, much less than that around curves. The rabbit cut in front of her at the first corner and was gone.

The blast of static startled her. She quickly snapped off the radio then realized that the sound wasn't coming from the dash. It was higher, overhead. She stuck her head out the window and scanned the sky. Could they have put high wires, electrical transformers of some kind out this way? But who were "they"? The tribe wouldn't have tried to electrically annex this part of the Rez, miles of sheep camps and the once-in-awhile hogan? It wasn't economically feasible. And since Anglo-introduced, bottom-line thinking had invaded the reasoning of the elders, she knew it had to be something else.

Flashes of light danced across the eastern horizon. Lightning? She didn't think so. Lightning didn't move horizontally, zigzagging along the top of a mesa in short-lived bursts of illumination, like little explosions. She'd never seen anything like that before—well, maybe, on the Fourth of July.

Now, she was curious. She slowed until the pickup

rolled to a stop. She tugged on the emergency brake, shut the engine off and just sat there. Something didn't feel right. The air was prickly, charged like before a rain. But there wouldn't be rain; there wasn't a cloud in the sky. And this was the end of the normal monsoon season. Any moisture was highly unlikely. Yet, there was a feeling, something in the atmosphere. The windshield was too bug-laden to see clearly; so, she stepped out into the night.

She felt herself frowning and tried to relax as she listened. Nothing seemed really out of sync. The sounds of chirping insects were melodious and soothing. But it struck her that their cadence was hurried, frantic even, much too fast for a normal night—a night that wasn't overly warm. In fact, there was too much activity in general. She should never see rodents scurrying about in the open. Normally, they would seek the camouflage of low bushes. But there were no owls, or nighthawks. With all this furry food out in the open, not one winged predator swooped down to take advantage. It was like someone had taken a giant stick and stirred up the ground around her but didn't tell the birds of prey.

She gasped and clapped her hands over her ears as a sound, faint, high above her, difficult to define but not unlike the hum of a tuning fork, reverberated across her eardrum in a finely modulated shriek. Then as she scanned the moon-bright sky, an object, black wings aimed backward along its sides, glided across the broad flat surface of the moon that was suspended above the mesa to the east, and for one microsecond in time its shadow looked for all the world like the Batman insignia.

She burst out laughing. Could she be lucky enough to have Val Kilmer or George Clooney pop out of the sagebrush needing a ride to town? Probably not. And the smell. The air was filled with the pungent odor of fuel. She cupped her hands and hooded her eyes to rake the horizon. The hum was so distant now that she didn't trust her ears. Could it be only the remembered sound that seemed to vibrate in her head? Certainly the mysterious aircraft had been swallowed by the night. Or maybe it hadn't existed at all.

Her gaze swept across the horizon to the east, angled to the west, then she froze. Squarely in her vision was this . . . thing. What could she call it? It had to be a plane of some sort. But not one that you'd see everyday. It was just a wedge, a black triangle with chopped angles and a sharp, pointed nose flying low, maybe five hundred feet above her. She watched it bank slowly to its right before leveling, wings dipping slightly, then straightening to accelerate toward her, lower, and lower. . . . She screamed and dove under the truck.

Even sticking her fingers in her ears couldn't deaden the sound, this whining roar that felt like an axe was splitting her skull. Then the sound stopped in a grinding screech of metal and whoosh of wind that peppered the hood of the truck with sand. Then this, too, stopped. She waited. The silence was stifling but she didn't dare move. Not until she was certain that the thing wasn't coming back.

Finally, she inched her way on her stomach toward the front of the truck. She tried not to think of scorpions or centipedes or snakes—the desert's normal inhabitants that didn't take kindly to intruders crawling across their territory. Taking a deep breath, she peered out.

In the distance the air was cloudy with dust that swirled upward in a rolling blanket of grit obscuring her view. But one thing was certain, something had landed just beyond the rise at the edge of the arroyo.

She rolled out from under the truck, pulled herself to her knees and stood as a flare burst above her, the reddish phosphorous glow hanging only a second in the desert sky before quickly blinking out. Was someone in trouble? The pilot. Of course. What if he'd been injured?

She half crouched but ran the thirty feet to the edge of the embankment, then scrambling upward she threw herself under a thick green mass of chamisa, rabbit brush thick enough to hide her flattened body as she stretched against the sandy rise.

There it was, and it was a plane. Probably, a Stealth Fighter. She'd bet anything that she was looking at the radar-defying plane that was usually kept under wraps. It was awesome, even with a twisted mass of cholla cactus hanging rakishly from one swept-back wing. The pilot had landed in a belly flop that had torn the undercarriage, peeling away the sheet metal and tilting the plane to the right. He'd been lucky not to have gone up in flames.

But where was the pilot? He must be close by. Someone had sent up a flare. She started to stand when the muffled but persistent chugging of an engine pushed into her consciousness. Instinctively, she crouched before looking to the west, away from the plane. A large, closed-bed truck was slowly picking its way down the arroyo opposite of the way she had come.

Brenda watched as it bumped over foot high rocks and flattened cactus and brush. The star and circle Mercedes emblem, centered on the grill and big as a pie plate, bobbed and ducked then popped into view as the truck collected its strength to push over the arroyo's rim and roll to within reach of the plane. Its hooded headlights cast light directly in front of the front wheels and nowhere else. Brenda absently wondered at such a unique feature. Certainly not standard issue, she guessed.

She shrank against the sand. Doors on the back of the truck flew open and five figures jumped out and ran toward the aircraft. Their excitement was apparent. She didn't need to see their faces to know that. And she couldn't see their faces, anyway. Flexible black suits that looked like ribbed rubber covered every inch of their bodies ending in hoods pulled well down over foreheads. Their goggles were some kind of wrap-around type like the shades favored by senior citizens. Boots and gloves were also black and snug fitting as skin. And not one person was under six feet tall.

Yet, it was the language that stumped her. She couldn't understand a word they yelled back and forth. Then one person vaulted up a slanted wing to the cockpit, but it was quickly apparent that he didn't find what he'd expected. It was also apparent that he was angry. Gesturing wildly with a large hand-held weapon, the man yelled at the others until two men quickly scrambled up beside him.

Then the man with the gun repeatedly slammed the butt of the weapon against the canopy but to no avail; it didn't budge. Finally quieted by whatever the men said, he slid to the ground leaving the two to work on the Plexiglas—but he wasn't quiet for long. He paced up and back in front of the plane and shouted at the others.

Brenda strained to understand. Surely she would recognize English, Spanish—a little French or German—but this language was unintelligible. She propped herself on her elbows, brushed her bangs out of her eyes and continued to listen to words that had no meaning.

But there was very little talk now, just grunts and pointing as four men formed an anthill assembly line to pass along pieces of the instrument panel. There was one man inside the cockpit now who dismantled what looked to be gauges and display screens and handed the pieces quickly to waiting hands who in turn passed the chunks on; the last man in line racing with his parcel back to the truck. They worked fast; Brenda had to give them that. They were redefining the word efficient. She'd heard that carjackers could do this—strip and run in less than two minutes.

She pulled her body in close to hug the sand. She didn't quite let the thought surface, but at some level she wondered what would happen if someone saw her. She risked a peek over her left shoulder. She could clearly see her tan pickup bleached by the moonlight to blend with its environment, and she almost laughed out loud. From this distance, Elmo looked like he had been junked, dumped out on the Rez like a hundred others to rust, ashes to ashes, dust to dust. With the drooping bumper, missing tailgate, crumpled fender and primer-spotted paint job, who would think he had gotten there under his own power, and recently, even? She was suddenly absurdly happy she drove a vehicle that wouldn't attract attention.

A burst of rat-a-tat-tat brought her head back with a snap. The one who was so angry was spraying a 180-degree area of the ground with bullets. He stood in front of the plane pointing the machine gun away from where she was hiding but he was turning slowly, his body spasmodically jerking with each round of fire. She pulled her elbows into her body and willed herself to become small and one with the embankment as bits of rock skipped and zinged through the brush coming her way. She'd been right. Her life depended upon not being seen. Then abruptly the shooting stopped.

She was afraid to even breathe. Had she given herself away? Were they walking toward her right at this very moment? Her heart thudded in her ears and she squeezed her eyes shut. Time dragged and even in the cool night, perspiration formed on her upper lip and at her hairline and her underarms were clammy. She practiced taking soft, shallow breaths, exhaling with her mouth open.

But the quiet wasn't interrupted; even the talking had stopped. She inched her left arm to within a few inches of her face. The luminous dial on her watch said ten forty-three. She fought an urge to peek over the edge. Then she heard the slam of a door, once, twice . . . and the hiccuping start of an engine. They were leaving. Could that be? Slowly she raised up. The truck was backing at a snail's pace, angling away from the plane while two figures dragged a third man, someone not wearing a head-to-toe black cover-up suit and flopped him face down under the cockpit. Had they found the pilot? But why were they leaving and not helping him? He was unconscious.

Or maybe he was dead. She sharply sucked in her breath. Yes, of course, that made sense. The man with the machine-gun killed him. Brenda felt a stab of dread. But what if he was only wounded? She watched as the men jogged back to the truck and jumped into the back. The last man in lowered a black, fringed skirt that skipped across the sand-packed arroyo and flicked up bits of gravel erasing all evidence that they'd been there. Suddenly, the truck accelerated, turned and jolted over the arroyo edge picking up speed as it disappeared.

She didn't move until the chugging persistence of its motor had faded to a low-decibel, diesel throb. Then carefully she stood, dusted off her jeans, tucked in the tail of her chambray shirt and all the while eyed the ransacked plane and its limp companion. She looked around her. Things seemed to be back to normal. The frenzied activity of wildlife had slowed, only a Coahuila scorpion scuttled out from under a boulder to disappear under another one. Still, she couldn't make herself move toward the man on the ground.

She rolled up the sleeves of her shirt, slipped the ribbon off of the heavy knot of hair drawn back at her neck and tucked the wisp of plaid into her pocket. Then she fluffed her hair, running the fingers of both hands up and through before hooking the thick mass behind each ear. There'd better be enough water to wash when she got home or she'd look like a mess tomorrow—the kids would tease her unmercifully. But wasn't there an old saying about only ghosts washed their hair after sundown?

Why was she stalling? She knew she had to help—try at least. She glanced again at the man on the ground. He hadn't moved. She couldn't leave without seeing if he was alive. Yet, she was reluctant. She couldn't get the picture of the black-suited man with a machine gun out of her mind. She knelt and retied the laces of her right Nike running shoe, then stood and surveyed the plane again. Oh, this was being silly; she couldn't put it off any longer. She took a deep breath and stepped out of the shadows.

In the next instant she was flying through the air. The explosion was so powerful that she was thrown backwards into the brush, blinded for a brief second by an apocalyptic flash that could have heralded the end of the world. The tongue of heat that rolled out from the plane seared her forehead and left her gasping on her knees. And her ears ached from a sound so shattering that Brenda feared permanent damage. But she was alive. Black oily smoke swirled above the flames that had burst from the mid-section of the plane. She could still see the man on the ground. He wasn't touched by the fire, not yet, anyway.

Without giving her safety another thought, Brenda sprinted toward him. The heat was staggering but she dropped to her knees and crawled the last ten feet, her face just inches above the ground. There was a burp of sound and she covered her head with her arms and braced for another blast of fire, but none came. So far she was lucky, but she had to hurry.

The man was stretched out on his stomach. She tugged at a shoulder but couldn't roll him over; he seemed stiff and the flesh was puffy above the collar of his shirt. She didn't expect a pulse, but she placed two fingers on the carotid artery. Nothing. That was no surprise. Yet, there was no apparent cause of death, no blood anyway. He was just a man, mid-thirties, Anglo, clean-shaven in a crisply pressed blue shirt and slacks, parts of a uniform sans jacket . . . and he was very, very cold. There was nothing she could do— she had to get out of there. She didn't even want to think about the taboos of handling the dead. Had she upset the man's spirit? She'd seek help later.

She backed away, still crouching, then stumbled in haste, her hands stinging from the blistering heat of the sand. She clapped her hand back over her mouth. She didn't dare look up and risk breathing in any more of the toxic fumes than she already had. She should have tied something around her mouth and nose. But it was too late now. There was a rumble somewhere above her, and the plane lurched to its side in a shower of sparks.

She stood to run but was rooted to the spot by a hand

that clamped down on her shoulder. She jumped and screamed, throwing her head back hoping to connect sharply with her captor's chin, as strong arms crushed her chest pinning her arms to her sides. She wiggled forward and aimed a couple well-placed kicks upward and back that only served to make her lose her balance. But she didn't fall. Her assailant simply picked her up and didn't flinch at lifting one hundred and fifteen pounds cleanly off the ground and running with it. Her screams died in the rough glove pressed against her mouth while terror rode up the back of her throat in vile-tasting phlegm.

Her captor slipped down the lip of the arroyo and threw her face down knocking her breath out, then slammed his body full length on top of her. The popping and crackling of the fire seemed close. She gasped and tried to turn over but she was pinned to the ground. Behind them a series of blasts rocked the earth, and she could feel his hot breath on her neck and his chest heave as he fought to breathe evenly.

Brenda spat sand and sputtered to get the dirt out of her mouth; then, she suddenly wrenched her head to the side, looked into the eyes of her captor and almost fainted. She blinked, willing her heart to stop pounding. How could it be? This sort of thing only happened in movies. But this wasn't Hollywood. Were her eyes tricking her? Couldn't this just be her imagination? With a moan she let her head drop forward and didn't feel the hand encircle her neck and squeeze the pressure points that brought on blackness.

TWO

Amos Manygoats slept outside because his wife was a capitalist. And a shrew. But it was his daughter he blamed— a graduate of a business school whose senior project was to offer her family's traditional hogan as a bed and breakfast. At first, he couldn't believe his wife would even listen to such irreverence. But there had been a business plan, a budget, even a forecast. Her professors had praised her as "innovative, daring, entrepreneurial in spirit." So, as a sacrifice for his daughter receiving an "A", he left them alone.

He didn't even help with the second outhouse. Or enlarging the cold box in the juniper that acted as a fridge in the winter. She named her family hogan, Tse Li Gah Sinil Hospitality—Two White Rocks Hospitality and sent out flyers. His daughter advertised that the traditional Navajo hogan was built around four posts, each representing one of the sacred mountains of her homeland. She'd added that the door of the hogan faced east; men sit in the south; women, north; and guests, west. Her professors encouraged her to add other bits of lore—whatever she could say without incurring censure. So she chose the story from the *Blessing Way* of how the first hogan came into being.

Reluctantly, Amos helped her with it. Wasn't it better to know what was being told? To make certain she didn't over-step boundaries? He helped her tell the story of how the first hogan was built by Coyote who had gotten the logs and instructions from the Beaver People. The first hogan had a fork-stick frame. The first two logs were a fork-tipped and a straight one. The male straight log was joined at the top with the female forked log. This symbolized a strong union of husband and wife. This first hogan was a very holy place. Precious turquoise, white shell beads, obsidian, jet and abalone were buried under the frame and songs were sung in its honor.

His daughter's professors were thrilled with the flyers. They assured them that the hogan and breakfast idea would be popular, a one-of-a-kind experience that hundreds would want to try. Amos wasn't so sure. He'd balked at the hand painted sign above the door but lost.

The first to come were anthropologists, strange lanky men who wore pants with many pockets. And like tonight, had kept him busy with questions. A man and his son had wanted to make Navajo arrows and learn about the rites of passage. The two other men were foreign. Even his daughter had trouble understanding their English. But each had paid $125 and extra for the child to sleep on piled sheepskins, in the octagon shaped hogan of rough-cut logs bonded by cement. The roof was covered in green tarpaper; the opening for the stovepipe allowed a glimpse of sky. The winter nights were often bitter. Yet, their visitors came all year round. One hundred and twenty-five dollars. Amos marveled at the money.

Dinner was almost always a savory mutton stew and warm fluffy fry bread. He had to admit that he ate better on weekends. One Saturday night he'd come into the hogan to share the evening meal, and a visiting anthropologist got him talking about the squaw dance, a coming-out ceremony that his daughter had taken part in. The man even knew that originally it had been an important ceremony, the *Nda* or Enemy Way—a celebration for warriors returning from contact with the enemy. Since the man had known so much, it hadn't seemed wrong to correct him here and there. After that, his daughter subtly advertised that Amos was part of the package. Conversation with an elder. Better than a textbook—wasn't that what his daughter had said?

The mornings would usually bring blue-corn mush but sometimes bacon and eggs—he guessed this group would want the latter. He licked his lips. He almost didn't care that he'd have to throw down his bedroll behind his sweat lodge.

Tonight everyone had gone to bed early. No talking until the sky stretched pale across the earth's edge. Even his daughter and wife retired to the half-finished hogan behind the house—the one he'd started to build for his daughter and her husband. Then the husband got a job in Albuquerque.

It didn't help his arthritis, this sleeping on the ground, but it helped his general constitution. He was seventy years old—or young as his daughter would tease. He didn't really feel old. Still, to have to stay outside, it wasn't right.

He rolled his blanket, tucked it under his arm and walked past the entrance of his hogan. Outside he motioned four times away from his body and toward where the sun had set. He'd been instructed to do so as part of the Blackening Way, a ceremony that would restore *hozho*, the balance between harmony and peace.

But how could there be peace? It was unnatural, a hogan

and breakfast. And the money didn't make anyone happy anymore—not Pansy, and, most of all, not him. His daughter stayed away from her husband longer and longer. That would bring no good. But the worst? The business was making Pansy crazy. She was having spells.

When he'd mentioned her problems to his daughter, she'd insisted that her mother see a doctor. What she called "a real doctor" over at the clinic. Amos knew she didn't believe in the tribal rituals. She didn't even speak the Navajo language very well—her own language by birth—at least not as well as Amos thought she should. When she didn't want to take the time to explain something in her native language, she'd just throw in an American word. It hurt his ears. But she'd offered to come all the way from Albuquerque to take her mother to Crownpoint. And Pansy had agreed to go. That in itself was an achievement.

The doctor gave Pansy some pills, but she'd fed them to the Billy goat when she got home and the goat colicked. So Amos had to agree with her that maybe those little pale pink pills weren't the answer. That big black and white goat could eat anything. But it still left Pansy with her spells.

When he traveled the forty miles to the IHS clinic in Crownpoint and told the young *bilagaama* doc from back East what had happened, he'd just laughed and said not to worry, they were placebos anyway. Placebos. Amos had looked the word up in a dictionary from the library on wheels. But then he knew for sure that the doctor had lied. There was no way on this earth he would believe that "nothing" had made that goat sick.

The doc had joked that that's what he got for marrying a younger woman. But Amos didn't think that twenty years made that much difference. But it was obvious the doc wasn't going to be able to help. So Amos stayed away from the hospital even when the young doc suggested he make an appointment for his wife to see Ben Pecos, the doc who worked on your mind. If a real doc's nothing-pills almost killed a goat, what could a doc do who only talked to you? It didn't sound good to Amos at all.

And then the doctor said he wanted to try hormones. That Pansy's problems might just be menopause, and then had poked him in the arm, winked and said something else about a younger woman. Amos had looked up that word, too, menopause.

But it was confusing. If that's what she had, the sickness that made her scream and throw things and stay up all the night, then she needed a cleansing, a ritual that would cost five goats and a couple hides. And Amos better set about finding someone to do it and not waste his time running across the country getting bum information.

Then things had quieted. Pansy had taken to ignoring him. Sometimes she'd fix food for the two of them, sometimes she'd just wander off. She'd closed the hogan & breakfast and his daughter had taken her into Albuquerque for a week. That seemed to work wonders. Pansy had dressed in her best skirt and blouse, took her squash blossom necklace out of her chest of clothing, and fastened thin polished slabs of turquoise to her ears. She'd already been back ten days, and her good humor was wearing off. But she still stayed to herself, didn't bother him much. She did all the cooking for the guests but never stayed to chat.

There was lots of work to be done around the hogan—haul water from a nearby well, keep the cooking fire going, tend the goats—Pansy still kept up. It was just the moods she got in. Like she was possessed. Which always seemed to bring him full circle. He needed to inquire about a cleansing and not put it off. But didn't he already know what was wrong? And wasn't it possible that it could never be righted?

Pansy had sold a sand painting. Guests had been curious about one they had seen and had asked how such a painting was made. She demonstrated and made a small painting for them. But its theme was sacred—holy to the Old Ones and now they had made her sick. Sometimes if he needed money, Amos would also sell a painting. But he knew how to make changes. Only exact reproductions of ancient designs invoked the anger of the deities. So he would leave out a snake, or a lightning rod or a *kokopelli*—usually he just put in the wrong number of feathers or changed the color scheme. But to sell a sacred sand painting, correct in every detail, robbed the Holy Ones of strength and drained power from their religion. It was a serious offense.

Tonight was a quiet night. Pansy had gone out to bring in the small herd of sheep that she doted on. Amos waited. She was gone overly long, he thought. Sometimes their guests would trudge along—experience bringing the flock to shelter. But not tonight. Their visitors had begged off.

Amos picked his way around the cars parked to the right of the hogan. One a black, bullet-shaped oddity like he'd never seen before; the other a rented SUV—like the hundreds he saw in Crownpoint. Both expensive. He knew that. He'd had an old truck one time. Ran until it just gave out and he'd walked home. He'd never needed another one.

He peered into the darkness. There wasn't anything that should be keeping Pansy. The night was warm and clear with a full moon to guide her. Yet, he worried and gathered up his bedroll to follow. It was always possible that an animal had gone lame and had to be carried.

The going was slow, but he was only a mile from his hogan when he saw it. Well, heard it first to be more exact. But the shape—he'd recognized those swept back wings that could flutter at the tips, a beak turned toward the earth. Black, proud, swift as the eagle, and magpie-clever in its dealings with man.

And the noise. Amos grinned. Nothing on this earth could make noise like the Thunderbird. The sound of the wind with the force of a storm behind it that made his ears tingle. He watched the bird fly overhead and paused. Should he go back and wake the visitors? This would be something they had never experienced. But what if he lost it? No, it would be better to follow.

He saw it dip low in the distance and he struggled to keep up. Lightning skittered across the top of a mesa to his right. Yes. Male lightening. He could tell. Then the huge bird popped up on the horizon, seemed to wobble and dive toward the earth. Food. It must have swooped down to catch something. Amos hurried toward the point where he'd last seen it.

But he had trouble finding the bird. Even in the moonlight, he was confused. Too many ravines and places for the bird to hide. He called out assuring it that he meant no harm. And he got an answer. A clucking beckoned him toward a clump of piñon some thirty feet away.

"I greet you." He spoke the words of his ancestor's, sending them out and up to the tops of the scrubby piñon.

He hitched up his new, board-stiff jeans and stumbled forward over the dry sand only to stub his toe on the point of a half buried chunk of granite. He tried to imitate the sound that he'd heard by clicking his tongue against the roof of his mouth, but his tongue managed to slip out the hole left by the loss of an incisor and its two neighboring teeth; so, the sounds he made were little more than saliva punctuated sputters.

He paused and waited to hear the clucking again. And there it was coming from a knoll with five small pines growing together at its top, trunks gnarled and twisted. He leaned his bedroll against a low branch and sank to his hands and knees and crawled forward. It was a good place for a bird to hide, a canopy of short thick needles overhead and a cushioned mat of dry grass underneath.

He didn't see the blow coming. He simply felt the wind leave his lungs as the blackness swept over him. And he lay there—a long time it seemed to him because when he awakened, there was no bird. A hundred feet to the west was a smoldering mass, wisps of black smoke lazily drifted upward before dissipating in the night sky.

And the smell. So acrid that his eyes were burning. Had lightning struck something—brush stacked and waiting for someone to claim it before winter? But that didn't explain the smell. Maybe an old sofa or tires. All kinds of things were dumped out here. But still . . . Amos didn't have a good feeling about what had happened. He thought about looking for the Thunderbird, but concluded that wasn't a good idea. Hadn't the great bird thumped him a good one when he'd gotten too close? It was obvious that the bird hadn't been calling to him. He stood, but wobbled when he took a step. Then the first coughing spasm rocked him, and he grabbed a branch to keep from falling while he spat and sputtered trying to clear his throat. His lungs ached. The air was unhealthy. He couldn't even smell the fragrant piñon with his nose an inch from the branch. His head seemed clogged and it was difficult to think.

THREE

The night was perfect. He chuckled when he thought that he might be mistaken for the *chindi*. If someone saw him in his black cape, running close to the ground, twisting erratically, sometimes tripping over the suede booties that engulfed his shoes—and then looked for prints in the morning, they'd find none. He was thorough. He never left a trail. But he didn't venture onto the reservation often. Tonight there would be multiple incidents. That's what the paper would call them—incidents. As good as anything because they wouldn't have a clue.

His bag of instruments jangled unnervingly. He didn't have time to stop and repack the scalpels and hemostat, wrap them in the yards of gauze neatly tucked into his pockets.

He needed to make good time. In and out in under an hour. That was almost a motto. It'd worked over the years. No one suspected. And he'd profited handsomely from the hoax.

Yet, tonight he was vaguely bothered by something— something he couldn't name. Just a prickly feeling, some sixth sense warning that shivered up his spine. He slowed to a walk and then stopped. The air felt different, close, deadly calm. He never carried a flashlight, didn't want to tempt himself to use it. He relied on moonlight and the cover of darkness to protect him. But what he wouldn't give at this moment to scan the brush, pierce that curtain of dusk that masked the road and all that loomed around him in shadowy outlines.

A skyward whine pricked the silence, the sound intensifying as a dark triangle screamed overhead.

"Whoa."

Low, circling, obviously a Stealth on some kind of maneuver. This was interesting. Perhaps, he should investigate and get to his work later.

FOUR

Colonel Hap Anderson eased off the gas and felt his lips pull across his teeth in an involuntary smile. Give 'em a thrill. Wasn't that his motto? A muffler would steal this pleasure, bridle the roar of the engine, six in a row, dual overhead cam . . . he swung the D-type Jag into the lane leading to the entrance of Kirtland AFB. A briefing at three fucking o'clock in the morning and he'd been summoned to take part. But it was big. Not something he could ignore. The phone message had used the emergency code—on the cell devoted to business, the one he slept with.

The salute was snappy but the eyes of the young guard at the gate roamed over the sleekness of the black bullet-nosed front end and open cockpit of the antique racecar, stopping for a moment on the black fin that protruded in back of the driver.

Right-hand drive was always a stopper, too.

"How are things in Gotham City, Colonel?"

The young man looked pleased with his own humor. Hap had heard that one before, the Jag compared to a bat-mobile, but didn't steal the thunder from the youngster. Let him think he was original.

"Just dandy, son, thanks for inquiring." He grinned, then returned the dismissive salute and gunned the engine. The rumbling response was music to his soul. He didn't drive the car much. But nights like tonight when he had an excuse to be out on the back roads . . . well, it just didn't get any better than this.

He made an arc in the parking lot in front of the two-story brick building that housed the "war room" on a secured floor entirely below ground. Precautions. His whole life had been one of playing the game and being careful. And now he was close to retirement. Forced retirement. And he didn't have one bat's eyelash of an idea what that meant. He was scheduled to start transitioning sessions at the end of the summer. Three months and all this would be history.

He eased into the parking space with his name on it. His wife had stenciled a similar sign on the wall of the garage at home. Just a little something to duplicate what he'd been used to, to assure him some things didn't have to change. But he hadn't appreciated the gesture and let her know. It was painted over the next day.

There was going to be a star on the old epaulets before he hung it up. But fat chance now. And all because of some yahoos who took their oxygen masks off, donned cloth caps forty thousand feet above ground at five hundred miles an hour and posed for the pilot of a jet flying nearby—and then, of course, lost control of their own aircraft.

Stupid, stupid youth. It had cost the lives of two young men and surely and finally capped his own stellar thirty-year career. The Air Force was changing. There had been a time when the powers who be would look the other way. There wouldn't have even been a wrist-slapping. But the Air Force's chief civilian safety officer got a hair up his ass and told everyone who'd listen that the kids had disrobed and bared their buttocks for the other pilot. Mooning at forty thousand feet. Hap had made damn sure that those boys—what was left of them— had been found in their flight suits and damn sure that everyone heard the story about the snapshots.

But the damage had been done. Terms like "incompetent" and "poor leadership" floated around. The safety officer smelled blood and ranted and raved about the military repeatedly failing to punish senior officers whose supervision, or lack thereof, managed to cost the taxpayers millions of dollars—not to mention human life. Hap had been admonished to "lay low" for awhile and let it blow over, but it had been three years. The handwriting was on the wall. He was a has-been, passed over, ignored when his expertise could have been beneficial—no, he had to get out. The sooner, the better.

"Got any idea what this is all about?" A man leaned out the window of the car parked next to him. He had to yell above the Jag's engine.

Hap shook his head. He resisted the urge to gun the Jag just a teensy bit and simply shut the engine off. He hoisted himself out of the rounded, egg-shaped opening and paused to pull off his helmet and the stocking cap he wore underneath. Now he had "helmet hair". At least that's what his fifteen-year-old son would say. And if he could trust his expression, it had to be worse than just plain "hat hair".

He ran his hands through the short, graying, brown curls on top of his head, coaxing them to separate and stand upright. Then he dragged his palms over the close-shorn sides above his ears. He still had his hair and a thirty-four-inch waist on a six foot one frame—and could get it up twice a week whether he needed to or not. If all that was any consolation, and maybe it was at fifty-eight.

"You got any fix at all on what's going on? You hear anything over at the lab?" The man asked stepping out of a 911 Turbo 4 Porsche. Hap's eye skipped over the sleek contour of the car. One hundred thousand dollars worth—maybe then some. And he'd been waiting on Hap, hadn't gone in until he made sure Hap saw the new baby in "arrest me red".

"Nope. Thought someone like you'd have the skinny." Hap couldn't ignore the man any longer, but he could ignore the intent of the comment about the lab. He turned his back and busied himself pulling a briefcase from under the passenger seat. Hap had been "loaned" to Sandia National Laboratory since the incident. Just routine, act as a consultant—the title that covered a multitude of sins. He'd been detailed to a group that worked on frequency jamming devices and more recently had been tasked with trying to figure out why the Stealth Bomber couldn't tell a mountain from a gathering of cumulus clouds. Interesting work.

And he meant that. It had put him on the cutting edge, exposed him to technology that the man on the street wouldn't believe existed. The lab had teamed with Lockheed Martin and the Air Force to bring the F-22 to reality—a fighter so agile and fast and electronically sophisticated that it ran the risk of outsmarting the pilot.

Now a scant year from production, simulated flight decks had yielded to the real thing. And a prototype featuring this latest technology was currently being tested in fighters. But the fine print in his contract screamed "don't rock the boat; float this one right out the door". He still had a child to get through college. One of the back-east schools wouldn't be cheap.

"You coming?"

Hap sighed and fell in step. He disliked Rolland "Rolly" Bertrand, another "full-bird" equal in rank but someone who hadn't fucked up. This was a man who could still revel in his "fair-haired boy" status—someone who was on base and hadn't been loaned out . . . but someone who had lost his hair and had added a few inches to his waistline nevertheless. And someone who had to be one-up at whatever cost all the time. The Porsche was a good example. But Hap would be damned if he'd comment on the car.

"I think we lost one." Rolly leaned conspiratorially close slicing through Hap's reverie.

"You know that for sure?" Hap felt a quickening of his pulse. The "one" he was talking about was an F-117A, the Nighthawk Stealth Fighter. Forty-six million dollars worth of aircraft and carrying another fifty million in prototype electronics.

"Not one-hundred percent. But this was the night of the test." Both men walked crisply toward the building in front of them.

"I hope you're wrong. Maybe it's good news—gather us all around for a little 'job well done', a few slaps on the back," Hap offered.

"You're a dreamer. Nothing good happens after midnight unless it's got its legs around your neck. I learned that a long time ago." Hearty laughter, then Rolly pushed the door open after he carded it and held his badge to the scanner. "No, trust me on this one; we got problems."

The war room was bunker-safe and fortified, down one flight of stairs from the main floor. Divided into two levels, the upper deck was a sitting area with work tables and chairs surrounded by a pipe railing, a mezzanine of sorts that might lack something in esthetics, but made up for it in sturdiness. The walls of the room contained maps, a viewing screen descended from the ceiling to Hap's right and all of the lighting was florescent and dimly yellow. The paint was rose-beige, walls matched railings, and white acoustical tile overhead deadened any sound that might escape. Not exactly a party atmosphere, but Hap was used to it. He'd held meetings in worse places. He wasn't knee-deep in mud in some god-forsaken jungle.

A couple majors and a captain snapped to when Hap and Rolly walked in, then went back to their computers on the lower level. Hap poured a cup of coffee at a portable cart just inside the door and tapped a full packet of powdered creamer into it, stirred, then added a second. The damned stuff was brackish. Which supported his guess that some of these people had been there for a couple hours already.

"Let's get this show on the road." The master of ceremonies was a one-star general, Alex Stromburg, a man in his sixties, fair, but one not known to mince words. "We've got a lot of material to cover."

Hap followed Rolly up the short set of stairs, nodded his "hellos" to the assortment of brass already gathered and took a seat at a table in back. This had the feeling of something big, all right; there was a manila envelope of materials in front of him, the red Top Secret stamp almost jumped off the paper.

"Page one should be a map. I'd like you to have that in front of you." General Stromburg waited until the shuffling of the six-man audience died down. A copy of the same map was now visible on the overhead screen. "I'll get right to the point. We have been notified that an F-117A has gone down somewhere here." The pointer stabbed at an area of northwest New Mexico then trailed a tight circle just this side of the Continental Divide. "We believe that the crash occurred at approximately twenty-three hundred hours. At this time we do not anticipate finding any survivors."

"But you haven't had a ground crew in there yet?" Hap asked.

"Not a crew exactly. At this time we're operating mainly off of film shot by a TV news team who just happened to be in the area. We estimate that these photos were taken some fifteen minutes after the crash."

"I don't want to be no dummy, but why are we still waiting to send in a ground crew some three and a half hours later?" Hap didn't try to conceal the edge to his voice. One thing about being a short timer, he had nothing to lose. But if General Stromburg was pained by the interruptions, he didn't show it, Hap thought. And the question was a good one; one he'd bet half the room wanted to ask.

"This area . . ." General Stromburg turned again to the overhead screen and now traced a larger circle with the pointer. "All this is Indian land which has slowed our investigation—"

Now Hap's anger spilled over. "It's a goddamned part of the United States, isn't it? Let's get in there, make something happen. It isn't like they're going to ambush us with bows and arrows." He had a short fuse lately when it came to incompetence—someone else's fuck up.

Hap was a little irked when his querulousness didn't ruffle the general. If the truth were known, Hap was sick and tired of the "new" military. You had to take courses in interpersonal relations for God's sake. Men were born leaders—either you were one or you weren't. These guys were better suited to boardrooms, than in-the-field tactics. And all these warnings about what you could or couldn't say—women this, minorities that. The military could hand down whatever edict it wanted concerning "special groups", but the majority of old-timers would never change.

"Indian land is sovereign territory," the general continued. "We do not have jurisdiction over this area. We are forced to tread softly, follow protocol, seek direction from the Indian leaders. It is our understanding that this area is sacred to the Navajo. These people have a proud history of service in the United States military—"

"So we're just pussy-footing around waiting for the right moment to saunter over for a look-see? And whatever we find out tomorrow morning or next week will be just that much more stale for the waiting?" Hap continued his bullying.

"Not exactly."

Hap marveled at the general's constraint. He wasn't sure he'd have that kind of patience.

The general took a deep breath before he added, "Bear with me on this. We may not have a thorough ground report, but we do have a preliminary one, and we're lucky enough to have some aerial film that will help put the crash in perspective. Some of the shots aren't half bad. Ready, John?"

The general signaled to the man in the projection booth behind the wall at Hap's back. He proceeded to fold down the protruding neck of the overhead projector and scoot the machine to one side just as the lights in the room dimmed. A screen descended from the ceiling.

There was a "no smoking" sign on the back of the door but three people lit up anyway, their smoke hanging in the soft light, wavering upward in layers sucked ceilingward by the ventilation system. In times of stress, rules could be broken.

The crash site flickered across the screen, then steadied as the projectionist focused.

"Who'd you say filmed this?" Hap asked.

"Part of a TV crew out of Farmington. We have their tape. When they realized what they had, they got it to us right away. These guys came up with some pretty good footage—not that the tape doesn't raise questions, but we're lucky to have anything at all. It was plain ol' blind luck. These jokers are flying around in a twin-engine Cessna trying to verify the report of a UFO some viewer had called in when they see what looks like a flare—apparently it was so short-lived, it took them a while to pinpoint the site."

"Sounds like someone was alive out there," a colonel in back noted.

"Initially. But this frame shows the plane and surrounding area. As you can see—John, blow up this shot for the group." With a whine of equipment, the blackened mass in the center of the photo grew until the outline of an aircraft emerged. "Here and here you can make out the wing and cockpit of the F-117A. Due to the smoke it's difficult to clearly see anything else. . . ." The pointer tapped away on the screen. "Notice that fire is coming from the mid-section, the forward fuselage, and from this angle the underside of the fuselage."

"Explosion upon impact?" Hap asked.

"We don't think so. But more on that later. Let's have the close-up of the cockpit." Again the whine from in back of him and Hap saw a different, clearer view showing an empty cockpit—nosecone intact. Almost intact, that is. Hap leaned forward. It looked like someone had taken a can opener to the metal skin, then neatly pulled it away from the forward fuselage in chunks. And the pilot? Hap couldn't be sure but from the obscure grayness of the shot, it didn't look like there was anyone in the cockpit. Before he could ask, the general pointed to what might have been a pair of legs, from the knees down, sticking out from under the plane at the bottom of the frame.

"This would appear to be feet; again, we presume they belong to the pilot. It would appear that he was able to reach the ground and release one flare before collapsing."

The next series of shots had captured the plane engulfed in flames. As new and larger balls of fire were recorded on film, the F-117A seemed to melt frame by frame. The kid in the booth let the film run then quickly worked back through the shots until there was only billowing black smoke drifting across the desert.

The general stepped to the right of the screen. "From this point on, I don't think there's any new information. Nothing, that is, that will shed light on why we lost the plane. But that's the singularly odd thing about all this. Other than the fighter being tipped on its side, there is no evidence of it impacting the earth—not in a way that would suggest a crash. John, hold on that shot, please."

The general pulled out the pointer to its full extension. "For instance, there . . ." The tip of the pointer trailed along the lower left hand side of the screen under the mass that had been the fighter. "There's no crater gouged out by con- tact." The general paused to let this information sink in before he added, "The pictures seem to indicate a crash landing, maybe something intentional, possibly a fuel prob- lem or some malfunction that gave the pilot time to assess his options and bring her down."

The room erupted with rapid-fire questions.

"Are we assuming then that the pilot didn't have time to get away? Leave the area before the plane went up?"

"Surely he would have known his options while in the air and once on the ground could have reacted accordingly."

"Or was there a problem with the pilot in the first place—maybe leakage of toxic fumes and he was overcome?"

The assemblage was acting like a think-tank, brainstorming their hypotheses.

"All possibilities, gentlemen," the general said. "The one thing we can be thankful for is that this region is so remote. If we have to lose one, it might as well be out here—little or no threat to human life. We're hoping we won't have to deal with anyone succumbing to chemicals, anyway."

General Stromburg shuffled some papers in front of him before picking up one sheet and clearing his throat.

"However, we can't be certain about that. I'd like to add that we were able to deploy a single scout to verify what you've just seen, a little search and rescue mission that must be kept under wraps. We cannot, I repeat, cannot indicate to the leaders of the Navajo that we trespassed. We need their cooperation. This is not going to be a simple in/out investigation."

Hap blinked trying to adjust as the lights in the room came up. The general took a chair on the dais next to the audio-video control panel. His tightness of jaw belied his otherwise calm exterior.

He cleared his throat before adding, "The initial report of our person on the ground verifies the death of the pilot. We'll dust the area in the morning with the Navajo's permission, but the fire looks to have made easy answers impossible. The lab will have a challenge on their hands." Then as an afterthought, "Oh yes, our boy found a pickup parked about fifty or sixty feet from the crash site. Engine was still warm, but no driver. The truck is registered to a Brenda Begay. Nothing turned up on a background check. However, we're not taking any chances. We'll try to locate her. Our guess is that she's an eyewitness. But it's also possible that this woman was injured."

Hap tilted his head. "You don't suspect any direct involvement?"

"You know the answer to that, Hap. Keep an open mind. At this point in time, there's nothing to suggest that she was more than an innocent bystander. We found these school materials in the cab." The general held up a spiral notebook and two texts. "Nothing in here to indicate she was anything but a student on her way home . . . wrong place, wrong time. Of course, we'll want to interview her and possibly the family."

Hap straightened. This made things sticky—a dangerous new wrinkle and one that was potentially damaging. One that could quickly put an end to tests over the reservation. An unaccounted for possible eyewitness? What had she seen? Had she died trying to help?

The general leaned over to punch the button that would raise the screen then hesitated and asked, "Anyone want a repeat of any shots?"

"Rerun the beginning of the tape," Rolly called out. Hap thought the general's glance Rolly's way was appreciative, a little knowing nod. The general also must have thought there was something to see in those initial frames.

John quickly stopped on the first frame, focused the equipment and then enlarged the shot. Once again the hazy cockpit of the fighter filled the screen.

"I'm not sure I really saw anything. Smoke seems to have risen level with the rubber seal on the canopy. But what about that bare spot in front?" Rolly asked.

"Good question. That sheared piece in front of the cockpit suggests that the pilot had some difficulty in the air." The general added, "If he did lose a part of the forward fuselage, it would explain a lot. Hopefully, tests will get us closer to an answer. Wouldn't you agree, Colonel Anderson?"

Hap nodded slowly. He knew what the general was getting at. This was the first test of the electronic package that boosted the plane into the year 2010 when it came to know-how, but if something went wrong there'd be no time for correction.

"Any timeframe for when we can have a closer look?" a colonel in the front row asked.

"As I said earlier, a lot depends on the Navajo. I'll have a team out in the morning to talk with their leaders. In the meantime I've asked Colonel Anderson to share with you just why this crash is such a loss."

Hap reached for his briefcase. He'd given this same presentation a number of times—at the Pentagon, for the CEO's of various companies, the biggies at the lab—all the time jockeying for an ironclad position in someone's budget, someone who would see the potential, realize that this technology meant the difference between winning and losing in the future.

Hap walked to the back and handed John a disk—the top secret PowerPoint presentation. Now it was show time. His show. And it would be good, impressive; he knew that. And this was just one more part that he'd miss in retirement—the front and center attention. He paused for dramatic effect and then began.

"This could be a busman's holiday for those of you who have had men go through the cockpit demonstrations here on base. We'll continue to run groups through this training over the winter. But we've also started to incorporate certain aspects of the F-22 prototype electronics in F-117A fighters, and yes, the plane that was lost tonight was fully equipped with computer and display technology not previously tested in flight." Hap poured a paper cup of water, took a sip and quietly added. "We cannot rule out the possibility that it was the equipment that caused the accident."

Hap nodded at John in the control booth and turned to the screen now filled with three range models simulating an air battle. The left-hand mock-up was marked defense display, followed to the right by a tactical display and lastly, an attack display. Lines of red, blue, green and yellow sharply outlined the symbols that set up the playing field against a black background.

"This, gentlemen, is exactly what the pilot sees on his control panel. His onboard receivers collect radar signals from fighters in the area and any surface-to-air missiles or SAM sites are identified with a red pentagon." Hap pointed to the two symbols in the first display window. "Not only are threats identified, but the distance at which those threats are likely to detect the F-22 is also calculated. I might add that the F-22 is not as stealthy side and rear, and the pilot needs to know this range to give him an advantage."

"In the second panel you'll see three targets on the hit list while over to the side these four aircraft are shown as 'friendlies'. We refer to this bit of heads-up information as 'situational awareness'—the ability to spot potential danger while it's still out of range. I don't need to tell you how this can separate the men from the boys and tip the old playing field in someone's favor very quickly."

Hap waited for the appreciative murmurs to die out then continued. "The best, however, is yet to come. In the far right panel, the attack display gives the pilot the data needed to take out a threat in a forty-mile range. The bar on the left shows the target's altitude while the notches on this scale . . ." Hap ran the pointer down the right side of the screen. "This shows the maximum range of the F-22's missiles and the distance at which he can fire and break away in safety. This graphic also gives a read on the range of the hostile missiles." Hap paused and scanned the audience for questions before moving on. No questions and they were in the palm of his hand. What he was presenting impacted every person in the room. It felt good to be up front with all eyes center.

"You'll notice that the display symbols differ in shape as well as color. Pilots wear an anti-laser visor which blocks certain colors. This allows for instant identification and a low rate of confusion."

"Are you saying that all three screens use identical symbols?" Rolly asked.

"Exactly. And show the scene from the same orientation unlike today's cockpit displays. Look at the symbol representing the plane in each of these screens. The pilot always views his own fighter from the God's eye view, top down, with its flight path pointed straight up through the center of the screen."

"What's the power behind all this?" the general asked.

Hap grinned, "Nothing small. Try two banks of 32-bit computer cards packed into the forward fuselage—the calculating power of a supercomputer."

"And this is the package that we lost?"

"Sorry to say that it is." Hap brought up the lights in the room and took a chair to the side of the dais close to General Stromburg. "I think it puts new emphasis on the first aerial photo that shows what appears to be a part of the fuselage torn away. That rip in the skin is directly over the guts of the computer and could have wreaked havoc with managing the plane in the air. If, in fact, that's what happened—and we may not be able to prove it conclusively—I believe it warrants grounding any further test efforts."

"I second that," the general broke in. "I'll speak to the labs in the morning. Of course, the 49th Fighter Wing at Hollomon has been notified and successive tests put on hold. Any other discussion?"

Rolly's head perked up. "Well, the dead of night probably rules out the pilot trying to moon someone." The laughter that followed was entirely his. Hap didn't even flinch. The son-of-a-bitch wasn't worth causing a scene over. But it did strike Hap that now might be a good time to offer his assistance.

"I'd like to volunteer to lead the evaluation team. I've been working on the Lab's transfer of rights to state-of-the-art video technology with two Navajo owned companies out of Window Rock. I've made a few friends in the area. At least, I'm a familiar face—maybe I can expedite things."

"Good idea. You've got the job. I'll name someone to work with you. In fact, let's set this up now."

"I'd like in," Rolly volunteered.

"Col. Bertrand? Good by me. You'll support Hap on this one. Be in my office at 0600. I'll notify everyone present of our progress, in the meantime, gentlemen, get a good night's rest, what's left of it."

Hap didn't look at Rolly but he was relieved when his new partner didn't follow him out to the parking lot. He'd had enough of him for one evening. It rankled that Rolly had been assigned to the project—volunteered no less. He didn't need him tagging along. Watching his every step. But it might work out all right. It was better not to speculate. He'd deal with having to work with him in the morning. At least he hadn't punched him out, and he had given a good presentation that placed him right in the center of the action; this had the smell of redemption about it. All in all, it had been a good night's work. He patted the Jag and didn't stop the grin that pushed back the corners of his mouth.

FIVE

Pansy was home when Amos half crawled, half walked up the dusty lane that wound back around the pens and the well to their hogan. She was sitting in the rocker that he'd bought at the high school rummage sale that raised money for new football uniforms. Pansy had dragged it outside and sat there pushing back and forth. She couldn't really rock. The rockers had been worn smooth. And that was just one more thing that Amos had intended to do—replace those curved pieces of wood so that she could work up some momentum. But Pansy didn't seem to notice she wasn't going anywhere, and she seemed soothed.

He put a hand to his head. The blood was dry now, caked at the crown but the pain dulled the vision in his right eye. In fact, the right side of his face twitched involuntarily when he tried to focus. It had been one heck of a wallop.

He sat down by the rocker on the dry sandy earth. He felt better when he didn't move. He told Pansy about the Thunderbird but something told him she'd seen the bird, too—a slight nod of the head, maybe, but she didn't stop her almost frantic movement. Amos looked closely at her face. She sat transfixed staring into nothingness.

He pulled himself onto his knees. Pansy was never one for inactivity. Even the spells of late were loud, filled with yelling and arm waving. But the wife in front of him was in a trance. He pulled back. What had happened out there? What had the Holy Ones done to his wife? Was she being punished for selling the sand painting? He thought so. Or maybe the money from the hogan & breakfast. The Thunderbird had spoken to her and had rendered her a statue.

It was like the lesson last Wednesday night at the Hosanna Pentecostal church, the white trailer with a wooden cross-nailed above the door. God had turned Lot's wife into a pillar of salt for not following his bidding. Amos almost wet his finger and touched Pansy's arm, but he didn't.

He leaned against the rocker and closed his eyes. He awoke with sunlight washing over his body. He was stiff and cramped from sleeping sitting up. Pansy was nowhere in sight, but Amos smelled the piñon scent of a cookfire wafting from the hogan. His head throbbed and felt heavy on his shoulders. He slumped down, then rolled out flat with arms outstretched, soaking up the sun's warmth, and watched the mesas turn pink while his thoughts drifted to the night before.

There were no cars parked by the hogan. All their visitors had apparently left early. He turned his head. The scent of bacon floated on the morning air beckoning him to its source. Since the visitors were gone, was the meat for him?

Then Pansy appeared in the doorway and motioned for him to follow as she took off around the hogan down toward the pens. With an effort Amos pushed himself upright and sucked in his breath as the pain traveled down his arm. He swayed for a moment, then started out in the direction Pansy had taken. When he caught up with her, she was standing inside the makeshift corral that housed the Billy goat. She pointed to the ground in front of her.

Amos gasped. Pansy was standing there calmly, but he felt his stomach lurch toward his throat. He couldn't help himself. It was the work of the *chindi*. He could feel the evil. What had the poor goat done to deserve such a death? But who else would skin an animal like that? Risk becoming a wolfman? Amos had to think. The night had been a bad one—the Thunderbird, now this. Had he seen a ghost fire? He shivered.

Then he stepped closer and peered at the goat's head. Whatever it was that butchered his goat, it had only taken meat from the goat's left side. He pointed that out to Pansy, but she just stared trance-like. That goat had one fierce-looking, milky, blue-white left eye that he'd fix on you just before he charged. But that eye could witch you, too. Amos would have killed that goat long ago had it not been for that eye and the waste of a good half of the animal because, of course, no one could eat from the spoiled left side. Amos chuckled, then held his sides in devilish laughter. Whoever did this would pay. Already he felt better knowing that the goat's killer would go blind.

S I X

"Ben, step in here a minute," the Assistant Tribal Chairman called through the open door.

Ben Pecos had a half-hour before he was expected at the hospital. He'd left his DayTimer in the car but he didn't have patients until ten, and then he was booked solid until five. Six individuals, if all showed, who wanted to share their problems—who expected advice from someone they considered one of them. Which was sort of stretching the truth but it got him more appointments than the Anglo shrink the tribe had hired last year. Ben's mother was Pueblo and his father unknown, but it gave him some leverage.

He paused long enough to sling his jacket over a chair in the hall. The cement block building that housed the Tribal offices was warm. It was that tricky time of year when one had to choose between air-conditioning and heat, and a wrong call could mean you sweltered or froze for half a day. He'd guess someone had erred on the side of heat overnight.

He hadn't planned on spending the morning. He'd stopped by the Tribal offices in Crownpoint to check on the funding of a grant. He'd submitted the paperwork in May. The federal government worked slow, and he'd wanted to hurry things if he could. Fat chance. It looked like the alcohol program would start up minus a counselor. Maybe he could volunteer; it was only one night a week—but a night that he didn't have to give. He taught two nights, worked the evening clinic in Gallup one night, was on-call for the community council . . . he desperately needed another twenty-four hours in his week.

The moment he crossed the threshold to the Assistant Tribal Chairman's office, he felt the tension. Three men in uniform—a major and a couple of Air Force colonels—sat tersely in front of Ernie Old Talker who leaned forward with hands folded on his oversized mahogany desk. Somebody wants something and negotiations have broken down, Ben thought.

"Close the door, please."

The colonel nearest him gave the order. Not even his office and he's calling the shots. And then Anglos wonder how they tick people off. Ben shut the door and waited for the assistant chairman to indicate where he wanted him to sit before pulling up a chair.

"I'm Colonel Anderson."

"Rolly Bertrand here," the man next to him followed.

Ben leaned across to shake hands. The men seemed relieved to be talking with someone they obviously considered "one of their own". And now wasn't the time for Ben to mention his ancestry. He'd just see where this would lead. Seemed odd to have two full-birds on a project. Stakes must be high. The one who introduced himself as Rolly cleared his throat.

"I don't know if you're aware that we lost a fighter last night somewhere on the reservation."

"No. I hadn't heard." Well, that explained the tension. The Air Force needed permission to investigate, take troops across what was probably sacred land. And if Ben guessed correctly, it would take numerous trips before the case was closed.

"Was there loss of life?" Ben asked.

"We have reason to believe the pilot landed the plane but didn't have time to escape before there was some type of explosion. All the more need to get in there today," Colonel Anderson added curtly. He seemed to be the one without patience.

"Where did this happen?"

The major stood to lean over the assistant chairman's desk. "With your permission, sir?" The major paused to look at Ernie, and waited for a nod. Good, Ben thought, at last a little deference for local rank. The young man moved a pencil holder and stapler, then unfolded and smoothed a map across the felt blotter.

"Approximately here."

Ben leaned close. The map was the one issued by AAA entitled "Indian Country" and probably was as good as any he'd seen when it came to pinpointing back roads. The colonel was pointing to an area between Crownpoint and Chaco Canyon above Standing Rock. Desolate country. A few sheepherders but not much of anything else.

"Sir, we have a team on standby to go in. . . ." the major offered after getting the nod from Colonel Anderson.

Still Ernie Old Talker didn't say anything. He just pushed back, stood and moved to the window behind his desk. Ben could see the elementary school playground in the distance. Bright dots of color grouped around the swings or slipped down the slides. Ernie took his time, then turned back to the group and nodded.

"I will have our people lead you. But I must ask for

silence. I want nothing written down about any shrines or sacred places; I want nothing photographed—nothing disturbed. We will decide what road you will use to enter the site and will post sentries to check your vehicles coming and going. Our laws will not be violated. There are those who say that the air space above a sovereign nation under treaty with the Federal Government should not have to worry about this sort of thing—that maybe you overstep your boundaries as it is."

Rolly started to say something but seemed to reconsider. "As you wish."

"I will expect full restitution for any injuries to our people. Ben, I want you to canvas the area within a mile radius and seek out anyone who might have inhaled toxic fumes from burning plastics or other materials. We need to be represented by Indian Health Services on this one. I'll let your boss know that I've borrowed you for a few days." Ernie made brief eye contact with Colonel Anderson before looking away. "The Tribal Council will determine what payment is due for damage to life or the grounds. It's eight fifteen; I will expect a report by early afternoon." He rose. "Gentlemen," Ernie walked around his desk. "Any questions?"

"We'll reconvene here at one thirty." Colonel Anderson turned to Ben. "Ready to go in five minutes?"

Ben nodded. He resented the interruption in his morning. But it wasn't exactly something he could turn down. And it wouldn't do any good to tell the assistant chairman that he was a psychologist and not a medical doctor. But he agreed, IHS should know what's going on. Contamination of any kind—water, food stuffs in the area, not to mention possible toxic fallout—could lead to serious medical problems. Ben was a "floater" for the time being anyway.

Assigned to the hospital in Crownpoint and surrounding area after the clinical director in Hawikuh had requested his transfer.

Ben stopped at the secretary's desk to use the phone. He pushed a wayward lock of dark brown hair out of his eyes, squinted at the numbers on the phone and vaguely wondered if he needed glasses. He was only thirty-one; did that make a difference? The receptionist at the Crownpoint clinic answered on the second ring and took the message that he'd be tied up until late afternoon.

The parking lot was crowded with vehicles and Air Force personnel—a lot of milling about and looking officious, Ben thought. This wasn't going to be an easy day. He sensed that the two colonels disliked each other. There was a wariness, not to mention a feeling of one-upmanship that made him give the two of them a wide berth.

Why'd he let himself get roped in? Then he saw Tommy leaning against his Bronco. Always the observer, arms folded across his chest, the ever-present tribal police uniform looking crisp and spotless, mirrored sunglasses hiding inquiring eyes. The term "good cop" came to mind—far wiser than his twenty-six years—young, eager but with a good head on his shoulders.

"Tommy." Ben waved and started toward the Bronco.

"Hey. Want a front row seat?" The grin hinted of relief at seeing a familiar face.

Ten minutes later a regular convoy pulled out of the parking lot in front of the tribal offices. Three white Broncos with four-wheel drive and the tribal seal on their sides led the way followed by two jeeps and an air-conditioned sedan driven by an airman, first class—probably some flunky assigned to the colonels, Ben decided. He wasn't sure how far the sedan could go; they only had so much paved road before it would be cross-country, across arroyos—rougher terrain than the Buick was used to from the looks of it.

Tommy led the way. The first stretch of washboard after they left the asphalt rattled Ben's teeth so badly that he clamped his jaws shut, and it took an effort to keep them that way. The road was worse than he remembered. He watched Tommy lock onto the steering wheel and keep the car close to the right side of the road, one wheel in soft caliche powder. Thank God it didn't look like rain. Ben would hate to be caught on roads like this during a gully washer. Slick and treacherous before they turned to muck that would mire all but the best four-wheel drives. The ankle deep ruts that jolted the Bronco attested to the fact that rain had stranded a few people out here—and not too long ago.

They rode in silence since talking might prove injurious to their health. Ben glanced back through the clouds of yellow dust to see how the Buick was faring. It was keeping up. The young airman was pushing it. Something to be said about how you drive when the vehicle isn't your own.

Tommy loosened his uniform collar. Ben thought briefly of the threesome in Ernie's office. Uniforms did things to people. He hoped that he wouldn't have to interact with the men after today. Neither colonel had seemed particularly sympathetic to issues of culture.

And then his thoughts slipped to Julie. Didn't they always? He teasingly told her they needed to get married so that he could concentrate. And they would have been married by now if her mother hadn't had surgery and begged them to wait until Christmas. Julie was with her now in

Arizona. But she promised to be back next week.

He had thought of asking her what was wrong with the picture? They get engaged and dear ol' Mom suddenly has a medical crisis. Actually, elective surgery—something that could have waited. Absolutely page eighty-seven text-book perfect. And Julie refused to discuss it. The conversation, one-sided as it was, escalated into hurt feelings and a not exactly romantic evening before she caught the plane in Albuquerque.

He needed to change things, say he was sorry but most importantly, lay off criticizing. Wasn't he being insensitive? He'd never been in her position. His mother was dead by the time he was five. His adoptive mother was restrained, never one to meddle. Julie's upbringing had been so different—banker father, socialite mother. But like him, an only child. In a peculiar way that was a bond.

He thought of waking beside her, reaching out, touching, then drawing her to him warm and soft, sleepy but willing . . . and how much he missed her. She'd called from Phoenix, but things seemed strained. He guessed it was up to him now.

A sudden jolt snapped Ben out of his reverie. His head had just grazed the top of the Bronco's roof. "Hey, you're going to lose your passenger."

"Sorry about that. Tough to see some of these boulders embedded in the road."

The road, Ben noticed, was now an arroyo, wide and winding, banked by four-foot sloping sides. The going was easier on the hard-packed sandy bottom and somewhat smoother. But the day was heating up. Nine thirty and the temperature was already in the 80's. Unusual, but then the whole summer had been a hot one. And the tribal car was without air-conditioning. Ben cranked down the window. Better. There wasn't as much dust and the breeze felt good.

"Is somebody stuck up there?"

Ben pointed through the windshield at a truck parked in the middle of the makeshift road about a hundred yards ahead.

"Looks like a junker."

Tommy seemed so sure. Ben wondered how he could tell. He had seen some pretty sorry looking vehicles on the reservation that were still making it around under their own steam.

"Stop anyway, just in case someone needs a hand."

Tommy pulled up alongside the tan truck and pulled the brake after he shut off the engine.

"If I didn't know better, I'd say this is ol' Elmo."

"Elmo?"

"Brenda Begay's truck. It was her dad's."

Ben got out, walked around the truck and had to admit it didn't look promising. This vehicle had seen better times but it had all its glass. Didn't that indicate someone hadn't given up on it? He looked in the windshield, then opened the driver side door. The keys were still in the ignition. So, it wasn't a junker. He had been right. Maybe someone was taking a leak. Ben shut the door and walked around to the front and scanned the surrounding area. Strange. Who would leave his vehicle and hike out of sight to attend to a call of nature? You'd have all the privacy you'd want standing right here. He leaned back against the hood. Then on impulse walked to the front of the truck and raised the hood. The engine was cold. This truck hadn't been driven in a while.

Ben went around to the passenger side and opened the

door. The seat was empty. He checked the glove box. Insurance, registration, proof of purchase—all in order. The owner's name was Brenda Begay. Tommy was right.

Ben walked back around the truck and leaned in the Bronco. "This is Elmo."

"What?" Tommy was out of the Bronco, door slamming. "There's no way she'd come this way. The highway cuts through right above her mom's place. This makes no sense. She's fifteen miles, at least, from home. Brenda has a daughter. She's probably three now. Her mother takes care of her when she's gone, but I can't imagine Brenda not wanting to take the shortest route home."

Ben passed him the registration. He could feel the dread, the fear start to intrude upon his thinking. She had left right after class as far as he knew. He hadn't kept the group late. But if what Tommy said was true, why was her truck here? The truck could have just given out. Maybe she had no choice. Maybe she had to take her books and walk home. But fifteen miles. . . .

Quickly, Ben jumped into Elmo's cab, pumped the gas pedal and turned the key in the ignition. One turn and the engine roared to life. It even sounded pretty spry for its age. So it hadn't left her stranded. The blast of country/western music attested to a working sound system—new and expensive from the looks of it. Brenda wouldn't park her truck out here and leave it.

"Get out of there."

The arm reached in the open door and yanked Ben sideways.

"You've just contaminated possible evidence." Colonel Anderson glared at him seeming reluctant to drop the hold on his arm.

"Evidence? Of what?" Ben was furious. What gave this man the right to jerk him around?

"Anything this close to a crash site is treated as suspicious until proven otherwise."

"How do you know we're that close?" Tommy pushed between them.

Colonel Anderson dropped his hand and stepped back, "According to the aerial photo—"

"You've been here before, haven't you?"

Tommy lowered his voice as the others walked toward them led by Colonel Bertrand, but he didn't try to disguise his anger. There was no answer as the colonel turned on his heel to confer with the group of Air Force personnel.

Ben watched Tommy chew his lower lip. Tommy was furious, but so was he. All this bended knee, please allow us to search for our missing . . . all a sham. Apparently, the military only needed permission in the daylight. But Brenda. What did they know about her?

"Are you sure about how far it is to Brenda's house?" Ben asked. It was still difficult for him to estimate distance when the landscape didn't have markers—at least not ones that he was used to.

"About fifteen miles, maybe a little less. She wouldn't walk from here. But there's got to be a logical explanation for her leaving Elmo."

"Such as?"

Tommy just shrugged his shoulders. He looked stricken. Was there something personal between him and Brenda? Could be. But Ben couldn't remember seeing them together.

"I saw her about ten. We were supposed to go for coffee but then I got this call for backup. She left just after I did which means she'd reach this point at about the time the aircraft was supposed to have crashed."

"Over here!"

The yell interrupted their discussion. An excited Colonel Bertrand was beckoning to them.

Ben and Tommy hurried to the edge of the arroyo and climbed up the sloping, sandy side and there it was—the charred mound of debris. Ben hung back as the military team swarmed into action. They would take samples, measure, document—it would take hours, days even.

"I'm calling in." Tommy turned back. "The dispatcher will know if there's been a report on Brenda. He can call her school for me to make sure."

Ben followed Tommy to the Bronco. It took Tommy a minute to clear the static. On a reservation that covered almost eighteen million acres and had over two hundred thousand people, a two-way radio was a lifeline. A cell phone was usually worthless. The officer in the Crownpoint tribal police station boomed out over the wireless.

"Yeah. Report just came in. Brenda Begay didn't show up at home last night and she's not at work. Mother's real upset. Says something's happened for sure. You got information?"

Tommy said he thought he might and then explained. When he'd hung up, Tommy sat for a moment leaning forward, arms draped around the steering wheel.

Finally, he said, "It might make the family feel better if they knew local law enforcement was on top of things. You up for going by the house?"

"Good idea."

"Unless you think we should wait here . . . in case they find another—"

"No. Let's get going."

Ben didn't know what to do to be helpful. Would they find another body in the wreckage? That was possible. Brenda had seen the crash and tried to help or . . . ? Ben didn't know what the "or" was, but maybe he should alert the salvage crew. But then didn't they already know? Hadn't the Air Force already been out here to look things over? Someone had probably already gone over Brenda's truck. How much did they know that they weren't saying?

"Give me a minute." Ben intended to find out.

He quickly covered the ground between the Bronco and the thick knot of conferring brass.

"I'm going to agree with you that the owner of the pickup may be involved with the crash somehow. The owner, a woman named Brenda Begay, is missing." Ben had approached Colonel Anderson first and the two of them stood some twenty feet from the wreckage. As a precaution, everyone wore molded paper masks that cupped over nose and mouth. The colonel handed one to Ben.

"Let's talk over here. These damned things are a nuisance." The colonel snapped his off and led Ben back toward the cars. Out of earshot, Ben noticed.

"Listen son, I might have overreacted back there earlier. I've just been in charge of things like this more than one or ten thousand times—what'd someone tell me you do for a living? Shrink, isn't it? Well, I can't expect you to think like an investigator, now can I?" The smile wasn't exactly sincere, Ben thought. "We'll watch for . . . anything unusual. Shame if this Begay women was only trying to help and there was some kind of accident."

What was the man trying to say? That he knew that something had happened to Brenda?

"What happened to Brenda Begay?" Ben hadn't heard

Tommy walk up behind him. Could the colonel hear the anger in Tommy's voice? He seemed to study Tommy a moment before he responded.

"I don't know. Believe me. But if I did, that kind of information would be classified—at least for the time being."

"I don't want to butt in, but I could use the help of one of you." Colonel Bertrand approached. "We have a situation here that calls for a tribal decision."

"What is it?" Tommy stepped forward. "Maybe I can help."

"We need to take some samples of vegetation, say, up to a hundred feet of the plane—maybe, farther out. Who would be able to okay that?"

"I would. I'll assign a Navajo officer to work with you. If for any reason your guide cautions you against continuing in a particular direction though, you have to honor his request."

"I understand. You have my word we'll follow his recommendations."

It was good to hear Colonel Bertrand acknowledging some restrictions. Ben wished that Colonel Anderson showed as much deference.

"Let me find someone to act as guide. Show me where you want to start." Tommy turned to follow the colonel.

Ben watched the two men return to the site.

"What will they look for?"

"A little bit of everything. We need to determine if the pilot dumped fuel. If he did it at altitude, we won't find a thing. Stuff will have evaporated. But if he lost the JP-8 at a lower level, there'll be traces on the brush—it'll take a lab to tell us for certain. It might indicate there was a leak in fuel line or tanks. Hell, we've got to come up with some reason that we're looking at a pile of rubble."

There was something in his voice—concern, frustration? For a moment, Ben almost felt sorry for the man. Maybe he was selling him short. He was obviously under pressure to come up with answers.

"Colonel!"

The yell startled both of them. An airman was waving for them to join him some one hundred and fifty feet to the east of the plane. Ben took off at a trot, the colonel on his heels.

"This could be nothing or it could be something," the airman apologized. "But to be on the safe side, I thought you ought to see, Sir."

Tommy and Colonel Bertrand were standing next to the airman. Tommy was tightlipped and Ben could see a muscle in his jaw involuntarily twitch.

The airman pointed at a hair ribbon. At least that's what Ben would call it, a piece of material, a plaid of sorts—pink and yellow streaked against turquoise, two feet long and one inch wide. But the remarkable thing was it was tied in a bow. Someone had taken the time to tie it on the end of a piñon branch about four feet off the ground and left it there to flutter in the breeze.

"When was the last time we had rain?" Ben asked Tommy.

"Yesterday afternoon."

It probably hadn't been necessary to ask. The ribbon's crispness and unfaded color was proof that it hadn't been there for long.

"I can't think that it would mean anything. But let's get pictures." Colonel Anderson didn't seem interested.

"I suggest that you have your lab analyze the fibers, any hair particles—it might be able to tell us a lot," Tommy stammered and seemed ready to explode. "Who are you to say what's important and what's not? There could be lives at stake."

"I agree. We need to be treating everything as priority," Colonel Bertrand chimed in, then patted Tommy on the back. "Officer Spottedhorse, I can't tell you how sorry I am this has happened. It isn't easy for anyone."

"At least someone is using his brain." Tommy glared at Colonel Anderson. "You will have your men take samples and have them analysed."

Ben didn't trust the situation. Tommy was barely under control. He'd just insulted the colonel and now he was giving him orders. That wasn't going to earn him any points. The look on Colonel Anderson's face assured him of that. It was obvious that the disappearance of Brenda Begay was consuming Tommy but was of little importance to the colonel.

"Over here. Colonel Bertrand, Colonel Anderson, this looks serious."

Another airman and an Indian officer were squatting on the ground next to a clump of piñon some thirty feet from where the ribbon had been found. The airman was pointing to something on the ground.

"Blood. I'm sure of it. Used to do a little flunky work in hematology. This isn't that old, either. Ten, twelve hours at the outside."

"And this just might be the cause."

The Indian officer slipped on transparent rubber gloves and moved to pick up a piece of granite about the size of a large paperweight; its serrated edge was covered with brown stains. Ben and Tommy bent forward to look.

"Must have caused one hell of a head wound judging from the hair caught along these edges." The airman indicated tufts of hair stuck to the rock.

"Shit." The colonel uttered the expletive under his breath, but Ben had heard.

"Sir?" The airman looked up.

"Nothing. Bag the evidence and give it priority." Was the look of disgust meant for Tommy? Ben couldn't tell.

Ben watched the man carefully slip the rock in a plastic bag, seal it and make notations on a tag fastened along the top. The wad of hair caught along the edge of the rock was thick and black. But the strands were short. From a man's head? It would seem that way. Brenda had long hair. That ruled her out as the victim, but could she have been the assailant? He was tempted to run his idea by Tommy but thought better of it.

"Looks like this could have belonged to whomever got clobbered." Tommy held a rolled up blanket caught with twine around the middle. "Bedroll."

"See if there's anything inside." Colonel Bertrand stepped up to hold one end of the bundle.

Tommy quickly undid the string and opened the blanket to reveal another tucked inside. The inner blanket was a Pendleton—old, much used, frayed around the edges but its pattern in golds and reds and blues was still bright. The outer blanket was cheap, a faded cotton, maybe acrylic, Ben guessed.

"Doesn't tell us much," Colonel Bertrand said.

"Only that there might have been another observer," Tommy said. "That's pretty important, I would think. Looks to me like someone was out here tending his flock and got clobbered. I'll be checking for another missing person."

Colonel Anderson shook his head and without saying anything turned to walk back toward the cars. The three of them watched him go.

"Look I don't want to make excuses for Hap's behavior, but he's not as callous as he comes off. He's been a leader of men for thirty years." Colonel Bertrand paused, "There was an incident, well, not exactly an incident that should have been blamed on Hap, but it was. He'll be transitioning out first of the year. It's hard on him—facing a new life. This investigation is important to him—important for him to have command of something. Try to help him out when you can and overlook his testiness."

Tommy didn't say anything, just offered a noncommittal shrug.

"Thanks for sharing the insight. We'll try not to be judgmental." Ben looked at Tommy but there were no reassurances, so he added, "I'm going to speak with Colonel Anderson. Meet you at the Bronco in five minutes."

Hap had almost reached the Buick when Ben caught up with him.

"Colonel, I—"

"Let me tell you a little something." The colonel turned to face him. "Last thing we need is a bunch of cry babies who think their lungs got scorched. I hope for all our sakes there weren't any observers. If there were, we'll do right by them, but that's what's wrong with our government today. A handout here, a handout there—I don't need to know your politics, but I'd like to think you agree with me."

Ben stiffened, "That's tough to do when the Navajo haven't sanctioned aerial maneuvers over the reservation. Any injuries happened to innocent people who shouldn't have been put in danger."

The colonel stared at him. Choosing his words? Wondering how far he could go? Ben couldn't tell. But the man could be a tyrant. It was tough to sympathize with him. Finally, the colonel turned away.

"At least, you can make eye contact. Someone said you're half Indian; you must have been raised on the white side."

Ben didn't answer. It wouldn't make any difference. The comment was meant to needle him, not gain information.

"Tommy and I are going to run by Brenda's house. I'll be back for the meeting at one thirty."

The colonel nodded, opened the back door of the Buick and sank back heavily against the seats. Suddenly, the window whirred down.

"One more thing, Dr. Pecos. You find any observers—anyone alive and able to talk—you call me first. Do you understand? The Air Force is in charge here. And I'm leading this show."

Ben didn't even turn around, just kept on walking. If some poor unsuspecting herder had been injured—let alone Brenda—his first inclination wouldn't be to ring up good ol' Hap.

"Let's get out of here." Tommy already had the Bronco's motor running when Ben climbed in. "The investigation is in good hands. Colonel Bertrand seems reasonable and willing to check every lead." There was no way that Ben was going to share his conversation with Colonel Anderson.

"He seems to know how to run an investigation."

"Yeah, too bad he's not in charge."

Ben left the window down. The "road" twisted and turned back on itself so that it seemed for every mile forward, they had gone two backward.

"This would really be a long way to walk."

"Too long." Tommy maneuvered the Bronco around a narrow turn in the riverbed. "That's why I didn't recognize old Elmo to start with. It just doesn't make sense that she'd abandon that truck."

"You know the family well?"

"Graduated Crownpoint High with Brenda's older brother. Her mom's pretty old now. It's good she's got help. Brenda's dad died about five years ago. But it's a long ways from nowhere to live with a baby. My sister's kid gets ear infections once a month. Seems like they're always in the emergency room."

Ben watched the bleak landscape roll past. Cholla cactus, chamisa, sage; not inhospitable, but you had to know how to make the land work for you. Brenda and her mother were isolated this far out. So many of the younger generation gravitated toward living in a community, shunned the isolation that had been an important part of their grandparent's lives. IHS had released statistics on the number of elderly that no longer had help with chopping wood or carrying water or transportation to a clinic. Thirty-three thousand old folks fending for themselves when just a few years back, family would have taken care of them. What did it say about Brenda? Was living out here necessity or preference?

"Start looking for a hogan over on your right. We've got to be close."

Tommy bounced the Bronco up the side of the arroyo and slowed once they were on level ground.

"Yeah. I was right. Haven't been here for years but there it is. Her mom's place and Brenda's trailer in back. I helped her brother put in the septic tank that summer."

As they neared, a Navajo man ran toward them.

"Any news?"

Tommy shook his head and slipped the Bronco alongside the hogan. The man looked so hopeful, Ben hated to see him disappointed.

"There's been no word," Tommy said quickly before Ben could comment, then introduced Brenda's brother, Sam. An elderly Indian woman stood in the doorway of the hogan with a toddler clinging to her long, blue velvet skirt. Sam turned and shook his head and the woman disappeared inside just as the toddler bolted on chubby unsteady legs toward her uncle.

"Ma-ma. Ma-ma." It was a gleeful cry and Sam quickly scooped her up, hugged her and smoothed the perfectly pressed pink dress with heart-shaped buttons.

"No ma-ma yet, Mariah. Can you say hello to our visitors?"

Small, round, black eyes studied Ben thoughtfully. The child was beautiful. Dark bangs dusted her forehead and strayed to the corner of her eye. She swiped the strands away with a tiny-balled fist, then abruptly twisted around and buried her head in her uncle's denim shirt.

"She's usually not this shy."

"There's been a lot of excitement."

Ben was about to turn away when he found himself staring at the end of Mariah's thick, shiny braid. The bow was plaid—the identical pink, yellow and turquoise material found tied to the piñon. If he'd wondered whether it had belonged to Brenda, now he had his answer.

SEVEN

"It's a sign."

"How can you know that?"

Tommy was pacing around the boxes stacked in the middle of Ben's living room. He'd planned to finish unpacking this weekend. But it looked like it wouldn't get done.

"I guess because I'd do the same thing. I'd leave some kind of message that would tell the world that I was still alive. It was obviously left where it could be easily found."

"But it doesn't necessarily mean that she's safe. How can you know that she didn't put the ribbon there and then go to help the pilot?"

"Because that makes no sense. It was found on the other side of the wreckage, quite a distance from her truck. Why would she go out of her way to tie a ribbon to the tree and then backtrack toward the plane? I'm willing to bet you that there's only one body discovered."

"So, where's Brenda?"

Tommy shrugged. "Something very real happened to her out there. She'd never leave that baby for one minute that she didn't have to."

"I agree. But there doesn't seem to be any plausible explanation."

"What if the plane was shot down?"

"That's crazy."

"What's so crazy about it? Think for a minute. Maybe she saw something she shouldn't have. And she's in hiding—or worse, what if she's been taken captive?"

"Come on, Tommy, we don't have proof. Give me a ride to the Tribal Offices. I need to be back by one twenty."

If Brenda was alive, she'd be happy that Tommy was looking for her, Ben mused. If, that is, she wanted to be found . . . what an odd thought. But one, Ben supposed, that had to be considered.

Ben hurried up the walk to the Tribal Offices. He'd parked next to a news van with a rotating satellite dish anchored to the roof. Must be a team out of Farmington. Maybe the same ones who shot the footage of the F-117A wreckage. He was a few minutes late, but it didn't look like it was going to matter. Some twenty people milled about outside the closed door of Ernie's office. Ben caught sight of Colonel Anderson and instantly gathered that the man was not a happy camper.

"Lunacy," the colonel hissed when Ben took a chair beside him in the hall. "The idiots are going on about a UFO sighting. Says they were eyewitnesses. Can you believe? They're saying that the plane was sabotaged by aliens."

"Do you have better information?" Ben asked but realized quickly that the colonel wasn't in a joking mood.

"Did you see that crap in the truck outside?"

Ben shook his head.

"Go take a look but hang onto your lunch."

That raised his curiosity a notch or two. Ben walked back

outside. A crowd had gathered at the back of a pickup parked next to the TV news van. The bed was enclosed by stock bars and something was covered by a tarp just inside the tailgate.

"I'm getting ready to charge a quarter for gawking." The man sitting on the tailgate appeared to own the truck.

"I think you'd get it," Ben said acknowledging the ten or so people around him. "Does this have something to do with the sighting last night?"

"See for yourself." The man pulled the tarp back and Ben understood why the colonel had warned him about his digestion.

The mound in front of him had once been a calf—until it was mutilated. The skin around the face was neatly cut away, so was one eye and an ear. The wounds were blood-less—just clean, precision-perfect incisions including those around the anus. The young bull's testicles were gone along with his tongue.

"Where did this happen?"

"Farmington area. Over by the Chaco Gas Plant. I run about two thousand head on a ranch over that way."

"Has this ever happened before?"

"Between you and me?"

Ben nodded.

"About ten times in the thirty years I've been ranching. And it's always the same, always happens on a night when someone sees lights or hears this giant whirring noise."

"Could predators do this?" Ben asked, already knowing the answer.

"Not likely. I know that's the story for the general pub-lic. But look for yourself. These cuts were done by someone who'd practiced. They're perfect—here, see that? And here." The man pointed first to the eye socket and then the rectum. "This here area is just cored out. These aliens would make hellish good veterinarians."

"Is there someplace you can report it?"

"Local Farm and Livestock Bureau and my insurance agent. But I don't want this to happen again. Now, you tell me, what can I do about that?"

Ben had no idea.

"How serious a crime is this?"

"Felony or misdemeanor depending on the animal's worth. Cutting or marking an already dead animal is considered vandalism."

"Vandalism?" Ben didn't think he heard correctly.

"Yeah. Can you beat that? It's treated as criminal trespass."

"I suppose this animal was valuable?"

"You only lose the best."

The man moved to pull the tarp back across the carcass.

"I don't know what good I'm doing over here but the news guys wanted to get some shots, broadcast from here if they can. I hear a fighter crashed out there somewhere. That's an awful lot of coincidence, if you ask me. People report strange lights, a plane goes down, my calf gets cut up—say, anyone on the reservation report any mutilations? This sort of thing seldom happens to a singleton."

"Not that I know of."

But I probably wouldn't know if it did, Ben thought. There was secrecy on the reservation. Something like mutilation wouldn't be broadcast. More likely it'd be chalked up to the *chindi* and life would go on after atonement had been made.

"You know when the meeting's going to be over?"

"It hasn't started yet." Ben paused, "I don't mean to be asking a hundred questions here, but what will you do with the carcass?"

"Put it in the freezer until I get something settled with the insurance."

"I wish you luck." That seemed lame, Ben thought as he turned to walk back inside. Couldn't he have said anything more cheerful or understanding?

"So what'd you think?" The colonel met him at the door.

"I suppose an alien theory is as good as any. The precision of the slaughter certainly raises questions."

"I didn't see anything out there that a good coyote couldn't do."

Ben looked up to see Ernie Old Talker motioning from the door to his office. The colonel followed Ben back inside.

"It's my understanding that we may be dealing with loss of life." Ernie motioned with his chin including Ben in the discussion.

"Let's not be hasty, Mr. Old Talker. I don't think we have anything conclusive, anything that pins anybody's death on the crash of the F-117A other than the pilot."

"Ben?"

"I think we should keep an open mind. At this time we know that Brenda Begay has disappeared and that someone, in all probability a Navajo man, was hit over the head near the crash site. However, we have no evidence that this person is also missing."

"What should be done about them?" Ernie motioned toward the door, a slight twitch of his lips to the left. He didn't need to give a name to the TV crew.

"I don't see the harm in an interview. Maybe, Dr. Pecos here could set them straight. The Air Force has already released a statement. There's nothing more for us to say at this time." The colonel sat back.

EIGHT

Tommy had promised the Begays that he'd return, sit awhile. He wasn't certain who would feel better—he suspected that he would be the one comforted. If he hadn't answered that call and the two of them had gone for coffee . . . it was no use beating himself up over it. He only swore to himself that he'd find her, make it up somehow. But what if . . . no, he couldn't even think that way.

Sam handed around cans of warm root beer. Tommy sat on the edge of a chrome plated kitchen chair. They had invited him to sit with them in Brenda's trailer since Mariah was taking a nap. He felt Brenda's presence—a vanilla scented candle on an end table, pictures from the elementary school, a dress hanging behind the door with the hem in pins. An elementary school picture of a young Brenda with short hair smiled out from the top of a bookcase. It seemed she'd just stepped away and he couldn't shake the sadness that settled over him.

If the trailer was shabby, it was also neat and clean and bespoke of care—the kind of compulsive thoughtfulness that made a home. Some women were good at that. Others? Well, he'd dated enough of the others. He concentrated on his root beer and tried not to think of what he thought could have been.

Mariah awoke and toddled into the room. The child was exceptional, Tommy thought, as she peeked out from her grandmother's skirt. Perfect features just losing their baby-roundness—she was truly a miniature of Brenda. It didn't take long before she had edged her way along the sofa to stand by Tommy.

"No ma-ma." The eyes that looked up into his were solemn beyond their years.

"Ma-ma will be back." Tommy fervently hoped that that wasn't a lie as Mariah climbed onto his lap.

Brenda's mother said something and Sam offered to take Mariah.

"She says if you don't want her climbing on you to just put her down."

Tommy smiled broadly. "It's fine, really." In times like these he wished he spoke Navajo. But he didn't even speak his own tribal language. His mother had been a rodeo groupie. She'd given him the last name of the bull rider she thought was his father and had raised him in a Pueblo some sixty miles from where they were sitting. He'd stopped worrying about his heritage years ago.

"Brenda likes kids." Brenda's younger brother, Tony, had pulled up a matching chrome and plastic kitchen chair to the edge of a circle made by two sofas and a recliner. None of the furniture was new and the recliner sported a wide swath of duck tape over one Naugahyde arm. "She can't wait until she's a teacher."

"She'll be a good one," Tommy added. "That's why it's so difficult to think that she just disappeared."

Everyone looked at the floor.

"She wouldn't leave Mariah," Sam offered. "I know that."

"But what could have happened?" There was an edge to Tony's voice.

Sam's shrug said nothing and everything. They think it's witchcraft, Tommy thought. No one offered anything and from that point on, the small talk seemed painful. They talked about Brenda's plans to teach. Her mother was very proud of that. And then conversation moved to Mariah when she squirmed down from Tommy's lap and disappeared into the narrow hall at the end of the cramped living room.

"I suppose I should be going," Tommy said finally. "It's probably getting close to Mariah's lunchtime." It was difficult to disguise his disappointment. Other than a nice chat, the visit hadn't produced one clue as to why Brenda might disappear—only a lot of reasons why she wouldn't.

"Da-da."

No one had paid attention to Mariah's return until she dropped an 8" x 11" gilt-framed picture on the floor at Tommy's feet and plopped down beside it.

"Is this your daddy?" Tommy squatted beside Mariah and watched her head bounce up and down.

"Da-da." A chubby finger pointed to a man in an Air Force uniform standing next to a fighter. He didn't need to look closely to see that the close-cropped haircut and striking features belonged to someone he knew—and might envy just a little. Almost too handsome—wasn't that what his mother had always said? Tall, light-skinned—wasn't his nickname, Mr. Hollywood?

"Ronnie Cachini." He hadn't meant to say the name out loud. He remembered when he'd heard that Brenda was pregnant and Ronnie was the father—almost four years ago—he'd wondered then about the two being together.

They seemed to have such different values. Ronnie had always been the daredevil and there had been lots of girl-friends—with broken hearts, Tommy supposed. But what about Brenda? If she kept a picture, was she still in love with him? Had she ever been? But Mariah seemed to attest to that. He stood and hoped the sick feeling in his stomach wouldn't spread.

"Has he been notified about Brenda's disappearance?" Tommy asked Sam.

"Doubtful. He doesn't come around much. I guess he was here one Christmas. But they're not married or any-thing. Anyway, he's stationed in Germany," Sam added.

"I see."

And there didn't seem to be anything more to say. Tommy picked up Mariah and hugged her and promised to come back. Then he said good-bye to Brenda's mother. He stood for a moment on the doorstep and looked at the packed sand front yard. Desolate. Wasn't that a good word for it? Ronnie Cachini would never live out here. But Tommy Spottedhorse would. And then it struck him maybe Brenda wanted to get away. He shuddered. His grandmother would say someone had just walked on his grave.

Forty-eight hours had never seemed like such a long time before. But like they taught you in school, the longer the elapsed time between crime and capture, the more diffi-cult it became to reach conclusions. Tommy had talked his supervisor, Leonard Tom, into letting him continue as investigator. Things were quiet and there was pressure to solve this one. Anything that happened this close to home involving human life took precedence over missing livestock or the occasional break-in.

There seemed to be such a lack of evidence, he couldn't help but think there was something right under his nose, something he'd missed—or maybe he just hadn't asked the right questions of the right people. And that included Colonel Hap Anderson and Colonel Bertrand. Tommy needed to "touch base" as they say. The colonel probably had the lab reports back by now. He bristled at having to talk with Colonel Anderson, but the man was in charge. In his own mind Tommy tied Brenda's disappearance with the crash of the F-117A. But did the colonel? Somehow he doubted it. The hair ribbon proved she was out there. Was the military trying to duck responsibility?

The question was should he call first or just show up? It was a long drive but Tommy didn't have anything else to do. He turned onto Interstate 40 and headed for Albuquerque.

Tommy noticed it immediately—the guarded, less than warm welcome even though the colonel said, "Call me Hap" as Tommy stepped into his office. He'd been the last person the man wanted to see. Tommy was sure of that. Civility was strained. And Colonel Bertrand was nowhere to be seen—Hap seemed to have accepted full responsibility of the investigation.

"I suppose you're interested in our progress to date as to probable cause of the crash."

Tommy nodded. The man was more into posturing, perching on the edge of the desk with a leg swinging free, periodically brushing fingers through his short curls than answering questions. There was a distinct scent of old testosterone in the room. And maybe he should put feelings aside and play along with the good old boy act, butter the guy up, show him he played for the same team—but he didn't. He hated this kind of man who probably abused his power and was compelled to act superior to others.

"Well, at this point it's too early to be definitive. I can say that only one body has been recovered—that of the pilot."

Tommy sighed. But hadn't he known that, felt that Brenda was alive?

"Was the pilot an experienced man?"

"Ten years in. An up-and-comer from what I'm told with a bright future serving his country."

"I'm sorry . . . ." And he was. Tommy felt for the family that would have to be told. Maybe a wife and children left without a father.

"Losing a man never gets easy. I don't care how much combat you see." The colonel paused, toying with a pencil. "We suspect that the crash was caused by pilot error. The man was testing state-of-the-art electronics, first time out, in fact, and it's possible that something went wrong—something that would have made the plane unmanageable."

"Any idea why he didn't eject?"

"First inclination of a good pilot is to save the aircraft if he can. There's every indication that the pilot felt he could land and do just that."

"The explosion occurred after he landed?"

"It would appear so."

"Is that normal? Maybe, that's not the right word."

"There's nothing normal about losing a pilot and craft in any situation."

Tommy chose to ignore the colonel's testiness. He changed the subject.

"Have you found the Navajo to be cooperative? Given that a member of the tribe has disappeared?"

"Yes." The colonel abruptly stood. "I feel like I'm wasting your time. I can guess why you're here. I'm afraid I can't be helpful with the Begay woman. But there's no reason to think her disappearance is in any way connected with the crash."

"I know that the hair-ribbon found at the site belonged to her—and the truck—those are two strong connections."

"There could be a hundred explanations—none linked to the crash."

"Coincidence seems pretty convincing." But it was useless talking to the colonel. The interview was over. Tommy stood. "Is there information on the F-117A? Some brochure, maybe? I want to get the facts right when I report to Mr. Old Talker." The colonel was trying his best to dismiss him. Tommy wasn't sure what he'd come for, but he knew he didn't have it.

"Yes, yes. Give me a moment." Colonel Anderson walked around the desk, pushed the intercom button and barked an order to someone at the other end. "Sgt. Farley will have a package for you on your way out. Now, is there anything else I can help you with?" The smile was back in place.

"What was the pilot's name?" Tommy had almost forgotten to ask.

The colonel quickly shuffled through a stack of papers.

"Just checking to see if next-of-kin have been notified. Yeah, we're clear on that. The pilot was an Arthur Ronald Cachini."

Tommy started, his thoughts tumbling over one another. Ronnie Cachini. Brenda and Ronnie. . . .

"Cachini sounds like an Indian name. I believe someone said that he's from New Mexico. Don't suppose you knew him?"

"Better than that. Ronnie Cachini is the father of Brenda Begay's child. Now, tell me that these investigations aren't related." Tommy was instantly sorry that he'd sounded so triumphant when he caught the hardness in the colonel's icy stare. He was a poor loser on top of everything else.

"What are you saying?"

"That Brenda Begay was romantically involved with this pilot at one time. I don't think they've been in touch recently but he's visited before. And he is the father of her child."

The colonel walked to the one window in the room and stood with his back to him. He was quiet for a long time.

"What's your read on all this?" he finally asked.

"I don't know really. But I'm not sure I believe in coincidence of this magnitude. There was no good reason for Brenda to be on that road if it can even be called that. Why would she take that way home if she didn't have a reason?"

"Are you saying that some kind of rendezvous was planned? A ten year man is going to crash-land an F-117A out in the middle of nowhere to see his girlfriend?" the colonel exploded.

Tommy realized how preposterous it sounded. And he realized how much he didn't want to believe it. But where was Brenda now? If there was a meeting planned—maybe he was only going to fly over low at a certain time—but instead she saw the crash, the death of Mariah's father—it would have been devastating. But why would she disappear?

"The crash could have been a mistake. Maybe he just wanted to say hello," Tommy suggested.

"Wiggle the wingtips of a forty-six million dollar fighter

just to impress some broad on the ground . . . risk his life and lose it?"

"That's not unheard of. There was an incident just a few years ago involving some guys mooning each other at—"

"I know about that incident," the colonel barked.

"Well?" My God, the man was snappish. "It proves that my theory could be correct."

"I really don't think so, Mr. Spottedhorse. And I don't want to hear about that theory on the news tonight. All the speculation stays in this room because it is just that. There's not one shred of evidence that what we're saying is even remotely true."

"Come up with something better."

"I don't believe that's my job. I am in charge of the investigation into the crash of an F-117A and the death of its pilot—no more, no less. I don't give a big rat's ass about your Brenda Begay, who just might have been obstructing Air Force testing that night."

"That's ludicrous."

"Think what you want. But I'm warning you to be careful. I don't want you to go back to the reservation and get everybody all riled up over nothing. We don't have any facts. If you want to stay investigating this case, I suggest you be circumspect—"

"Do I detect a threat?"

"Let's just call it a caution, and now if you'll excuse me."

Tommy let himself out, picked up the packet of material waiting at the desk outside the colonel's office and continued out into the parking lot. He'd struck a nerve. But Brenda had witnessed the death of the man she had loved or still did, he didn't know if it was past tense. What would that have done to her? Did she identify the body? And then what? Would she have harmed herself? There were too many missing pieces to the puzzle.

"Did Hap give you a hard time?" Colonel Bertrand was leaning against the Bronco. "Between you and me, I don't think he's following up every lead, you know what I mean? Just taking a scrape at the top of things—not digging for the real truth."

Tommy waited, almost uncomfortable under the colonel's stare.

"Listen, any chance you knew this Cachini fellow?"

"Vaguely. Mostly by reputation."

"What was his reputation?"

"I don't know, daredevil, ladies man." Tommy took a step toward the Bronco. He thought of telling him about Ronnie and Brenda but didn't. The colonel would find out soon enough, and Tommy needed to think, not spend time discussing Brenda Begay's love life with this man.

"Sounds like every other airman. Any feel for his politics?"

"No." What did that mean?

"Well, thanks. Better let you get going."

Tommy watched in the rearview as the colonel stared after him not moving until distance blurred his image.

NINE

Edwina Rosenberg slowed to the posted twenty miles an hour and rounded the last twist in the one-lane road before pulling into the Visitor's Center at Chaco Canyon. She'd come out this way almost twenty years ago and when the degree in anthropology was completed, she'd stayed. Moved her mother out from Chicago, bought a modest stucco and frame house in Farmington and was still here.

The jobs had been ones she'd dreamed about—sifting for potshards among the Anasazi ruins of Chaco Canyon, building a history of these ancient people one miniscule chunk at a time. It had been her life and when the research money dried up, she'd stayed on to conduct tours and work for the personnel at the park she'd helped to create.

She often came to work at the crack of dawn—that time of day when the sun pushed up over the east rim of the rock cliffs. It was her favorite time of day. She always knew she was watching something that these ancient peoples had watched and marveled at—the beauty as streaks of purple and rose and pink licked along the top of the canyon, then dipped down to touch the stone houses before stretching across the valley.

Summer or winter, she would get out of her car and stare. She often drove the arduous, slow-going washboard road into the ruins in near darkness just to see this spectacular sight.

There was never any doubt in her mind why the Anasazi chose this canyon for their home. Even the ruts that challenged the government four wheel drive vehicle never dampened her spirits. Mornings were special; her time to be close to antiquity and a God that she believed existed for all mankind. She loved her time alone with all the beauty around her. But this morning she was almost late. A fight with good old Mom about the sack full of books on the front seat had cheated her of any morning splendor.

She nosed into the parking spot with her initials on a white plaque—third one down from the path that led to the front door. Edwina brought the Bronco snuggly against the railroad tie boundary. She sat a minute gathering her thoughts, another day, another dollar as her mother would say. She sighed, gathered up her lunch and the argument-causing sack of new romance novels, slipped from behind the wheel and turned to lock the Bronco. There had been a time when she wouldn't have had to do that. She tucked her thermos under her arm and stuffed her lunch sack into the satchel purse slung over her shoulder then shifted the books to her free hand. She sorely missed not seeing the magic of the sunrise.

She turned forty in one month and knew in her heart of hearts that ice cream and cake with dear ol' Mom just wasn't going to cut it. She'd sent off for several cruise brochures before deciding on the Caribbean—all those islands with white beaches and shopping. She'd worked with a travel agency in Albuquerque and hidden the tickets when she got them.

She'd bought two after reading a book on visualization—picture what you want, prepare, and it will happen. So far the second ticket lying in her bureau drawer hadn't conjured up the companion she hoped for.

And what mom didn't know wouldn't hurt her. Edwina wasn't up to a lecture on being wasteful or worse yet—her mother would insist on going, too—just assume the second ticket was for her. That was decidedly not in Edwina's plan. A fling was more like it. One thousand dollars worth of a good time. If a companion hadn't materialized by the time she left, she'd just find someone on board. She'd heard that the ships hired escorts, at the very least, dance partners for women traveling alone.

And why not? She was prepared to absolutely haunt the ballroom. She'd taken a month's worth of tango lessons in Albuquerque last year. A warm spring spent one Saturday at a time with her sweaty cheek pressed against Gerald's. But he just wasn't her type—polyester shirt and cheap shoes split along the outside hinting at corns on the little toes. They'd had coffee a few times but the shoes bothered her. Surely the cruise ship would have a different caliber of men.

She set the sack of books down and stooped to pick up a candy wrapper beside the walk. Three feet from a receptacle and two feet from the front door and someone litters. She stepped quickly to the tightly covered can to the right of the front door, lifted the lid and held her breath. They were emptied once a week, every Friday, to be exact, so this one had another day.

"Ma'am?"

She whirled; the thermos flew out from under her arm and banged with a sickening thud against the side of the building. The man stepped from the shadows and blocked her path.

"Please, I didn't mean to scare you."

Edwina didn't trust her heart not to simply explode; it was beating so wildly. But for a strange moment she thought she had conjured this man. He was almost too good-looking to be real, six foot, muscles that pulled his Khaki tee-shirt flat across his chest and arms, baggy fatigues tucked into boot tops, short black hair, large dark eyes, tanned to perfection . . . this could be a beer commercial.

"Ma'am? I'd like to go inside."

"We're not open."

"I'm camping in the area and I'd like to use the facilities."

"At eight, come back at eight—that's when we open." Edwina clutched her purse in front of her and wondered at the breathy sound of her voice as her eyes traveled from his face to his chest, stopped at the canvas belt in his pants and darted back to his eyes.

"I'm sorry about the thermos." He picked it up and held it out giving it a shake. "Oh no, the liner shattered."

"Old, it was incredibly old." Why couldn't she think of something else to say? Something witty, entrancing. Then she made an executive decision. "Did you say that you just needed to . . . wash up?"

He nodded.

"Well, we open in twenty minutes anyway. Come on."

There were no facilities in the park. Water and wood were available only at the Center. A few scattered port-a-potties remained—most had just mysteriously disappeared—but no running water anywhere. Camper-trailers had to be self-contained. If he'd ridden a bike in, he'd be at a disadvantage. The park was just not user-friendly. Wasn't that the term used at the last manager's meeting? There were plans to improve . . . but that took money. She was always glad that year to year, she was still employed.

She was all business now and stooping to pick up the sack of books moved in front of him to the door.

"Let me take those." He lifted the sack from her arms with a smile that sent her stomach leaping for her throat.

"No, I can—"

"I insist."

Again, that smile. She had to turn away and finding her keys in the bottom of her purse, unlocked the front door, but he pulled it open and held it for her. Their arms touched and she shivered, then swallowed hard. She couldn't believe this was happening. She was alone with the most gorgeous man she'd ever seen.

"The restrooms are in back. Give me a minute to turn the lights on." She smiled at him then went behind the counter and pushed the buttons that brought the shelves of books and maps on the walls into bright focus.

"Thanks."

His smile stayed in his eyes, she noticed, before she watched him walk to the back around the vending machines to the restrooms. Those incredible eyes, and it dawned on her that she wasn't the least afraid to be alone with him. But a ranger would be along any minute. However, a lot could happen in a few minutes. Was she being stupid?

She hadn't moved from behind the counter when he came out.

"I'm afraid I need some change." He held out a twenty. "Thought I'd load up on some carbs as along as I'm here." He gestured toward the vending machine that held an assortment of packaged cookies, chips and nuts.

"Oh, sure. Just a minute."

Well, this could be it. What if he thought they kept cash on hand? Was this a ruse to rob her? He probably wouldn't have gone to the bathroom first. That's what her practical side said. She dug the cash box out of the drawer and gave him 5 one's, a five and a ten.

He handed her back the ten. "Could you spare another 10 ones?" A smile still played around his eyes.

She could, but how odd. He must be planning to make a meal from the machine.

As if he'd read her thoughts, he added, "Got a couple pals who are bottomless pits. Especially after hiking. Do you know of any good trails?"

"No. Well, yes. I guess I do. I better." She laughed self-consciously. She couldn't seem to get a handle on her nervousness. She forced herself to look away. "Let me get you one of the park's maps. At least then you'll know where you can go and where you can't." Edwina reached into a drawer and handed him a folded map of the area.

"Thanks." He tucked it into a pocket and moved to put the first dollar into the machine. Finally, after amassing a pile of brightly colored sacks and wrappers, he turned back. "You wouldn't happen to have a bag? I wasn't thinking how tough it'd be to carry all this stuff."

"You should have brought one of your buddies."

"Yeah. But getting them out of the sack at this hour is impossible."

"I'm not sure what's around here . . . oh wait, I always carry a tote." Edwina dug to the bottom of her purse. "Here. It's sturdier than it looks." She unfolded the mesh, straightening some of the knotted strings before handing it across the counter.

"This is great. I'll bring it back." He didn't seem in any

hurry to go, and she stood expectantly wondering what else he wanted. "I couldn't help notice that the pay phone's out of order. I really need to check in at home. My mother's sick and I promised I'd let her know when we got here. Is there any possibility that I could use the Center's phone? I'd gladly pay. It's only to Albuquerque."

Edwina felt—actually felt her heart melt. His mother ill and here he was out for a good time with friends but thinking of her all the time. What a dutiful son.

"Ma'am?"

"Oh." Edwina snapped back to the present. "Yes, use my phone in here." She held open the swinging gate that let him behind the desk and then proceeded toward the back. Was her office tidy? What had she left out? A quick surveillance of the room showed a neat, if sparse 10' x 10' space, its walls covered with maps. And one Fabio poster. Would he notice? For the first time ever, she wished the life-size chest and abs weren't gracing the north wall.

"Take your time." She discreetly backed out of the room once he was seated behind her desk, sitting in her chair, and closed the door. She knew she'd never think of her office in the same way again.

She toyed with trying to listen in. Instead, she just hovered by the door. She could hear that he did a lot of the talking. A couple times he had raised his voice. Must be trying to get his mother to do something—maybe she was like Edwina's mother who only went to a doctor as a last resort. She'd have to be on her deathbed to spend money on a diagnosis. They probably had lots in common.

The call seemed to be taking a long time. She began to worry about the other rangers coming in. That wouldn't be a good thing. She was almost ready to tap on the door when she heard him hang up. The end was so abrupt she hardly had time to rush to the front desk and appear busy.

"Is she all right?" Edwina hoped she didn't sound too breathless.

"Yeah. As right as she can be." He smiled. "Well, thanks again. Here's two dollars. Will that cover the call?"

"Yes. Uh, you really don't have to. We're allowed two personal calls a month out of the area. I haven't used mine." She waved off the two crisp ones he held out. It was a lie, of course. The government wanted you to be accountable for every penny spent—but she'd think of something. A call to Albuquerque wasn't too out of the ordinary. But you were required to report it.

"I insist."

"Well, OK." She plucked the bills from his fingers, very careful not to accidentally touch his hand. She was already having to control her breathing.

Then, that smile, and he was gone. She clutched the one dollar bills and berated herself for not asking him how long he would be in the area. Camping. He'd said that he was camping with friends. So, maybe he'd be back. Wouldn't he need to call his mother again and didn't he promise to return her tote? She had to see him again. What if he was a movie star? He looked exactly like that guy who did the run-away bus movie.

And when he came back, she'd be prepared. Tomorrow she'd wear the short sleeved, cerulean cashmere sweater and her tightest jeans. She could always change to her uniform later. And she'd get the gray out of her hair, pick up the dye on the way home . . . maybe some red highlights. She hugged herself and walked back to her office. His scent still lingered. A crisp citrus-clean smell just edged out by the aroma of good, honest body sweat. Edwina breathed in deeply and swiveled in her chair, the dollar bills pressed against her breast, staring at the Fabio poster, but not seeing.

When he knocked on the glass partition that ran along the side of the Center's front door, Edwina had already been behind the desk for a half-hour. She'd missed the sunrise but she'd had time to adjust and readjust the blue scarf that pulled her hair into a bun-like pouf at the neckline. And she'd thrown on a strand of pearls, the good ones that had belonged to her grandmother.

"Great sweater."

That was his only comment on the way to the bathroom, but Edwina clutched the counter to remain upright. His smile filled in all the blanks as to what he was really thinking. It was exactly like that time at the Fabio book signing when Fabio had looked up at her, one foot from her face, and said, "Your eyes are so incredible" in that melodious accent and instead of saying a simple "thank you"; she'd fainted.

She couldn't think of a thing to say as her mystery friend loaded up on food from the machines (corn chips seemed to be a real favorite), and then he was gone. He'd brought the tote back but she'd insisted that he continue to use it.

She acutely felt the void—like someone had punched the wind out of her—the minute the door slammed shut behind him. She walked to the back window and watched him lope out across the hiking path. Then he turned and waved. She was so embarrassed. He'd felt her stare. Did he think she was checking up on him? Making certain that he took the path designated for visitors? She waved back. Or was he so conceited that he'd known she'd check those tight glutes below that narrow waist? She didn't mind a man who knew he had what it took to be admired. And this man seemed so unassuming.

The third morning she brought sandwiches—ham and Swiss on rye, with mayo and mustard, four dills wrapped separately. She'd left the lettuce and tomatoes off. In the heat they could turn easily and go limp and brown. She'd toyed with making a side salad, tossing it with her orange-raspberry vinagerette dressing and packing it in a Tupperware container. But there was a chance she might not get the container back. And dear ol' Mom had every piece of Tupperware numbered. No, she didn't want to arouse suspicion. The less known the better. And not everyone liked salad so she'd stuck with the sandwiches and an economy package of corn chips.

"This is great. I can't believe you did this. Let me pay—"

"No. Don't be silly. I won't take it." She pushed his hand away that held a twenty and almost gasped at the contact of skin. She swayed slightly on her feet then thrust her hand out and said, "My name's Ed—Eddy."

"Eddy?" He took her hand and held it (overly long she thought) before letting go. "Like in Edward?"

"Edwina. My grandmother's name."

"Oh." And it wasn't until he'd turned to go that she realized he hadn't said his name.

"Wait. I don't know your name."

"What do you think my name would be?" He paused and nonchalantly leaned against the doorjamb. He was teasing, but she could go along.

"Something like Jacques or Ian or Sean. . . ."

"Yeah. Something like that. Let's go with Ian." Then he laughed and pushed through the heavy front door and was gone.

Ben Pecos had been able to work in Amos Manygoats right before noon. Amos was a reluctant patient, but his daughter had brought him in complaining of headaches and memory loss. The physicians had asked Ben to do a neurological work up—nothing in detail, but they wanted him to offer an opinion as to whether Amos's problems were physiological or mental. A barely scabbed-over crease across the crown of his head would seem to indicate the physical.

Amos's daughter stayed with him to interpret. Almost all of Ben's older clients needed help with the English language. It didn't do a lot for patient/therapist confidentiality but it was better than not reaching these people at all. Ben began with a few simple questions testing short term as well as long term memory. Everything seemed all right. He sat back.

"Do you know how your father got that head wound?"

"Some accident while he was out with the stock. I think he said a tree branch fell on him."

Plausible, Ben thought, but couldn't bring to mind any trees out on the mesa big enough to crash down that way and leave a gash. . . . Abruptly, Amos suffered a spasm of coughing that racked his thin body and left him wheezing and red in the face.

"How long has he had that cough?"

The daughter turned to her father, said something and got a shrug in return.

"I'm not sure," she interpreted. "I don't remember it, but I haven't been around for a couple weeks. He's had one bout with pneumonia but that was a couple years ago. I don't think his lungs have fully recovered. Anything out of the ordinary seems to bother him—dust, the pollen when we come to town. It could have just been the exhaust from my car."

Something was bothering Ben; he just couldn't quite bring it to the surface—

"Ask your Dad if he's lost his bedroll?"

"Bedroll?"

Ben nodded and knew even before the translation that Amos understood. The cut on the head, the cough, this was the man who was on the mesa that night. He must have seen the crash of the Stealth Fighter. Ben sat forward. Amos was twisting in his chair and looking at the floor. He's uncomfortable about something, Ben thought.

"He says he doesn't know." The daughter looked perplexed. "What's this about a bedroll?"

Ben explained, leaving out the possibility that her father might have been attacked.

"If he saw the death of that pilot, that explains a lot," she said but didn't offer what exactly. Ben waited. As modern as the daughter was, she still can't discuss the dead with ease, he thought.

"I'd like your father to stay in the hospital a couple days for observation. I don't want to alarm you but with a history of pulmonary problems—"

"He won't want to do that. That would leave my mother alone." She paused. "I guess I could take my mother back into Albuquerque with me . . . ." She turned to Amos and discussed the matter. Ben didn't think Amos would agree but the daughter turned back and said, "Two days, only."

"Great. I'll get him checked in." Ben reached for the phone.

"Ummm, Dr. Pecos? My father wants to know if anyone's come into the hospital who's—" She conferred with her father again before finishing, "gone blind."

"I don't understand."

"Well, this crazy thing happened. An old goat that my father's had for years was killed the other night. Someone skinned it in this strange way—pulled its skin away from the head and carved around the back end. It was just a mess. But the person also took meat from the goat's left side, the side with the goat's walleye. It's a superstition but my father believes that person will go blind."

Ben sat back. A goat was mutilated the same night that fifty miles away a young Hereford bull was sliced up? He wasn't certain what it meant but he couldn't ignore the coincidence. And he'd have to be careful with this information. It would only fuel the argument that UFOs were involved. All that was needed now was for someone to have seen an alien. He picked up the phone to make arrangements for Amos to be admitted.

He hadn't come on Sunday morning. Edwina put the sack of sandwiches in the fridge in the lunchroom. And brooded. She'd had her hopes up, even worn a new silk blouse and short khaki shorts with beaded belt that matched her earrings. Her mother had warned her not to bend over.

Where could he be? Her practical side said that no one had hired her as his tour agent and he could have very well gone home. She had no idea where home was, maybe Hollywood like she imagined. But she wasn't going to rest until she found out. After all, he still had her tote.

"Hey, Edweener, you want to pull some shit detail this morning?"

The man in the door was more or less her boss. At least, he had the seniority among those who were on duty today. He'd transferred in from someplace back east and let everybody know he considered this park a real step down.

"Such as?" She wasn't about ready to jump at latrine cleaning.

"We got some signage down up on the ridge. It's been awhile since anyone rode fences, so to speak. I need you to take the Jeep and do a perimeter shot, put things back in order. It'll take the better part of the day."

Yes. She almost yelled out loud. This was perfect. She could snoop, check the campground. . . .

"Sure, I'll go." She caught the keys he tossed her way in mid-air.

The Jeep whined up the first incline behind the Information Center in third gear. Edwina had chosen this shortcut to the top of the mesa because it overlooked the largest row of hand-chiseled stone houses and was closest to the campground—the one that she assumed he would use. Actually, for him to easily reach the Center every morning on foot, it was the only campground he could be at. The other one was some twenty-five miles away just this side of Nageezi. He wouldn't be there.

But calling this a campground was somewhat of a misnomer in that there were no amenities—like all the others in the area there was no running water or sewer system.

Twenty by twenty spaces had been crudely marked off, bordered by rocks, and park personnel had placed a half dozen signs and boxes containing park pamphlets—the dos and don'ts and what to see—at the entrance. Each space sported an iron-solid pedestal grill, a picnic table and a few sparse piñons that offered neither shade nor privacy.

But those who stopped there overnight never stayed long and drove those big cumbersome self-contained units anyway. So, the grills were seldom used. This wasn't the type of camp for someone to spend much time. And he had shown up at the Center three days in a row. For some crazy reason Edwina had imagined he was riding a motorcycle, something sleek and expensive—European, with tent and gear tied to the back. She'd gone to a Harley rally once and Ian just wasn't the sort—heavy leather, facial hair, bandanas, potbelly.

She pulled to a stop beside the row of info-dispensers to the right of the drive that would take her back to the camping spaces. She'd fill the empty slots first and look official— just in case anyone was watching. The boxes were hardly ever vandalized and one unit even asked that people put in a dollar before taking a brochure. She almost always found more money than the number of absent materials could account for. At least somewhere in the world people were honest and generous.

Exactly three motor homes loomed up in the campground. All had a little old, mom and pop look. Probably because all three, aimed with their rears her direction, had lace-trimmed flowered curtains covering back bay windows. Not his style. And he was too old to be traveling with his parents. She smiled remembering the ill mother who surely cherished her caring son.

But hadn't he said something about buddies? Maybe, she was looking for two or three bikes. She'd check anyway—just do her friendly Park Ranger duty and see if everyone was finding things all right . . . and ask a few questions.

Edwina pulled along side the unit closest to the road, got out and knocked on the door.

"You're wasting your time. Nobody's home."

Edwina shaded her eyes and looked over her shoulder. A teenaged girl slouched against a picnic table two spaces over.

"Do you know whose unit this is?"

"I don't know their names."

Edwina walked toward the girl and held out her hand. "I'm Ms. Rosenberg from the Information Center, just doing a little survey to determine level of usage for the campground this month."

The girl was waving one hand as if to dry the bubble gum pink polish that decorated each fingertip and ignored Edwina's offer of a handshake.

"This place sucks."

Edwina laughed. "The campground or the ruins?" She thought she knew before the girl answered. The girl was probably thirteen or fourteen, Edwina thought. Old enough to have noticed a truly striking man if he had camped nearby.

"Campground. The rest of it is pretty cool."

"Are you traveling with your parents?"

"Grandparents. Their idea of seeing America. I'm from Salt Lake City." The girl tipped a Clearasil-dotted face upwards. "They're gone, took the car into Crownpoint for groceries. You need them to fill out something?"

"No. Maybe, you can help me. I'm also trying to locate a man about thirty, dark short hair, tan, very muscular—he left his wallet at the Information Center." A tiny lie but the girl was already shaking her head.

"No one like that has been here. We pulled in day before yesterday, and we were the only people here until last night."

"You didn't notice anyone riding a motorcycle?"

"Nope."

"Thanks anyway." Edwina turned to go. "And the people in these two units?" She gestured toward the motor homes to her left.

"Ugh. Older than Grammy and Umpa. Believe me there hasn't been a hunk within a mile of this place."

Edwina waved from the Jeep but the teen had already turned back to the magazine in front of her and drying the nails of her other hand.

"Attention span the length of a sparrow's tail," Edwina muttered to herself, but she believed the girl was telling the truth. He hadn't been in the campground. She sat a minute. Now what? She had no plan past finding him here. She'd been so certain, the disappointment was painful. She eased the Jeep into gear and bounced onto the dirt trail that led out of the camp and back toward the rim of the canyon.

But it didn't make sense. There was nowhere else for him to be. Legally, that is. No one was allowed among the ruins. Most were closed even to walking tours. Pueblo Bonita at the north end, the largest and most intricate still welcomed the curious. But he had left the Center and hiked up the trail that would put him up here, where she was now, some five miles from that particular ruin.

And then it came to her. Why was she thinking that he'd necessarily play by the rules? Didn't the rangers have to roust half a dozen campers each summer from caves or dwellings in the cliffs that were strictly off-limits? She felt let down. But it was her own stupidity to assume he wouldn't be involved in anything against the law.

Now she had a real purpose to find him; it put a slight blemish on her feelings—she'd wanted him to be perfect. But this gave a thrill of adventure to it. Unless he was illegally excavating. That was a different story. Climbing around the cliffs, camping, that was one thing; but if he was involved in—she braked the Jeep and sat there hugging the steering wheel. It hadn't been that long since a group had been arrested for digging and attempting to carry off two mugs, almost whole, both excellent examples of the Chaco black on white period some thousand years earlier.

She needed to be thinking differently. If he was doing something he shouldn't, he wouldn't be doing it in plain sight. Think. Where would the most likely spot be? One that might yield treasure, shielded from view, somewhat difficult to reach but still within hiking distance of the Center? A place very few would know about. . . .

She pounded the heel of her hand against the steering wheel. She had it! Just the place and somewhat of a climb to get there, but the hollowed-out rooms high above the valley floor were entirely secluded with only a rickety wooden ladder as access. A ladder that should be kept hidden for ranger use—but also kept in good repair for just this type of emergency. She slammed the Jeep into gear, made a half turn and headed for the rim. She even knew the road to take that would keep the Jeep hidden from view until the last mile or so. And she'd hike that; didn't she keep in shape for just this sort of duty?

Dust from the trail would herald her coming but stopping a mile back, she would catch the beginning of a ravine that wound below the sheer cliffs. It'd take binoculars to zero in on her activity. But no one expected her, she reminded herself. On foot she'd stay to the shadows and in broad daylight she'd be difficult to spot. If anything, she wished the day wasn't quite so warm. Sweat collected between her breasts—the ones she was still paying for. Her mother would never let her forget what she considered "extreme folly". The silk blouse felt like a rumpled second skin absolutely glued to her underarms. So much for looking like a fashion plate.

She pulled the Jeep behind a granite outcropping, stepped out, flattened her body against the slanting eight-foot rock and inched her way to the top. There she scanned a hundred and eighty-degree section of horizon with her own pair of field glasses. There wasn't one thing out of place—no animal or human movement, smoke, vehicles, nothing.

She tucked the glasses into their pouch and slid back to the ground. She felt vaguely disappointed but reminded herself that smart poachers wouldn't run up a flag. She pulled two bottles of distilled water from a box in the back of the Jeep, tucked them into a backpack along with flashlight, hunting knife, twenty feet of rope, and first-aid kit. Ready. She slipped down the rocky incline to the floor of the ravine and staying to her right in the shadows of granite overhangs, started out.

Thank God there was no one to hear her huff and puff. Could she be so out of shape or was it just the ninety-seven degree heat? Surely lifting weights and hitting the treadmill every morning accounted for something. She paused to drink from one of the bottles of water and splashed a little on her face and neck. The blouse was ruined already, might as well be comfortable. High, dry heat could sap one's strength without warning.

Feeling refreshed, she started out again. Her path was dotted with wildflowers in reds and yellows and purples. Some seemingly growing right out of rock boulders. She might be enjoying the hike if she didn't dread what she was going to find. Even if he was gone, she knew she'd find evidence that would place him where he shouldn't have been. Then what would she do? How would she feel about having made sandwiches for a felon?

She cursed as her heavy-soled, ankle-top boots dislodged a shower of pea-sized gravel that skittered over the side of the path and fell some ten feet. The climb to the cliffs was up and around on a path often no more than ten inches wide. Some of the niches had been carved out by the Anasazi themselves. If she wasn't so preoccupied she would muse on the world of a thousand years ago. But not today. Her focus was clear and centered.

And she was getting close enough that she needed to be extra careful about noise. The caves were set back, some fifty feet from the path. At the top of her climb, there would be a rounded open space of about seventy-five feet in circumference. A place where cook fires had warmed the gathering of Anasazi and strategic planning had taken place. Well, that last was her addition but, at least, the communal fires had been documented.

She paused to listen. Something had caught her attention, a scraping sound overhead; but the noise was probably not human. Predators and prey roamed these cliffs, hawks and eagles searching out rodents. And the sound wasn't repeated. At the top of the path, she waited to catch her breath. Or so she'd like to believe. The truth was, now that she was so close, she was having second thoughts. It seemed ludicrous to charge up the ladder and apprehend the wrong-doers all by herself. Of course, she might not find anyone. Yet, she *was* a Park Ranger. This *was* her duty.

She took a deep breath, exhaled, and marched across the open area. The ladder was always on the ground tucked behind the clump of scrub oak at the base of the twenty-five foot rock wall. Leaving it upright would only tempt someone to explore. But it wasn't there. Regulations stated explicitly that it was to be kept close at hand but not in full view of park visitors.

Perplexed, she backed up and searched the face of the cliff. Then she saw it, off to the left almost hidden from view balanced against the wall but nestling in a crevice. She felt a mix of elation and anger. This, at least, was the first bit of evidence that confirmed her suspicions. Someone had been up here and moved the ladder.

The anger gave her resolve. She yanked the ladder from its perch, walked it to the more secure flat ground of the open area, leaned it against the rock wall, gave it a wiggle with both hands to seat it in the hard sand and started up.

Edwina was not much for heights. Not on ladders. She could walk the rim of a canyon and look out, down, around and not be bothered. But straight up some twenty-five feet on wobbly, narrow wooden steps—in need of tightening judging from the third rung—this just wasn't her sort of thing.

She paused, then gripped the rounded sides, closed her eyes and made it to the top before allowing herself to even take a breath. She leaned her elbows against the sandy edge of the natural platform and cupped a hand to shade her eyes. She couldn't see anything that looked out of place—certainly there was no welcoming committee waiting with open arms—that was a relief.

But she'd have to investigate; she'd come this far. Balancing on the top rung and not looking down, she crawled over the edge and stood in an alcove of rock the size of a large living room with a rounded opening at the back which led to a catacomb of smallish caves. She'd been here before many times and knew the treasures that had been carried out—legally and illegally.

She smoothed her sweaty hands against her shorts and plucked her blouse away from her body where sweat had glued it to her skin, and waited for her eyes to adjust to the dimness caused by a gigantic granite overhang. At least it blocked the sun. She felt coolness by way of a breeze rustle around her. Suddenly the hair on her arms stood upright. She'd distinctly heard a noise, footsteps scraping along the rock floor, coming from the narrow entrance to the cave on her right.

"Who's there?" she called out, and listened. Nothing. It must be the wind playing tricks. She tried to relax. Would she feel better if she were armed? She slipped her backpack off and knelt on the ground to fish the hunting knife out of a side pocket. There. That was better. The honed steel with bone handle felt good in her hand. But wouldn't she look a little ridiculous if her mystery man suddenly popped out of one of the caves? She'd have some explaining to do.

But then, so would he. She couldn't lose track of that. He'd trespassed. She was sure of it. The wad of cellophane wrappers weighted down by a nearby rock looked strangely familiar—especially the large empty bag of corn chips still in the bottom of her tote. She pulled it out from under the rock and clutched it to her. He'd been here. She didn't know whether to feel ecstatic that she'd tracked him, second-guessed him and found his hideout or bitterly disappointed that he wasn't what he seemed to be.

She moved toward the back. How long had he been up here? There was a hollowed out, shallow pit close to the front of the cave. Had he or they risked a cook fire? She leaned over to scoop up a handful of ashes and feel the rocks piled around the sides. Cold. If he'd built a fire, it hadn't been recent.

And now he was gone. Edwina felt emptiness and acute disappointment like a stab of pain. She'd probably never see him again. Wasn't that the story of her life? Another opportunity evaporated before she had a chance to make something of it. She sat down on a rock beside the firepit. She'd have to check the caves in back but there was no indication of wrongdoing, no telltale trails of dirt or freshly chipped rock that might indicate someone had been excavating. He was apparently just a camper who with friends thought it would be more interesting to spend a few nights with the memory of the Ancients. She couldn't really fault that. It wasn't like he'd committed a serious crime.

At first the sound registered on her brain as the growl of a bear. Edwina leaped to her feet, straightened and frantically peered into the near darkness of the cave. A wild animal. But how could that be up here? Predators at this height either flew in or crawled up the vertically straight cliff sides—lizards and such. She shifted the knife back to her right hand and gripped the handle. Her breathing was ragged, and she shivered as a breeze dried the sweat on her arms.

Then she saw it emerge from the shadows, lumbering toward her upright, arms outstretched, staggering under the weight of its bulbous head. Rooted to the spot, she opened her mouth to scream. Then it lunged, hands raking the front of her blouse, tearing the silk, popping buttons. She dodged, then scrambled backwards on all fours forgetful of the cliff's edge, aware only that she'd dropped the knife. Then she was slipping, grasping the rim waving her legs to find the ladder. Digging with her nails into the shifting sandy edge realizing she was going to fall unless she had help. Looking up she found her voice, but her screams bounced from boulder to boulder as a foot came down hard breaking every finger in her right hand killing the screams as she was tossed outward and down to crash against the rocks below.

TEN

"There is no such thing as a universal symbol for aliens." Ben didn't try to hide his frustration.

"Then what do you call it? What is this a picture of—this something that was so important—so terrifying that a dying woman drew it using her own blood? You can't tell me she just slipped off the edge, a Park Ranger with years of exposure? She'd been here before; she knew the dangers." Tommy was squatting beside a rock staring at the lopsided circle, short neck and slanted eyes that Edwina Rosenberg had sketched before dying.

Ben shook his head. He didn't have any answers. A Park Ranger found Edwina's body around five. Ben was at the hospital when the call came in for an ambulance. A routine call, a tragedy but nothing out of the ordinary—a ranger fell from some cliff dwellings and was killed in the line of duty. He volunteered to help them bring the body down. He'd met Tommy at the site.

"What do you think she was trying to communicate, if not give us some clue about what happened?"

Ben didn't have an answer. She'd struck her head on a rock. How could anyone assume she was lucid after that? That the sketch even had to mean something? Couldn't it just be the aberration of a confused mind suffering from a tremendous concussion?

"How did she fall?"

Tommy had turned to question the young tribal police-
man who was taking pictures of the rock with the drawing.
Ben had helped two rangers and an ambulance attendant
carry the body to the van equipped to save lives and transport the injured back to Crownpoint. Only there had been
no question about saving the woman. Estimates put her
death at sometime before noon.

"Hard to say. Looks like she just backed up and slipped
over the edge, tried to hang on but lost her grip and broke
her neck."

"I saw a ladder. Do you think she fell off?"

"Ummm, not exactly. I'm not an expert but a couple
things looked funny."

"Such as?"

"Judging by the bruising to the right hand—I asked one
of the attendants and he agreed with me—the hand had
been broken, not just the fingers, the bones of the hand had
been smashed."

"How could that have happened?" Navajos would say
she'd pointed at a rainbow, Tommy mused. But he didn't
believe that way.

The cop shrugged. "I guess to my way of thinking, it
don't rule out foul play."

"Someone crushed her hand? Maybe as she grasped the
edge about to go over? Then you're saying she was murdered?"

"Nothing conclusive. But it's something we gotta look
at." The young man paused. "There were buttons ripped
from the front of her blouse that couldn't have happened in
the fall."

"So you think she was struggling to get away from someone?"

"Looks like it. Someone surprised her while she was investigating up here and rushed her before she could reach the ladder safely. She had some kind of open-weave sack on her arm, like she was prepared to carry something away. And, we found this." The man held out a clear plastic bag that contained a hunting knife. "Don't know who it belongs to but if it's hers, she was frightened of something enough to want to be armed."

"What do you make of the drawing?" Ben asked.

The cop seemed hesitant. "Hard to say. I don't much believe in aliens. Maybe it's a mudhead."

"A kachina?" Now Ben's interest was piqued.

"Yeah. Only mudheads are supposed to bring good luck."

Not this one, Ben thought. A murder. On top of everything else. Cattle mutilations, a downed aircraft, death of a pilot, a disappearance, now a possible sighting and murder . . . this would play into the hands of those fanatics who had been ranting and raving about a cover-up—the government refusing to acknowledge a visit from cosmic neighbors. So far their rhetoric had garnered the front page of both the Farmington and Crownpoint papers. It was like having the *Enquirer* delivered to his door on a daily basis.

Tommy was pensive when he joined Ben to take another look at the strange drawing.

"Something terrible happened up here. I can feel it. This is the part of the job I hate."

Ben knew he didn't have to comment.

"Are you in any rush to get back?"

Ben shook his head. He had some filing to catch up on but it could wait.

"I want to go up to the cave and look around. Want to come with me?"

They were by themselves; the tribal police had left but the rangers would be back. They would conduct an investigation of their own. The park would be closed until further notice. Someone had marked off the scene with yellow tape, winding it around boulders and scrubby brush, but the meaning was clear—don't snoop beyond this marker. Of course, Tommy was part of the investigation and Ben was curious.

"Sure."

He steadied the ladder and Tommy climbed up ahead of him. The ladder felt secure when he followed him, maybe a wobble on the third rung, but it was in surprisingly good shape, only a little messy from having been dusted for prints. They stood a moment at the top letting their eyes adjust. It was cool up here in the shadows, pleasant even, if one didn't think about what had just happened, Ben thought.

"This is interesting." Tommy knelt by a bunch of wrappers stuffed under a large rock to the right of the entrance to the cave.

"How did that much litter get up here?"

"Good question. Someone sure had a thing for corn chips and ham sandwiches. This is almost fresh." Tommy held up a plastic bag with a piece of someone's lunch, being careful to hold the corner with a Kleenex and then put it back where he'd found it.

"Any history of aliens coming to earth for a little ham and Swiss on whole wheat, hold the mayo?"

Ben laughed and watched as Tommy continued to sort through the thirty-odd candy and chip wrappers.

"Looks like someone hit a vending machine. There's a small fortune here in empty bags. Where would the closest machines be?"

"The Information Center, probably," Ben guessed.

Tommy sat back on his heels. "Do you think this Edwina knew her assailant?"

"I don't think they were friends. She wouldn't condone camping in a restricted area. Her fellow rangers seemed to think she came up this way to chase away illegal campers. I guess it's a problem every year."

"I'm betting she knew who was up here. And I'd also put money on the fact that it was male."

"What gives you that idea?"

"Did you see the way she was dressed?"

"What about it?"

"Short shorts, silk shirt, a beaded belt that matched her earrings? You can't tell me those are Park Ranger staples."

Ben thought a moment. He'd viewed the body and didn't think a thing about the way she was dressed. Must be Tommy's training. "Well, it's a warm day, the shorts were a good choice."

"Trust me. That was a outfit worn to impress somebody. And not another woman. I'm going to take a look around the cave. Maybe there's evidence of this mystery man."

Tommy paused at the five foot high opening at the back of the flat area where they were standing, then disappeared into the darkness.

"Hey, take a look at this." Tommy played the flashlight above their heads and stopped on each petroglyph. Stick figures of antelope and deer being chased by men with spears raced in place across the walls.

"It's grand. Think of the work to leave this history."

"I don't see anything with a round head and slanted eyes," Ben said.

"I'm convinced that woman was trying to tell us who her killer was." Tommy walked forward and moved the stream of light to the floor, then around and up and down, into crevices, past, then back to illuminate yet another wad of candy wrappers. "Someone spent a couple days up here, maybe longer. And lived on Snickers and corn chips. Tough diet. Must have been kids."

"Hard to say."

Ben moved toward the back of the cave. Another fire pit proved to be cold, unused for some time. Sustenance, if it could be called that, seemed to have come from the packages. But there was no reason to conclude that kids were the ones who pushed the woman to her death or attacked her. Even teenagers hiding out from their parents wouldn't have had a reason to be that vicious.

But maybe he was being naive—hadn't he read recently that murder was rising rapidly among that age group?

"What do you think this is?" Ben leaned over to inspect something spotlighted by Tommy's flashlight.

"It's a short piece of hose, looks like some kind of flexible rubber. Something off a vacuum cleaner, I'd guess," Tommy said.

"Well, I don't think she cornered an Electrolux salesman up here."

Tommy laughed. "I don't think we can rule anything out. I've seen some amazing things junked out on the Rez. I've found false teeth, plastic limbs, enough furniture and appliances to fill a dozen houses—human beings just discard things, collect and throw away. But I've never understood how trash gets to such out of the way places, weird stuff like this. A person wouldn't take a vacuum camping."

Tommy dropped to all fours and peered into an adjoining cave at the back, half the size of the one that they were in, and empty. Two other small rock rooms had entryways too narrow to squeeze through.

"Only a child could get in there. They must have been used for storage." He took two loops with the flashlight over the ceiling and a cursory glance at the walls. "No decoration back here." He stood and joined Ben by the opening to the large cave.

Ben could sense Tommy's frustration.

"You know I halfheartedly expected to find evidence that Brenda had been here."

"Brenda? What gave you that idea?"

"Maybe wishful thinking. I guess it's pretty silly to even connect the two incidents at this point. But something about the pilot being Ronnie . . . her finding him dead that way, maybe she'd go away for a few days, mourn privately."

"Are there any Indian ceremonies that dictate that?"

"No. I know it's stupid. She wouldn't have left Mariah." Tommy switched off the flashlight and walked outside. "Let's go back to the Information Center. Someone must have seen something, someone maybe, who didn't belong around here."

The Center was closed and the Park Ranger who opened the door was reluctant to let them in until he saw Tommy's badge.

"I have a few questions concerning Ms. Rosenberg." The ranger led them back toward the wrap-around counter.

"Don't think I can be of much help."

"Could you tell me what she was like?" Tommy took

out a notebook from his shirt pocket.

"A little odd, stayed to herself—but she was a good worker."

"Did she have a family?"

"A mother over in Farmington. Controlling old lady. I think Edwina liked to get away as much as she could."

"Now, you don't know that for a fact." A heavy-set man came out of what looked to be an office to the right. "It's gonna be hard on her mom. Edweener was all she had."

"Do either of you have any idea what she was doing up at the caves?" Tommy asked.

"I asked her to ride the rim and check the signage," the large man answered. "We had some information posts down to the south. I don't know how she ended up where she did. She must have seen something."

"Had she had any visitors here? Someone she spent some extra time with recently?"

"Naw. Not Edweener. Now I'm not saying she wasn't personable, she was—and attractive. Had a body that wouldn't stop, once you got past that horsey face—if you'll pardon me. But she was kinda ditsy. Read that romance trash every chance she got. You know, the kind with some half-naked body builder on the cover. There's a stack of twenty or so of those books in the bottom drawer of her desk." He gestured over his shoulder.

The officer who had opened the door stepped forward. "There was something—maybe you should know about. Took place the last three days or so. Could be something, could be nothing but two mornings in a row I see this man leave the Center just as I'm making the turn to go into the parking lot in back. It was early, a little after six thirty both times. Edwina had obviously let him into the Center. When

I questioned her, she just said it was someone who wanted to use the facilities. Said he'd been camping up on the rim."

"So it wasn't someone you recognized?" Tommy asked.

"No. Never seen him before. And at that I didn't get a very good look—mostly from the back. When Joe here mentioned the hunks on the front of her books, well, it reminded me of the guy. He was built pretty good. He could have posed for those covers."

"And she didn't mention a name?"

"Not that I remember. She did start bringing in sandwiches, though. There's a bread wrapper full of ham and Swiss on whole wheat in the fridge right now, 'bout six to eight of 'em. I can't say I know who they're for, but she didn't offer them to us."

"She must have expected to see him today." Ben turned from examining the rack of literature on the wall by the door.

"Yeah. But with the sandwiches still here, he must not have shown up."

"Surely she would have taken them with her if she'd planned on meeting him," Tommy said.

"Whoever she did meet up with out there did her dirty. What happened to her was despicable—shouldn't have happened in a park like this. And I overheard one of the cops say it could have been kids. That really makes me sick."

Tommy nodded but he wasn't eager to discuss the kid theory. So she had supplied someone with sandwiches, ham and Swiss exactly like the one he found. Was there a rendezvous planned? He needed time to sort through everything. He consulted his notes. "What do you make of the drawing?"

Both men seemed reluctant to comment. Finally the

large one who seemed in charge offered, "Overactive imagination, I guess."

"Yeah, she read all the time. Not that she shirked her duties or anything, but when we weren't busy she'd have her nose buried in a book. Next to that romance stuff, she read a lot of science-fiction. I used to trade off sci-fi with her once in awhile."

"It's going to fuel the controversy about alien sightings, that's for sure. But I don't think it meant anything," the second ranger said, leaning against the counter. "I got a feeling that whoever did it is long gone. And they didn't go up in the sky in a little silver disk."

I'm inclined to agree, Tommy thought. "How long will the park be closed?"

"As long as the investigation takes. My guess is we'll open in three or four days. 'Course if there's anything else you might need, give us a whistle."

The road into the ruins was one extended ribbon of washboard relentlessly jarring and bouncing the car across the shallow ruts. Tommy held the Bronco to twenty-five miles an hour—top out considering the conditions—and chafed at the time it was taking to go a mere nineteen miles. Patience. Wasn't that the virtue he most needed to work on? He hadn't planned on coming back the very next morning, but he couldn't help but think there was some clue out here to Edwina's death. He'd go out to the site—take another look, if he ever got there.

The sudden burst of light flooding the canyon made him forget any inconvenience. Peach and gold tendrils pushed over the rim then snaked along the ground until everything was bathed in a surreal, orangish tint. Tommy stopped to absorb the magic, then following the blacktop, wound around until he was in the parking lot in front of the Information Center. He hadn't expected the Center to be open, but there were two cars in the lot and a vintage Pace Arrow in addition to the two government vehicles he'd noticed in back.

The ranger who opened the door seemed irritated and looked distinctly relieved to have company. He ushered Tommy in without explanation.

"Mr. Spottedhorse. Good to see you. Still hot on our alien story?"

"More or less," Tommy laughed. "Is this a good time to talk?"

"I hardly think so," a querulous voice boomed up over the bookshelf of park pamphlets. "I do believe that I was here first."

"This is Mrs. Rosenberg, Edwina's mother, she's picking up Edwina's personal things. And the Stouts here brought in their granddaughter—"

"Thank goodness! You're the police, aren't you?" A smallish woman with thinning gray hair pushed in front of Mrs. Rosenberg. "Marian Stout, Mandy, my granddaughter . . ." She put both hands on the shoulders of a teenaged girl who looked like she wanted to be anywhere but where she was. ". . . and my husband, George."

Tommy shook hands with George but it was Marian who was spokesperson.

"We're leaving today. A murder not 5 miles from where we were camped and Mandy being the last person that poor ranger talked with before she died. I'll be surprised if this child isn't psychologically scarred for life."

"Talked with Edwina?" Ms. Rosenburg's voice rose.

"When?" Tommy asked.

"Just before . . . before it happened. Your Edwina stopped by the campground. We were gone but she talked to Mandy. Mandy, tell them what she wanted."

"Uh, she was like looking for someone."

"Did she give a name?" Tommy took out his notebook.

"No. She described him as a hunk."

"Chasing after a man. In my day they came to you."

Tommy chose to ignore Edwina's mother.

"Can you remember exactly what she said? Her description of this man."

"Um, I think she said he was muscular and, oh yeah, he was riding a bike."

"Motorcycle?"

"Yeah."

"Did she say why she was looking for him?"

"We all know why she was chasing after him." Ms. Rosenberg's voice rose in a falsetto.

"Well, she was doing the guy a big favor—it wasn't like she was chasing anyone. It was just her doing a good deed."

"Such as?" Tommy was intrigued.

"She had his billfold. He'd left it at the Center and she was trying to return it."

"That's a new one on me. She never said a thing about a lost and found item." The ranger shook his head, then shrugged.

"Did she say where she was going when she left you?"

"No. She was driving a really cool jeep."

"Did she seem upset? Stressed?"

"No. Like I said she was just doing this guy a favor."

"And you're positive she didn't mention his name?"

"Yes."

"I really don't think Mandy can be of much help. I'll make sure she gets back in touch if she remembers anything else. We really must be going. I can't believe our vacation in this idyllic place was just ruined. Isn't there anywhere safe?"

Marian seemed to be directing this last to Tommy but the question seemed moot. He watched as they walked single-file to the door.

It was Edwina's mother who finally broke the silence.

"I don't believe for a minute that there was a lost billfold. Plain and simple she was out to meet him somewhere—probably at this campground and she got stood up and then she followed his tracks to the caves—followed her murderer, hunted him down only to be brutally. . . ." Sobbing, she covered her face with her hands.

"I don't think we can—"

"He killed her, didn't he?" Rose's head jerked upright.

"There's no proof—we don't even know—"

"Will you find him? Will you make him pay for what he did to my Edwina?" Finally, the sobs stopped any more questions.

"You know, you might want to talk with Edwina's mother for a bit. I'll be available later." With this the ranger disappeared behind the counter and walked rapidly toward the back. Ducking out when things got a little emotional. This smelled of a set up but it might be lucrative to see what the mother knew, Tommy decided.

The woman who now stood squarely in front of him fumbling with a damp handkerchief was short, barely five foot, and almost as round as she was tall. Myopia was corrected by thick lens in enormous, square tortoise shell frames. Years of squinting had pulled her head forward giving her neck a pronounced "S" curve. She was wearing a waist-less dress in shades of purple and pink with a pilled green V-neck sweater on top. Maybe that was what was called a "layered look". Tommy wasn't sure.

"Would you be able to answer some questions about your daughter—I don't want this to be upsetting—if there's a better time . . . ?"

"Not at all. This has to be done." She seemed to perk up and stuffed the handkerchief into a front pocket of her black handbag. "Had you ever met Edwina?" She peered up at him with red-rimmed eyes.

The voice was hopeful, but Tommy felt it could dissolve into a sob at a moment's notice.

"No."

"Then how do I know that you're committed to finding this murderer? I mean this isn't really civilization. Are you really a police officer?"

This wasn't going to be easy. But Tommy had to sympathize with her. Her loss was overwhelming.

"I'm the investigating officer from Crownpoint. I want answers just as much as you do. We need to make certain nothing like this happens again." He reached out and touched her on the shoulder, just a reassuring pat but it seemed to work.

Her face brightened. "Call me Rose. Do you think you can catch whoever is responsible for this?"

"I believe we will." That wasn't a lie.

Rose dabbed at her eyes and seemed to be considering whether she believed him.

"You seem like such a nice young man. I want to be helpful. Let's go back to Edwina's office. We can talk while

I pack her belongings." She pushed past Tommy and without permission walked behind the counter and moved toward the back. A faint scent of perm solution wafted up from tight silver-blue curls that cork-screwed across her head. The "do" was obviously fresh. His own mother had adopted this same look and renewed it every four months. Tommy could remember a time when Indian women, even older ones, had straight hair to their waists.

"This is so much better. Those rangers would have just boxed things up and left them at the door. But this was something I needed to do myself. Men. I'll never know how Edwina could stand to work with them. Present company excluded, of course." Rose closed the door and squeezed behind the desk to take what once was Edwina's chair.

"Are you married?"

"No."

"Prospects?"

"Uh, no." Snoopy woman.

"It's no crime, you know, not being married. Our society puts too much emphasis on it, if you ask me. I always told my daughter that if God wanted her to be married, he'd find someone." Rose paused to blow her nose. "Are you dating?"

"I, uh, yes, I am . . . I was, sort of." Tommy looked at his shoes.

"How nice. I always encouraged Edwina to look above her station. It's so different for women. There's no reason to marry someone that you might have to support someday. Do you know last year, I caught Edwina with her dance instructor? Horrible little man. I saw them together in the grocery store. I could have died. They were walking hand in hand through the produce. It was then that I knew she was getting desperate."

"Desperate?"

"You know, some women will grab at anything late in life. I've seen it a number of times. Older women seeing life fly by, marry the first idiot they can corner. Edwina would have been forty this year. And in a panic—not that she would have admitted it—but I saw all the signs."

"What signs were those?"

"Well, among others, she was beginning to lie to me."

"About what?"

"She hid things from me. I found a packet of promotional material, brochures featuring cruises to the Caribbean. But that's not all—I found the tickets, too." She sat back smugly, arms folded across ample breast. "Can you imagine? She was going to take a cruise."

"When was she leaving?"

"Next month."

"You said tickets. She wasn't going alone?"

"No. Now, isn't that just the height of deception? She had planned this getaway. . . ." Rose's chin began to quiver. "Here I was the last to know. It wasn't like my daughter to keep something like this a secret. She could have meant to surprise me—we were very close until lately. But I don't know. . . ." Rose pulled out three desk drawers before finding a tissue. "She wasn't herself." She blew her nose and dabbed at her eyes.

Tommy waited a moment and then gently prodded, "Do you know who might have been going with her?"

"I don't know for certain, but I think the man was beginning to meet her out here—at work."

"Why do you say that?"

"She was fixing picnic lunches—every day for three days—and starting to dress to catch attention. I almost kept her from wearing those short shorts that morning. I told her what Ann Landers always says—dress like your going to be in a car wreck—and to think she was found in them, like a common—" Rose left the sentence unfinished and burst into tears instead. "She didn't listen to me anymore. When I questioned her, she'd get this dreamy look and say she'd met the most handsome man in all the world. Can you believe that? 'The most handsome man' as if looks was everything. But this is the same woman who was voted president of the Fabio fan club in Albuquerque last year. She'd just gone crazy, I tell you. Hormonal desperation."

Tommy sat back. Tickets for a cruise, kept secret from her mother—

"Did she mention a name?"

"Called him Ian."

"Just Ian? No last name?"

"Not that I can remember."

Rose had pulled open a bottom drawer and was stacking paperbacks on top of the desk.

"Trash. She had her nose buried in one of these all the time. Wasted money buying them. I told her to go to the library, that's what the place is for. But no, she had to buy every new book that came along. Her room at home is full. And these pictures . . ." Rose pointed to a particularly lurid cover that between breechcloth and ripped bodice left little to the imagination. "Can you believe that a grown woman spent time on this nonsense?"

Tommy hoped he wouldn't have to answer. He was getting a picture of Edwina's life and it wasn't pleasant. The woman in front of him would be very difficult to live with.

"How's it going?" The older ranger stuck his head in the door. "You two like some refreshment?" He held out two sodas.

"No thanks. I'm just finishing up," Tommy said.

Rose pointed to a copy-paper box with lid. "I need two boxes this size and an orange soda."

"I'll take a look."

Tommy followed the ranger out the door, quietly closing it behind him.

"How'd you know I needed a break?" Tommy teased.

"Just part of ranger rescue. Wonderful old biddy, isn't she? Caused Edwina no end of grief, I can tell you that. It's my theory that Edwina never would have had a life of her own strapped to mom the way she was. She needed to get away—about twenty years sooner than she did."

Tommy agreed but didn't want to be sucked into trashing dear old mom so he changed the subject.

"You said you saw a man at the Information Center a couple mornings back. You weren't in the office when he talked with Edwina?"

"Naw. I just saw him leaving. See over there?" He leaned across Tommy and pointed out the window. "That trail leads right to the ridge. I got a good look at his backside from here when he was maybe twenty yards up the path."

"Describe him."

"Like I said. Good build. Not fat, just muscle and he was jogging right along in boots, no less. Short hair, real dark, now that I think of it; khaki tee-shirt, camouflage pants—"

"Camouflage? Are you sure? Like the guy was military?"

"Yep, just like some guy on maneuvers."

"There's been a lot of Air Force in the area the last few

days. But no one would have been camping up here. At least, I wouldn't think so."

"Too tough to drive from here to that crash site everyday. This is tough terrain. Don't know how well you know the area but if you need to go out to the caves again, it'd be best to take one of us with you."

Tommy thanked him. He had been planning to go back to the ruins. But he didn't know what he was going to do now. A military man. Would an airman working the crash need permission to camp in the area? He'd ask one of the colonels. There were probably twenty men who met the "hunk" description all investigating the downed plane. He'd see if any of them rode a bike.

He picked up two empty boxes and walked back to Rose. Less than a half hour later, Rose was ready to leave. There hadn't been a lot of mementos. Tommy helped carry a box of books to her car.

"Mr. Spottedhorse, I know it's out of your way . . ." Rose was using her best wheedling voice, and Tommy automatically braced himself. "But if you could just take the time to follow me home . . . I'd like to show you Edwina's scrapbook. In fact, it might be important to have a photo of her—for your investigation."

The last thing Tommy had planned on was a trip into Farmington, still, it would be thoughtful to help Rose unload all the boxes and a look at the scrapbook might be interesting. . . . And it'd give Tommy the chance to interview the TV news crew who first broke the story about aliens. . . .

"Yes. I have the time." Tommy smiled at Rose. She needed the company. Grief therapy. Not in his training but he felt sure Ben would approve.

The Rosenberg home was tiny. Freshly painted wood siding sparkled with blue trim. Across the front and around both sides towering Cosmos and Mexican Sunflowers—the last of the late summer bloomers—dwarfed it in greenery. And lining the short walk to the front door was a knee-high picket fence completing the cottage feel.

"Welcome to our humble abode. It's cramped—well, maybe, not anymore, and a lot to keep up." Rose burst into tears but quickly recovered. "I just don't know what I'll do. Maybe I should move back home. I can't think of one thing to keep me here now that Edwina's . . ." More snuffling, then, "Well, this isn't getting these books inside, is it?"

Tommy followed her up on the porch, put the box he was carrying down and made three trips to Rose's car for the rest.

"I've poured us some iced tea." Rose leaned out the screened door. "You can just leave those boxes there for the time being and come on in. The scrapbook's on the coffee table." The furniture was far too large for the room's size. A heavy walnut sideboard bumped against an imposing hutch that was squeezed against a wall and still jutted three feet into the room. A divan covered in yellow damask and stacked with needlepoint pillows pushed into the center of the room from the opposite end. The coffee table, a dark, glassed-top oblong completed the obstacle course. He'd hate to navigate the center of the room late at night. But the rug was good. Something Persian, Tommy guessed.

"Sugar?"

"No, thank you." Tommy accepted the glass of tea and accompanying coaster and placed both on the coffee table.

"Sun tea. Edwina always made it. Even at her office, she kept a fresh pitcher in the fridge. You know, hers was always better than mine. If she'd forget to put the jar out when she went to work, sometimes I'd do it. And mine always tasted different, so I asked her what she did. You know the secret? She'd fill the jar half full of ice cubes. Can you beat that? Waste all that ice just to get something that has to heat up anyway. But it cuts the acid."

"It's good." Small talk. And there was every indication that Rose was good at it, endlessly good. Tommy opened the scrapbook and saw a smiling baby and a much younger, prettier Rose. The petite woman wore slacks and a scarf over long dark curls. She held the child on one hip and squinted into the camera. The child had her arms around her mother's neck.

"The Grand Canyon. That was taken at the south rim. Our first trip out west when Edwina was only one and a half. I always said she got the bug to come back on that very trip. Do you think that's possible? That our path in life can be set that early?"

"I think that's possible. I've probably always known what I wanted to do and where I would live."

Tommy flipped to more recent photos. A distinctly horse-toothed woman emerged, dynamite body, abundant auburn hair but an overbite that kept her from being really attractive.

"She was going to be a dancer." Rose settled in an over-stuffed arm chair.

That explains the first twenty odd pages of Edwina with stiff little net circles around her waist, Tommy thought.

"It was her aunt who encouraged her to go to college, loaned her the money, even."

"Was this something that you and Mr. Rosenberg supported?"

"Oh, Mr. Rosenberg had been long gone by then. He left when Edwina was three. He was in sales. Not an easy life, lots of travel. Men can't resist temptation when they're away from home." Rose dabbed at her eyes. "It's been just us girls for some thirty-seven years."

Tommy finished the scrapbook. A feeling of melancholy, pervasive and inescapable filled the room. He picked up his glass of iced tea and absently twirled the ice cubes.

"She'd never been boy-crazy as a girl. She was really quite popular in high school. There was even one boy, Francis something or other, who got serious. But we all encouraged her to think of herself first, establish a career. There was no warning she'd fall for someone ten years younger when she was forty."

"Ten years younger? When did she tell you that?"

Rose's head jerked upright, her eyes, distorted by her glasses, registered the terror of a cornered animal. "Well, I, uh, she, uh, had a diary." Then defiantly, "Why shouldn't I look? It's a mother's right under the circumstances. It could have told me about who would do such a thing to my little girl."

Tommy felt the excitement rise. Was this the break he needed?

"Can you tell me more about what she wrote?"

Rose dissolved into tears. "She never told me anything any more. I found out everything by reading about it after she died. It's all here." Rose walked to the hutch and pulled a smallish leather bound book off the second shelf. "This Ian and the sandwiches and how handsome he was. . . ." She sat back down. "Here. Do you want to read it? I guess it would be all right . . . if it finds her killer. But there's really not much, just what I've told you."

Tommy leaned forward and took the red leatherette book, made supposedly private by a single heart-shaped clasp. The lock had been forced. Tommy couldn't believe that they still made dairies like this. His sisters had the same model in middle school.

"Could I get you something? More tea?" Rose repeatedly blotted her eyes.

"No, thank you."

"Take the diary out on the porch where the light's better. In case you hadn't noticed, she wrote in purple ink. Scented purple ink. Strains my eyes something terrible to read it—not to mention my nose."

Tommy carried the diary to the swing, a suspended wooden slat affair that dwarfed the front porch. The sun was high now sparkling off the pink and fuschia Cosmos, but he couldn't seem to shake the deadening mantle of foreboding that pushed down around him. There was a sadness that surrounded Edwina in life and death—a death before dreams had been realized, untimely and brutal. . . . Tommy held the diary a long time before he opened it.

The book was almost full and seemed to chronicle the past year starting exactly on January first. There had been a fight with her mother about spending money to have a nice dinner out. Her mother had insisted on having a "nice TV dinner at home" so Edwina had driven into Albuquerque and had dinner with friends.

There was an account of dancing lessons in the spring and a man named Gerald. This was the man her mother had seen her with no doubt. There had been half a dozen "dates" or, at least meetings. But aside from doing a mean tango, it was quickly apparent that Gerald was not a love interest.

There were countless pages on Fabio—bylaws for the fan club, dates of personal appearances, those close to New Mexico were highlighted in pink. There was a play-by-play report of Edwina's fainting at Fabio's feet at a book signing in San Antonio and how he rushed to scoop her up and carry her to a lounge staying with her until she'd regained consciousness. Now that was a little hard to believe. But, maybe not . . . . There was a list of "little gifts" that she'd sent him. Mostly goodies from New Mexico, a chili ristra, a piece of Indian pottery, a silver bracelet with his name in coral. There was no indication that she'd ever heard back, not even a thank you. But this hadn't seemed to stop her from boxing up something else and taking it to the post office. By August she'd sent six gifts.

Suddenly, the last twenty pages seemed upbeat. A man had shown up one morning at the Information Center . . . . *I have always trusted my instincts. This is it. I just know it. I see it in his eyes and the way that he looks at me. I cannot ignore the wanting. He must be ten years younger but age means nothing when people are in love. And it was love at first sight. I will never forget seeing him standing by the door—and so sweet, imploring me to let him use the facilities, truly sorry that my thermos had broken when I'd jumped in fright at seeing him there. And to think that his first thought was of his ailing mother. How sweet to call her. Yes, yes, yes he was in my office, sat at my desk—I believe the essence of him is still there. How can I ever forget that image of a son who interrupts his camping trip to see if his mother is well.*

When I close my eyes I see him—that strong jaw and

tanned complexion that makes him mysterious. Is his name Ian? He didn't say that it wasn't when I asked. He said it was as good as any. I dream of those dark brown eyes and black hair and that powerful chest. I'll ask him how long he's been a bodybuilder. A long time I guess—no one ever made a tee-shirt and camouflage look so good.

"Camouflage." Tommy muttered the word out loud. That clinched it. This was definitely the same man that the ranger had seen. He turned the page.

And that tatoo. What am I saying? I hate tatoos, they're always so cheap, but on Ian the little bird on bulging muscle gives him virility. Maybe there are others. I long to strip away his clothing—there was more in this vein, and Tommy absently wondered what Rose thought when she read it. But he was bothered by something, something he couldn't quite put a finger on. He continued to read. *His pals must be men—to go camping and not bring adequate provisions. He loved the sandwiches and chips. Corn chips are his favorite. I'll bring more tomorrow. I must see him tomorrow. I want to talk. Not at the office but sitting out in the open air— maybe under the stars. I must find out who he is. I couldn't bear it if he's married. But I feel that he isn't.*

Today he said to me "nice sweater". I felt his eyes on me even when I'd gone behind the desk to answer the phone. He's so shy. I feel I'm going to have to be the one to break the ice, invite him out somewhere. But where? I'll think on that. Maybe a movie in Farmington.

Tommy quickly scanned the remaining pages. Nothing new, just lots more in the same vein, then abruptly nothing. The blankness of the white pages seemed ominous. Could this dark, mysterious stranger be her killer? Edwina was infatuated, a first rate case of puppy love.

Tommy closed the diary and sat for a moment. Had Edwina been lured to her death by this man? But that didn't explain the drawing of an alien head. Still, their first meeting was the morning after the plane incident . . . which some swore was caused by aliens. How ridiculous. This Ian seemed very real and very normal. It was a shame that Ian was probably not his real name. There wasn't much to go on. Yet, the man had made a phone call. Perhaps not much, but a lead of sorts if there was a record of it.

"Do you want to take the diary with you?" Rose leaned out the door.

"Yes. I want to show it to the authorities."

"Oh no. No one else needs to read it, do they? I hate to have people see Edwina as such a fool. She was a good girl in so many ways." Fresh sniffling.

"But if this man was her murderer—"

"I suppose you know what's right. Do what you have to."

"Could I use your phone? I'd like to call the Information Center, see if there's a record of the phone call he made from Edwina's office."

"Help yourself. It's on the kitchen wall." Tommy followed Rose back into the house. He'd call the Center and then drop in on KOAT, Channel 7—the station whose photographers caught the wreckage of the plane. Should he call first? Probably wouldn't make any difference. There was bound to be someone there who knew something about the night of the crash.

ELEVEN

"Hi. Don't I know you from somewhere?" The man held the plate glass door open, then followed Tommy inside. It was obvious that he'd been leaving and changed his mind.

Tommy recognized the fortyish man as an on again, off again anchor for Albuquerque's six o'clock news. Some years back rumors hinted at a drinking problem and forced removal to the hinterlands.

"Bruce Bartholemew." He held out a hand.

"Tommy Spottedhorse. We met four years ago when I investigated a mutilation over by Window Rock."

"Yeah, I remember now. So, what's up? Looks like you're still in the game."

Tommy nodded and handed a card to the receptionist, then as an afterthought gave one to Bruce.

"I'm here to talk with someone about the alien sightings—the filming crew, if possible."

"You working that Chaco murder, maybe?"

Tommy smiled, "Maybe." Bruce was irritating and didn't seem eager to disappear.

The receptionist slipped her headset in place and pushed at numbers on the panel in front of her.

"Jerry's in. Let me buzz him. He was the reporter on the scene that night."

"You might just want to talk with me." Bruce bent from the waist in a mock bow. "Resident expert on cattle mutilations, at your service."

"If you really want to be helpful, you can show this man to Jerry's office. He says he has a few minutes." Clearly, the receptionist wasn't one of Bruce's biggest fans.

But Bruce acted as if he were man of the hour and with a little too much flourish, motioned for Tommy to precede him down a short hall.

"Hey, are you lucky, or what?" Bruce leaned in the door of the last office on the right.

The man behind the desk moved to shake Tommy's hand and ignored Bruce. Jerry was the kind of man who could make seersucker look mussed. But Tommy instantly liked him—ponytail and all.

"The Air Force has just released my original tape. Would you like to see it?"

Tommy nodded and took a chair opposite the VCR. This was better than he'd hoped for. He leaned forward as the camera panned open ground, then a 360 degree view of the horizon.

"You'd gone up in answer to a call about UFO's, if I remember correctly?" Tommy asked.

"More like twenty calls. On a scale of one to ten, I'd say they were about a twelve in intensity. We get calls on a somewhat regular basis. The area west and south of Farmington is a corridor for sightings—most popular spot in the U.S."

"Do you check out every sighting?"

Jerry shook his head, "Can't, too expensive. But September 14 was different."

"Jerry's claim to fame is going to be capturing a little

green man on film." Bruce slouched by the door. A little too prissy to venture into a room stacked with plastic boxes of tapes that hadn't been dusted in awhile? Could be, Tommy thought.

A flash on the screen caught Tommy's eye. "What's that?" Ricocheting balls of green and pink fire bounced across the horizon. Then, just as suddenly, all was dark again. "That's amazing. Were those things on the ground?" Tommy asked.

"My measurements say some fifty feet above ground." Jerry said.

"What could make that kind of light?"

"Looked like a bunch of extra large Roman candles to me," Bruce said.

Jerry rewound the tape and pushed play. Tommy thought he saw a burst of light . . . a flare? He leaned toward the screen. It was over so quickly, the lights didn't hang in the sky long enough to fully to illuminate the ground below. "There were two distinct sets of lights? The group and then a singleton?"

"Yes. Both seem to be some kind of flare. The first set shows five balls of light—three green, two pink. The second flash of light, as you saw, was red."

"Do you think the color is important?"

"Don't know."

"But you sound like you think the lights could have been some kind of signal?"

"That's my guess." Jerry switched off the tape. "Look at this." He moved to a desk as littered as the rest of the room and unrolled a topographical map. "If I place the flare at this quadrant and the bouncing lights here, the point in between would be here." Tommy noticed the spot already had a mark. "And this is more or less where we found the F-117A. It took us awhile. Twenty-two minutes to be exact. There was a fire in the cockpit and then a series of explosions. The plane was engulfed by the time we got close."

Jerry turned back to the VCR and after fast forwarding, slowed the tape at the first sign of billowing smoke. Tommy watched silently as the smoke cleared, then once again obscured the wreckage. He had him go back to the frames showing the boots sticking out from under a wingtip.

Tommy felt like he was stalling. But he just didn't want to believe that Brenda Begay had stood out there in the desert, watched a plane crash-land and then realized her fiancé was dead. What would he have done in the same situation? Did it make a case for someone going a little crazy and just disappearing?

Yet, Tommy had seen the signals on the tape. He wasn't certain about the first ones, but the second came from close to where Brenda's truck had been found. So, what did that mean? Did Brenda have anything to do with signaling the plane? But what if there had been a rendezvous planned and she had signaled the plane, then watched her loved one die? But hadn't they set up a date to go for coffee? Well, not exactly a date but time to be spent drinking coffee . . . talking. He remembered her eagerness. She'd already jumped into the Bronco when the call came. No, she was not connected with the downing of the Stealth. He wasn't letting feelings cloud his judgement—he had evidence.

Tommy wished with all his heart that Brenda was safe somewhere. And the tapes gave no clue as to what had happened to her. Had he hoped that he would see some hint—something only he would recognize? It was foolish to get his hopes up. He leaned back, hands clasped behind his head and rocked back to balance on two chair legs.

"So what do you think happened out there? Any ideas what might have happened to the woman who supposedly witnessed the crash?"

"Alien abduction?" Jerry sounded half serious. And as completely as Brenda had disappeared, it almost made sense.

"Are you a believer?" Bruce asked from the doorway. Tommy'd forgotten that he was still there.

"Believer?"

"In little green men?"

"I don't rule anything out. But these lights seem very man-made."

"If you want to follow up the alien angle, let me give you the name of a guy here in Farmington—retired air-traffic controller who's made a life of studying this kind of stuff. He's been working on this sighting. I've got his card in my office." Bruce seemed intent on monopolizing the conversation.

Tommy didn't particularly want to spend more time with Bruce but as long as he was being thorough. . . . He thanked Jerry for sharing the tape. He hated feeling like he'd reached a dead end.

"Say, did you see my feature on animal mutilation? 'Bout six months back?" Bruce followed him out the door to Jerry's office and into the hall. "It got the local Pulitzer and all that—uh, I'd like to share my research if you have a minute or two."

"Sure." Why not? Tommy had been a cop long enough to know the good stuff sometimes came from the most unlikely sources.

Bruce's office was barren in comparison to Jerry's.

Plaques dating some ten years past lined the walls next to promotional shots—publicity done when Bruce was much younger, Tommy thought. Then there was almost a grotto, a shelf holding nothing but a statue and pictures of Bruce accepting the statue. Tacked to the wall behind was an enlarged copy of the article which included another picture of Bruce only this time kneeling and cradling the head of a grotesquely mutilated calf.

"Great article. Best reporting I've done. But to get the recognition it deserved—well, that doesn't happen too often. I was lucky."

"Tell me about the mutilations on September 14."

"Be glad to. Excuse me a minute." Bruce pulled out the center drawer to his desk, grabbed something and then leaned his head back as he squirted drops in each eye. "Allergies. If I don't do this once an hour, I could go blind." A hurried laugh. "Well, maybe not blind, just permanent damage to the cornea." When he sat forward, Tommy could see the red rims and bright red blood vessels that stood out sharply against the white.

"You know more than one animal was found that night?"

"There was a goat on the reservation and a calf over this way—closer to Farmington, I think." Ben had informed him about Amos's loss.

"Right. Those two carcasses were found some fifty miles from one another but both done by the same hand, well, that is, by whatever they have. Hands with six fingers, isn't it?"

"You support the alien theory?"

"Absolutely. Here look at these." He slid a scrapbook across the desk. "Start in the middle. These are from the past two years. Cases from Colorado, New Mexico, and Utah.

Now, compare the photos. What you'll see is that they're identical. Not one calf or goat or lamb looks any different from the other. All have those telltale, laser-perfect wounds."

Tommy had to admit that every picture looked alike—cookie-cutter perfection. "When did the incident take place that won the award?"

"My journalism was recognized six months back, but I've been photographing, keeping a log—that sort of thing for some years now. I was awarded for my diligence, really—my composite of events over a couple years' time."

"Did you say you were already under a doctor's care?" Tommy watched as Bruce leaned back and applied pressure to both eyes with balled fists, then extended fingertips.

"Well, not exactly. Pharmacist thought it was allergies. It's just that the itching is so bad."

"You might want to see a doctor."

"Thanks, but let me decide that."

Testy. Must be because he's so uncomfortable, Tommy thought.

He turned back to the scrapbook. "Why do you think the cuts are so . . ." He struggled to find the right words.

"Sex-organ specific? That bothers a lot of people." He turned the scrapbook and leafed through several pages, then stopped, and shoved it back. "Here, for example. Best photo I have of the anal coring. It looks like that, doesn't it? Just like someone or something cored out that heifer like she was an apple."

Tommy felt uncomfortable. The coring concept was just a little too real for him. He turned the page.

"How many mutilations happen in a year?"

"About thirty-five nationwide in cattle-producing states.

Most ranchers don't report them, though—obvious reasons, of course, the average person is just reluctant to believe."

"So who does keep a record?"

"New Mexico Farm and Livestock Bureau and the National American Farm Bureau—but when a case is reported there's usually a good sized insurance payment involved."

"Like the bull calf killed Monday night?"

"Yeah. I hear that one was worth around a hundred thousand."

"And you feel certain that it was aliens?"

"Look at the facts—there's never any blood, no tracks leading to or from the carcass, other animals avoid the dead one like the plague, like they can sense something unnatural about it."

"Still, coyotes, raccoons, insects even—I read once of cuts by a coyote fooling a vet."

"But these are precision-perfect. We're not talking random bites or chew marks. Here, look at this." Bruce flipped through several pages of newspaper clippings. "This is the one that's impressive. I wasn't there to see it, but I interviewed the reporter."

Tommy found himself looking at what he decided was a lamb, horribly grotesque, and barely recognizable. An eye was missing, so was the rectal area but the area around her was different. There was some sort of pattern on the ground.

"Crop circle," Bruce informed him. "First time an animal and a circle have been found together. Colorado, two years ago, July fifth. You know that summer there were more than two dozen mutilations reported in New Mexico alone. But Colorado took the prize. Look at these precise edges—the exactness of the design—the size of it."

"Wasn't this sort of thing proven to be a hoax in England some time back?"

"Depends on who you believe." Tommy thought Bruce would have winked if his eyes weren't already so swollen. "Did you ever see pictures of those found in Corpus Christi? Seven, if I recall correctly. Nothing too big, maybe twenty to fifty feet each."

"That seems awfully small. Aren't those things supposed to cover a football field? And only be detected from the air?"

"Or a second story apartment. Point is we're talking precision again. Big or small it's the way they're laid out—the symmetry of them."

"Have you seen one?"

"Well, matter of fact, I have. A field this side of Roy, New Mexico. Wide open spaces—filled with that knee-high prairie grass all cut different lengths. It was spectacular."

"Was this recently? I don't remember reading about it."

"Three years back."

"Any message?"

"In the circle? No, just some sort of geometric figure. I suppose if we could read their writing, it'd say something. That's the problem with Ufology—at the moment, it's now open only to interpretation. No one really knows. The mystery is beyond our understanding."

Tommy just nodded. He was a skeptic but needed to keep an open mind. Aliens did not kill Edwina. That he knew.

"Listen, I'd like you to have a copy of my article." Bruce reached in a bottom drawer and handed him a copy of the front page of the Farmington Gazette. "You know, you're holding perseverance right there in your hand. I can't tell you how long I waited for that day to come."

"Thanks." Tommy noticed the autograph in the upper right hand corner. Everyone measures success differently. It was obvious that the award had been Bruce's shining hour.

"Look, let me call my pal for you. There's nothing about little green men that he doesn't know. If you're in luck, you can run by his house this morning."

With a lot of posturing, Bruce set up an interview for him, then handed Tommy the phone to get directions.

"Just don't forget who got you this lead," Bruce whispered as he gathered up eye drops and a box of tissue and left the room.

Bruce's lead turned out to be a perfectly normal-sounding man who told him how to find his house and said he welcomed the chance to talk with a cop. He was even on the porch as Tommy pulled up in front of the modest brick ranch-style.

Tommy started to explain his interest in their discussion but was waved off.

"Hey, anyone Bruce sends by has got to be okay. All right with you if we talk on the patio?"

Tommy followed the short, rotund man who had introduced himself as Nate Stevens around the side of the house. He favored one leg and leaned heavily on an aluminum cane. It wasn't quite eleven but the morning was warm. It would feel good to sit outside. The covered slab that ran along the back offered dappled shade. A glass-topped table held a stack of journals. Books, some propped open, littered the area around an overstuffed chair and spilled over to a matching ottoman. All seemed to be on aliens.

"Welcome to my open-air office. Can I get you something? Soda? Tea? Maybe, a brew? My mid-morning snack is a splash of Johnny Walker's, gotta say I recommend it."

"No, thanks."

"Well, excuse me just a minute to freshen this up. I miss having a wife do these little things for me." He picked up a tumbler and managing the cane in his left hand, went through a sliding glass door.

Tommy looked up at the wife comment—was he kidding? He doubted it. But he couldn't fault the guy when it came to literature on the subject of aliens—the assortment was impressive. He picked up the book closest to him and turned to the picture section. The Roswell Incident. A lot had changed since 1947 but not people's fervent dedication to naming the U.S. government as cover-up agent. He read the news release issued shortly after the object was found. "The many rumors regarding the flying disc became a reality yesterday when the Army Air Corp was fortunate enough to gain possession of a disc through the cooperation of one of the local ranchers." Then later that same day, the Army Air Corp officials called a news conference in Dallas and insisted the debris was remnants of a weather balloon equipped with a radar reflector.

"Gives one pause, doesn't it?" Nate said, reappearing at the door with a fresh drink. "Now we know that one of the Army generals who was supposed to have given newspaper reporters the straight scoop about the weather balloon wasn't even in the area. He was fishing in Port Aransas. So all those comments—swearing to the authenticity of the weather balloon don't hold a lot of water. Too much fraud. No reason to go to that extreme unless there was something that needed covered up." Nate dragged a white plastic lawn chair out from behind the stack of books, put his drink down, pivoted with the help of the cane, picked up another text and turned back. "The 37th Annual National UFO Conference was held in Corpus Christi last weekend, by the way."

"Do a lot of people go to those sorts of things?"

"Hasn't Roswell's economy boomed with their museums and alien fairs? Wait. Maybe I have the James Moseley article here."

He pushed himself forward then leaned over the table without getting up. "Gout. Flares up every now and then. I don't know whether the Johnny Walker helps or hinders—but I'm not going to find out by abstaining." He sat back heavily. "I'm a supporter, if that's your first question—supporter and MUFON member. That's Mutual UFO Network in case you're a neophyte. To be frank with you, I don't know of a controller who doesn't believe. It's just tough to get them to talk. Did Bruce tell you I'm working on a book?"

Tommy shook his head. "Is your focus on New Mexico?"

"No better place. This state's a regular hot spot."

"Do you believe that the park ranger actually saw an alien? Might have been accosted by one?" Tommy asked.

"Absolutely. It's about time we started getting evidence of encounters. They've been biding their time."

"But the attack was brutal. That doesn't sound like an alien to me."

Nate hurumphed. "You've seen E.T. too many times. Why do you assume that any 'visitor' from another planet must be friendly? You've stepped on ants, haven't you?"

"I beg your pardon?"

"By accident, not knowing your brute strength or just not being careful—you've taken lives. Or maybe as a child, on purpose. Ever turned the garden hose down a mound, or tossed in a lighted match?"

"I hardly think—"

"But surely you see the correlation? Why do we expect them to know what will and will not kill us?" He sipped his drink. "We've killed them. That's the evidence right there in your hand."

"Roswell?"

"Biggest coverup in the peace time history of this country."

"But why? What was there to lose by going public—telling the truth?"

"Because they killed him. And nothing says the little guy was killed right away. Who's to say he wasn't killed after we'd gotten the information we wanted?"

"Information?"

"Mr. Spottedhorse, hasn't it ever made you wonder how the world became computer-literate so quickly? By World War II we had the know-how but we were clumsy—big rooms full of tubes that overheated and worked only a fraction of the time they were supposed to. But we quickly left all that behind, didn't we?"

"We gained computer information from aliens?" Tommy tried not to sound incredulous.

"Aliens helped us overcome Sputnik in '57. Gave us the knowledge to launch our own satellites. Later, we were first with manned exploration."

"But why couldn't the aliens have helped the Russians in the same way?"

"Exactly. Now, you've hit upon the premise of my book. It's my contention that aliens—not necessarily from the same planet—have worked for years to stir things up on earth."

"But for what reason?"

"Maybe they have a bet on. Who's going to annihilate the other the quickest—get rid of the major players and move in themselves?" The question was punctuated with a roar of laughter.

"Mr. Stevens—"

"Nate, please. I don't expect you to believe. But keep an open mind. They're out there, trust me on that. Why, the city of Hakui, Japan has announced plans to build a UFO research center. The library alone will house over 10,000 documents. But it's not all cut and dried research. There are documented personal encounters. You remember *Communion*, don't you? The Whitley Strieber book, latter '80's? It's around here somewhere." He hobbled toward the table by the overstuffed chair. "Aha. Here, take a look."

Tommy's intake of air was audible. Edwina Rosenberg could have been the graphic artist for the cover, the bulbous head, slanted eyes—dark without a pupil. People seemed to see the same thing, the same creature.

"Exactly what that ranger saw," Nate offered as if reading his mind.

Tommy opened the cover, leafed through the first few pages, then stopped and read aloud. "I know how it feels and looks to be with these visitors. I know how they sound when they talk and what it looks and smells like in their places. I know how they act and how they appear. I may even know something about why they are here and what they want from us." Tommy closed the book and sat for a moment. Could it even be remotely possible that Brenda had been abducted?

"So? Is that a hoax?" Nate gestured toward the book, ice tinkling in his tumbler.

"I have to admit first hand encounters sound authentic. Unless they're on the cover of the *Enquirer*."

"Even then, we need to pay attention. You can't ignore what that ranger saw. I wished I could have seen it—the being or the drawing." He ruefully added. "You know, we're having a meeting of Skywatchers here this afternoon. You're welcome to attend. We're a local group about twenty strong—Bruce is a member."

"Thanks, but I need to be getting back."

He was running late. He'd spent far too much time listening to babble about mutilations and sightings. Tommy was sure that both Bruce and Nate meant well, but they seemed a little out of touch. Or was he the one refusing to believe what was right in front of him?

He wanted to run the diary by Ben. Maybe, he'd pick up on whether this Edwina was . . . was what? Sane? He wasn't sure anyone could really tell, that is, know the inside story. From what he'd read in the diary, her mother certainly seemed to cause her problems. He caught up with Ben at the hospital just before lunch.

"You up for some grease?" Ben asked. "It's Navajo taco day in the cafeteria."

"My favorite." Tommy grinned. The sloppy meat, beans, potatoes, lettuce and tomato on a puffy piece of fry bread was a treat. He'd watch the calories next week when he started to work out again. But then that's what he'd promised himself last week.

They found a quiet corner and Tommy handed Ben the diary. Ben read the first marked page about her meeting this "hunk" and then looked up. "You think maybe she wasn't okay?"

"That's your territory, pal. But, yes, I think she was okay. Love struck, forty, living with mom, desperate for companionship—but okay."

Ben removed the paperclip and leafed through the remaining ten or so pages. "She gives a pretty good description of the guy. He could be her murderer. Ian sounds a little foreign. But he certainly was the guy she was tracking when she died."

"I doubt if it's his real name. But he's for real. You read the part about him asking to use her phone?"

Ben flipped a couple pages, then paused and scanned the page in front of him. "Nice guy. He calls his mother while he's out camping with friends."

"I've asked the rangers at the Center to get a copy of the records. Something tells me knowing who received that call could make a difference."

"You don't think he called his mother?"

"You know, I'm going to be disappointed if he did."

"What are you going to do with it?"

"The diary? Keep it for now. Make a copy, then turn it over to the tribal police in a couple days."

Ben didn't say anything. The diary could be a major breakthrough—the phone call, the description of this Ian.

Tommy leaned over to take back the diary.

"I think your morning's been more fun than mine." Ben said.

"I think strange is more like it. I spent a lot of time looking at pictures of dead animals." Tommy filled both their ice tea glasses at a side counter, then sat down again. "Tell me more about this Amos Manygoats. Didn't you tell me he had an animal mutilated the night the plane went down?"

"He lost his prize goat. I've only seen him once since we admitted him. He has an upper respiratory infection—the naggy kind that doesn't respond quickly to antibiotics. We need to hold him a few more days but he may decide to leave sooner. There's no doubt in my mind that he was out there that night. He could have seen the plane crash."

"But he hasn't said anything about what happened to him?"

"It's not that easy. First, he speaks very little English, and second, he probably has an Indian explanation about what went on."

"Could I talk to him? Through an interpreter?"

"It would be difficult. The daughter will be there this afternoon. I suppose you could see if she'd help. I'll try to arrange it."

Tommy had one more stop to make before he came back to the hospital. He'd been meaning to question Brenda's fellow teachers at Crownpoint Elementary. Now might be a good time.

"Brenda? Take off without a word to anybody? No way." Pam Black paused to take a sip of her canned pop. "Brenda has been my teaching assistant since the term started. Granted, that's only been five weeks, but I feel I know her. We have daughters about the same age."

"Did she ever talk about Mariah's father?" Tommy leaned against the fence. Maybe he didn't want to hear the answer to that, but he had to ask. He'd caught Pam during recess and standing out on the hard, treeless, sand-packed playground, he had to shade his eyes to read the woman's expression through the fence.

"Not really, not a lot anyway. You know he was going to be stationed at Holloman. Brenda said he was supposed to be here in October—guess he came a little early. That crash was so awful. Do you think she witnessed his death?"

"There's a chance that she did. But she wouldn't have known who the pilot was until she saw the body, and I have a feeling that she tried to help."

"It gives me the creeps. What do you think she would have done?"

"Go away to mourn?" Tommy watched the woman bite her lower lip.

"I don't think so. Mariah's a handful for Brenda's mother by herself. Everyday at three-thirty, Brenda used to dash out of here like she'd been shot from the proverbial cannon—in a rush to get home. No, she would have never just gone away."

"I agree with you. But do you think she was still attached to this Ronnie?"

"Attached?" Pam gave him a quizzical look. "Head over heels in love would be more like it. He was young when they first dated. He didn't want to get married—had to see the world. From what she said, he seemed to be really ambitious. I think he'd talked about them getting together after he'd saved some money. I know he was generous when it came to Mariah. There was a check every month."

"The shock would have been terrible—"

"Brenda's too sensible to just lose it though, run away or something. I could trust her with anything. She had wonderful judgement when it came to kids. A natural, if you know what I mean."

"Do you think there had been some planned rendezvous?"

"I'd never thought of something like that. It does seem odd that he was out this way and she was on her way home at the same time, had left the highway even. . . ." Pam's voice trailed off and she finished the can of pop. "No. I think she would have said something. Or at least seemed preoccupied. I would have sensed her excitement. I don't know how to say this any better—Monday was just another day. The week started like any other. Things were hectic but there was nothing out of the ordinary."

"How could someone just disappear? Nothing about it makes sense." Tommy leaned into the fence intertwining his fingers in the chain link and resting the bill of his baseball cap against the wire mesh. The comment was more for himself.

"Unless you believe in aliens," Pam said.

"Do you?" He turned to face her, surprised that she would bring it up.

Pam laughed. "I'd like to. Wouldn't it be great if there was another world out there somewhere? Offering a better job market?"

"Only if the world was friendly. What happened to that Park Ranger was brutal."

"I guess it's been proved that that wasn't an accident? She didn't just trip and fall over the edge?"

"She was pushed." Tommy left out the details about Edwina's crushed hand. Pam could read about that in the paper.

The shrillness of the playground whistle cut through the air. "Oops, that's me. Got to herd everyone back inside. Sorry, I couldn't be of more help. If I think of anything, where can I reach you?"

Tommy scribbled his new number, the one with voice mail, on the back of a business card and offered it through the fence.

"Thanks."

Pam took the card and jogged toward the center of the playground. Tommy watched as the children lined up in two neat rows, the younger ones holding hands, a mass of multi-colored sweaters and print dresses interspersed with small sweatshirts and jeans. Dark braids and ponytails mixed with caps barely containing unruly thatches. After a head count and admonishments to walk quietly and not run, the lines snaked into the squat brick building and disappeared.

A dead end? Maybe. But he had learned that the romance between Brenda and Ronnie was alive—at least, on Brenda's part. That ache he felt in his mid-section was real enough. She was "head over heels" in love . . . wasn't that what Brenda's friend said?

But if he stopped thinking of himself, didn't that put more emphasis on what a shock it must have been to have found Ronnie . . . or maybe more emphasis on Brenda's being out there for a reason. Just how far would a woman go if she were head over heels in love? Tommy sat in the parking lot. It was already two and time he got back to the hospital.

Amos's daughter was in the waiting room. She wore jeans and sweatshirt but sat beside a Navajo woman decked out in all her finery, velvet skirt and blouse, squash blossom necklace, and turquoise earrings. Ben introduced the older woman as Pansy Manygoats, and the daughter as Mary, then after explaining what Tommy wanted, excused himself to go back to his patients.

"We're just waiting out here until my father finishes his afternoon snack. He complains if we're there and then he won't eat."

"I hope I won't be intruding. I didn't realize that your mother would be with you. I'll keep it short."

"I don't usually bring her, but she's acting so strangely today. I didn't think it would be a good thing to leave her alone."

Tommy nodded. The older woman sat passively staring into space. There was something not quite right about her demeanor. Her quietness, the vacant stare . . . Ben had shared with Tommy that the mother was having medical problems—problems that Ben thought might better respond to psychiatric treatment. But for whatever reason, she hadn't come to see him. Tommy was surprised that Ben had any patients—not that he wasn't good—it was just that a "head doc" was an oddity. Would Tommy go to him? He honestly didn't know.

"Do you think your father will mind answering some questions?"

"You never know." Then Mary laughed, "You're Indian, maybe he won't mind too much. He's really tough on the Anglo docs around here." Checking her watch, she added, "I guess we can see if he's finished now."

Amos was sitting up in bed munching on a cookie, the empty peel of a banana and a folded newspaper lay on a tray beside the bed. The white gauze wrapping around his head stood out in stark contrast to his deeply lined, dark, weather-beaten, skin. He looked truly out of place, lost in the blank whiteness of the hospital sheets. The daughter spoke to him in Navajo indicating Tommy with a turn of her chin. He seemed to ponder what she said, and then waved toward the three straight-backed chairs lined up under the window.

"He says to take a seat."

The daughter led the mother to one of the chairs and said something that seemed to soothe the woman while she helped her to sit. Then the daughter busied herself pulling the tray away from the bed. She put the newspaper on the chair between Tommy and her mother and turned back to her father. Again, she said something to him in Navajo. Encouraging him to speak, Tommy thought.

Abruptly, Amos burst out in a long tirade in Navajo waving his arms, and his eyes carefully directed away from Tommy. Tommy sat quietly giving deference to an elder.

"He wants to know if you've come about his goat?"

"Well, sort of. I'd like to know everything he remembers about that night."

The daughter turned to translate, but Tommy could see the set of Amos's jaw. He had a sinking feeling that he might not get very far. If he wasn't there to offer restitution, Amos didn't seem interested.

"He says there isn't much to tell. He was following the Thunderbird and a branch fell on his head and that's all he remembers."

"The Thunderbird?" This was something new, Tommy thought.

"Personally, I think he saw the Stealth Fighter that crashed. Only he's attributed a mythical presence to it. He's probably telling the truth."

Tommy debated whether or not to share that the wound had been caused by a rock—wielded by a very unmythical person, no doubt. But he didn't need to make that decision because suddenly Pansy yelled out a loud "Hey" and Tommy and Mary both jumped.

"Mother, what's wrong?" Mary was so startled that she spoke to her mother in English.

Pansy had unfolded the paper and held it flattened across her chest, her chin resting above the headline. There under the masthead was an 8" x 11" photo of the head—the alien symbol drawn on the rock with Edwina Rosenberg's blood. Tommy hadn't seen the morning paper—in this case, the *Albuquerque Journal*, no less, and the enlarged photo was a shock. And, of course, the headlines were an inch high. PROOF OF ALIEN VISITOR? It sold papers—if that was ever an excuse for sensationalism.

Mary knelt beside her mother now and tried to quiet her, but the older woman remained agitated and insisted on talking. Finally, the daughter sighed and turned back to Tommy.

"My mother hasn't been well lately. I don't know what this means but she says that she saw this thing." The daughter pointed to the image on the front page.

"When?" Tommy sat forward. Saw it? How much of this was dementia and how much reality?

"That night. When the plane crashed, and my father got injured and the goat was killed."

"Can she tell us exactly what she saw?"

Mary spoke quietly, smoothed her mother's skirt, listened, and then sat there a moment before turning to Tommy. All the while Pansy clutched the paper and traced the dome-shaped head of the creature with her finger, back and forth, from one side to the other.

"I don't know what to make of this. It doesn't make

sense at all." She sighed. "My mother swears that she saw this, this alien at the crash site. He abducted a girl, an Indian girl, just ran off with her slung over his shoulder."

"What?" Tommy was on his feet. "Ask her again. Ask her to repeat what she saw."

"I don't know if what she says is true. It could be her imagination."

"I think she might be telling the truth."

Mary leaned towards her mother and spoke in a low voice. It took some coaxing, but once again the elderly woman pointed to the newspaper picture, gestured behind her and spoke haltingly in Navajo.

"She insists that's what she saw. Does this mean something? Do you know who she's talking about?"

"I think so." Tommy didn't trust himself to say more. A sense of foreboding made him feel sick. Had Brenda been injured? Was she already dead when someone carried her away from the crash site? No, he couldn't believe that—wouldn't allow himself to believe it. But why would she stay hidden? Or, why would her abductors hide her? What had she seen that night? Did she find the pilot dead or watch him be killed? Couldn't that be it? She was a witness to Ronnie Cachini's death? He didn't believe the abductor was an alien but he did believe that Brenda was probably expendable.

Tommy took a deep breath and asked Mary to see if Amos had seen the same thing. He hadn't, and Tommy believed him. His information seemed restricted to Thunderbirds, concussions, and goat-skinnings, not aliens. The mother had little else to say. She had gone out to pen the stock and had followed a great black bird but when she found it, the bird was in flames and this creature—maybe its spirit—was running across the arroyo carrying a woman away from the wreckage.

"Did she see where it went?"

Mary turned to Pansy and repeated the question, but Tommy could tell immediately that she hadn't seen much else.

"The thing just took off. It was running and disappeared in the dark."

"Did she see the thing attack the woman he was carrying?" Tommy almost held his breath until she answered.

"No."

"How did she know for certain that it was a woman?"

Mary asked her mother and listened to a rather long answer before sharing with Tommy.

"She says she found a hair ribbon. She saw it fall out of the pocket of the one being carried."

"Ask her what she did with the ribbon." But Tommy thought he already knew the answer. And he was right. Pansy tied the ribbon to a piñon branch in a large bow on her way back home.

There was no evidence that Brenda was alive, but there was no evidence that she wasn't. He believed she had been abducted but what should he do with his theory backed only by the sightings of an elderly woman in poor health? He needed to talk with Ben. Should Pansy be questioned? How sound was her reasoning? Ben's office door was shut, so, Tommy left a note telling Ben he was in the cafeteria.

"Hey, no chili fries?" Ben sat down beside him. "Did that diet you're always talking about start today?"

Tommy didn't acknowledge Ben's teasing but told him what Pansy had seen.

When he'd finished, Ben shook his head. "I'm sorry, Tommy. But I wonder how much credence we should put in Pansy's observation."

"I guess that's what I want to find out from you."

"I haven't examined her, but this alien thing bothers me."

They were sitting at a table in the corner. Mid-afternoon seemed a popular break time. The room was half full.

"Well, Edwina's no longer alone. We have two people who saw an alien."

"Are you trying to say you believe—"

"No," Tommy interrupted. "Whatever abducted Brenda wasn't alien but why keep her? What could she have seen? It had to have something to do with the pilot's death. I'm reluctant to share Pansy's sightings with the Air Force. She's obviously not all there—"

"Is that a clinical term?" Ben waited for Tommy to laugh.

"Hey, I'm kidding," Ben rushed to add, "I agree with you. Pansy appears to be disturbed and any hassle—even questioning by those investigating the crash might be too stressful."

"But am I doing the right thing? Could the information help find Brenda? Help the military find out what happened out there?"

Ben reached out and reassuringly patted Tommy's shoulder.

"I know this isn't easy. I wish I could be more helpful about Pansy."

"Can I have your attention?" A short round woman with heavy black hair threatening to burst the confines of the mandatory hairnet worn by kitchen help stood at the front of the cafeteria. She banged a large metal ladle against the bottom of a pan. The improvised tympanum did the trick. Slowly the room quieted and thirty some hospital workers turned her way.

"My cousin from Shiprock wants to say something." The woman from the kitchen stepped back and gave center stage to another woman, this one young with short-cropped, black hair that swung freely around her ears. She was neatly dressed in a navy suit, white blouse and low heels.

"Oh yeah, I forgot, my cousin's a lawyer." The older woman added, then sat back down at the corner of a nearby table.

"Well, thanks . . ." The young woman acknowledged her relative and seemed a little nervous, snapped open a briefcase that rested on a table beside her and drew out a long, multi-paged document. "I guess my being a lawyer doesn't have a lot to do with why I'm here. That is, it's not the first reason—I come as a community supporter seeking justice to an old problem for people who live in this area. As a lawyer I'm donating my services to get something done."

She waved the papers in her right hand. "This is a petition—a petition to change U.S. Route 666 to a less diabolical number and put an end to the strange happenings in this area that continue to plague us."

Chairs scraped against linoleum as the audience shifted to talk with one another.

"I think now is the time to take action. This matter has been brought before the American State Highway Transportation Officials before. Let's see, the first time was in 1964." The woman referred to her notes. "Yes, and three times after that but to no avail." Suddenly the woman hopped up onto one of the cafeteria's foldout chairs, teetered a moment, got her balance and continued. "In the Bible's Book of Revelations, 666 is the sign of the beast, the Devil. Anyone or anything portraying his sign belongs to the dark side and can expect trouble."

"You think Brenda's disappearance has something to do with this number thing?" a questioner called out from the back of the room.

"I do. There's no doubt. She left Gallup on that very highway before she cut over through Coyote Canyon. And now the death of the Park Ranger and that pilot . . . this area is tainted as long as we have the sign of Hell among us."

Louder murmuring from the audience seemed to stop the speaker but she started again speaking above the noise. "This petition will be presented to transportation officials from three states—New Mexico, Utah and Colorado—at their regional meeting one month from today. Your signature counts. Add your vote to the two hundred and ten people who agree that this must be done." The woman again waved the papers above her head this time. "Don't be left out. Make sure your voice is heard. This is not an easy fight. There are those who say the cost will be too much to change the signage along the 198 mile highway, maps in books, and addresses—things like that; but I ask you, isn't human life worth something? This highway has claimed the lives of too many of our people. Now is the time to act."

She hopped back down off the chair amid enthusiastic applause. Half the room, it seemed to Tommy, stood to push toward the speaker. Including Ben.

"Where are you going?"

"I don't want to miss out on a chance like this." He grinned.

"You're going to sign?" Tommy couldn't believe it. This was a man who disavowed any belief in aliens, yet at the mention of the devil pushes his way to the front of the room? "Are you kidding?"

Ben sat back down. "You called my bluff. But, honestly? It's probably not a bad idea. If people believe something is harmful, it usually is. And I haven't heard any better ideas as to why all this has happened. Why not let people believe they're being helpful?"

Actually, before he left, Tommy added his name to the petition. Even with a sharp Navajo lawyer on their side, it was doubtful that the people would get anything done. In this case the price of exorcism would cost three states dearly. And there were too many people who considered the fear of a number foolish. Just one more stupidity to pin on the tax-payer and make him pay for.

Tommy was restless. He had new information that sup-ported his belief that Brenda had been abducted and he couldn't use it. But there was more . . . something he couldn't put a finger on. What was he missing? He stopped by his apartment to check the mail and his answering machine. He could count on one hand the number of times he'd had messages. But still . . . it didn't hurt to hope. Maybe Brenda tried to reach him. . . . Should he try to stop thinking that she was alive? Was he just setting himself up for the unbear-able grief he'd feel if a body was found?

He got a soda from the fridge. One six pack of cream soda, a rounded wedge of yellow cheese, jar of salsa—extra hot, and a carton of eggs that might be as old as he was. In the door there was a tube of horse-wormer. He banged the door closed with his heel.

The apartment was really one side of a duplex and posh by Crownpoint standards. There were three rooms but each lacked enough furniture to make it look anything other than a transitory setting. He didn't have a bed yet and was making do with a large sofa. So the bedroom was empty other than for boxes. All those things in life that he felt he couldn't do without—trophies from athletic events long forgotten, ribbons from 4-H projects—the animals long dead, cleaning equipment, coat hangers, pots and pans, year books—he shut the bedroom door.

The cream soda had sweated a ring on the coffee table. He wiped it off and then sat down on the sofa. This wasn't home. It never would be. He'd moved himself and Harley into town knowing that. Even Harley acted like he'd rather be someplace else. Any thoughts of that big old paint horse brought a smile. His sister liked to call him his "next of kin". Well, that wasn't too far from wrong.

It had been two days before his sixteenth birthday when his Mom met him at school. He'd thought someone had died. She never would come to the high school if it wasn't important.

"I want you to come home with me," she'd said. At first that was all she'd say. He didn't even ask why she wasn't at work, wasn't at Crownpoint Security bank.

"I got football practice in two hours."

"There's a present waiting for you."

"What is it?" Tommy had wanted a motorcycle knowing it was impossible, but still he'd hoped and now, maybe, all that wishing had paid off.

"I think you have to see it first. And we've got to hurry."

So they drove back to the reservation mostly in silence. But his mother would smile now and again over nothing, just grin to herself and drive a little faster. That struck him as odd.

When they pulled into the yard, he noticed the transport. That is, how could he miss it. The truck blocked the front of his house.

"We moving?" It was the only thing he could think of to ask.

"No, silly. That's the truck that brought your gift."

A motorcycle, it was a bike, after all. He jumped out and raced toward a man leaning against the cab. A tall man, scrawny, weatherbeaten, old before his time who just watched him run up and didn't say a word.

"My Mom says you got something for me." It was then that he heard the first sounds of something angry—a big something angry that could rock that closed trailer bed just by stamping its feet.

"What's that?"

Finally, a smile. "That's your present, son. An' it's none too happy to be here from the sound of it. Come on, let's take a look."

Tommy trotted after him as the man rounded the back and deftly worked a couple bolts drawing back huge doors that swung to the sides. Then the man extended a ramp, dragging it backwards into the yard.

"This's the part that will take some doing. I'm gonna need your help, son."

Tommy stepped closer to peer into the darkness of the cavernous trailer. At the far end was a horse—a big, snorting, less than pleased piece of horseflesh that trumpeted and pawed the worn wooden floorboards and sent up clouds of dust from a bedding of oat grass.

"He ain't been cut. That makes him a little ornery. Meaner than a snake, I could say."

"You're saying he's a stallion?" Tommy's friends had had stock but never a horse like this. It wasn't a motorcycle but still. . . . He stared back as the horse eyed him then half reared and pawed the air.

"Anybody ever ride him?"

"Oh yeah. This here's your Daddy's horse. He's roped off of him some six or seven years."

"He doesn't act old."

"Old? He's coming nine. Eight's just about the time horseflesh starts developing some brains."

"Where'd you pick him up?"

"Durant, Oklahoma."

"This mean my father's dead?" Tommy realized that he didn't care. How could you get excited one way or another about someone you'd never seen? Someone who obviously didn't care enough about you to just say "Hi" every once in awhile. No, he could do without some traveling Indian-cowboy who followed a rope and half dozen calves that shot from a chute for a paycheck that wouldn't keep a woman and child. . . .

The man laughed and spit into the dirt beside one double wheel. "Naw. Just had some bad luck. I guess he wanted to leave you his most prized possession before he got tempted to hock it. This here spotted horse needs to go to the next Spottedhorse in line." The driver thought that was a lot funnier than Tommy did.

"So, is he going to come pick him up someday?"

"I don't think that will happen."

"How can you be so sure? He left, didn't he? Never cared

one way or the other whether I lived or died or what happened to my Mom. An' now he's giving me his most prized possession. Yeah, like I'm gonna believe that."

"I think your Dad's starting over."

Tommy could have smarted off but he didn't. He didn't care.

"Why don't you just get back in that truck and get out of here? And tell my father I don't want his presents. He's missed any chance he ever had to make things right."

"Can't do that, son. This here horse has been traveling sixteen hours. That's a horse's limit for standing in a moving trailer. I gotta leave him."

Tommy thought about this. He had never been cruel to animals. So maybe the big guy needed to stay. He looked at the horse. The horse stared back. Was he trying to communicate something? If Tommy hated his father, why couldn't the horse hate him too? He felt the beginnings of a camaraderie. But he also knew that his life had just gotten complicated.

"What do we do now?" Tommy asked.

"Well, you take this rope and halter and walk in there and get it on him, then you lead him out this-away. And I'll be getting on down the road."

"We don't have a place for a horse." Tommy said it loud enough for his mother to hear. But she didn't say a thing just leaned against the doorjamb of their house and watched the two of them. She wasn't backing him up. It was like she wanted this reminder of her past—even though she'd married after Tommy's dad had taken off. He'd always thought the house full of brothers and sisters attested to a good marriage; well, at least a busy one.

"I reckon he'll stay put in that there stock pen 'til

you get something better fixed up."

He was pointing at a pen to the side of the house that had recently held sheep until his uncle had sold them. It was made out of panels of pipe fence and Tommy guessed it would work but not for long, the horse would need more room.

"Get going now. He needs a drink and some exercise."

Tommy slung the rope and halter over his shoulder and walked into the truck. The interior was surprisingly cool but smelled of manure and hay and sweaty horse.

"What's his name?" Dumb. He'd forgotten to ask.

"Harley."

Tommy was now eye level with Harley and he just stood there a moment.

"You're not a motorcycle; I don't care what your name is." Had he wished too hard and this was some cruel joke by the Ancient Ones? "Do you hate my dad too?"

The horse nickered. In sympathy? He had certainly fastened two liquid brown eyes on Tommy's every move.

"Maybe we got a lot in common. You might like it around here."

Tommy slipped the halter over a long spotted nose, buckled it by the left ear, snapped the lead under his chin and then untied Harley from the tie-bar that anchored the feed bin. So far, so good. There wasn't room to turn him so he backed him out. And Harley let him. He clattered down the ramp and bunny-hopped in a half circle checking out his surroundings. Then spying the one clump of green grass, pawed the earth until Tommy walked him to it.

"You two are going to be friends." The cowboy leaned against the cab of his truck.

Tommy wasn't sure about that but the horse accepted

him. And he was a beauty—big for a paint and well muscled. He had a black spot around one ear that also took in his right eye, and a black blanket of a spot that stretched from withers to rump.

"Your Dad wanted you to have this, too." The driver opened a compartment on the side and dragged out a saddle. Not just any saddle but one encrusted with silver on black leather. "It was his parade saddle." There was a matching bridle and reins wrapped around the horn.

"Why you think he's doing this?" Tommy examined the saddle. If his dad was that down on his luck, surely this saddle would pay the rent for awhile.

"Probably just wants to give you something to remember him by."

"If you see him, tell him I have lots to not remember him by. An' I don't need handouts from some worthless piece of shit who never thought of anyone but himself."

"I'll see he gets the message."

Tommy thought a minute and then added, "Tell him Harley got here all right."

"Will do. You enjoy that horse now. He's just getting grown up like you are—the two of you got a lot of years together ahead of you. You do right by him; he'll do right by you."

And then the driver climbed up into the cab and started the truck, waved to his mother and then offered Tommy a half-salute before gunning the engine and backing up the incline next to the drive.

He'd found out later that the driver had been at his house all morning—had come just after he'd taken off for school. And his mother had taken a sick day to be with him. And he still hadn't thought to ask her about the man until later. But all she'd say was they'd had coffee and caught up on all the news. Whatever that meant.

Tommy roused himself. Enough daydreaming. He hated inaction and he felt an urgency—an undefined prodding to do something but he had no idea what. But there was the reoccurring, nagging thought that if he didn't act soon, there would be no chance of finding Brenda alive. He could go to his boss with the half-baked story about the alien abduction . . . but hadn't he promised Ben he'd leave Pansy out of things? But an abduction fit . . . or Brenda just ran away with someone—weren't there documented cases of the captured siding with the captors? Some weird mind-game reversal?

He could interview the Cachini family. They lived in the Hawikuh Pueblo. He wasn't certain of what he'd find out but it was better than remaining idle. He grabbed the car keys from the kitchen table. Besides, he needed to stop by the boarding facility at the edge of town and give Harley his daily treat.

TWELVE

"Come in."

Hap closed the door to General Stromburg's office. He didn't have to ask. This—whatever it was—was under wraps. He couldn't remember when he'd seen the general so grim-faced. He took a seat in front of the desk and waited. The general shuffled some papers, took off his glasses and rubbed his temples, then sank both palms into his eyes holding a moment. When he looked up, Hap was startled by his haggard, tired-gray pallor. This was a man who hadn't slept in twenty-four hours.

"First of all, I want to thank you for that report on the Begay woman. Her being out there that night away from the highway and then disappearing, well, it always bothered me. It just didn't add up. Finding out she was the fiancé of the pilot put a new slant on all this."

The general paused. So far, he hadn't said anything new, but Hap's sixth sense said the old boy had a kicker; knew he could sink the eight ball in the side pocket.

"Guess I need to just come out with it. It's hard knowing that young pilot who was one of our best, decorated, ten years in—a credit to his people—could be involved in some sort of duplicity."

Hap sat up a little straighter. What had they found out?

"It's a fluke really that we discovered it. The family was clamoring for the body, refusing any more defiling, religious reasons, I suppose. And certainly, we don't begrudge them that." The general fiddled with some papers in front of him. Get on with it, Hap silently urged.

"The lab guys here were badgering us to run some checks. I can't excuse why we hadn't jumped on it—the Native American thing, I guess, trying to be sensitive. About all we had was some dental work and a femur that had been broken in two places when the man was a kid." The general paused to look at Hap straight on. "But what that proved is that the pilot wasn't Ronnie Cachini. Or should I say the man we thought was the pilot. And I don't have to tell you we've got a giant can of worms on our hands. We haven't released any information to the family; we're stalling on the body but we can't do that much longer . . . I've scheduled a team to go out this afternoon and talk with the family."

Hap sat back, his mind racing. This put a new twist on everything. If they knew, how long would it be before—

"You've ruled out a co-pilot?"

"Only Ronnie Cachini got into that F-117A at Holloman. There was no second man."

"So the second man was someone on the ground. Someone the pilot caught up with later." It wasn't a question. Hap was thinking out loud.

"There appears to have been a nice little crowd out there the other night."

"Why?" Hap couldn't think of anything more to say, but he needed to keep the general talking. He had to know everything that they had found out.

"Want some educated guesses?" The general moved to a window that looked out over the parking lot. "There was some kind of rendezvous with the Begay woman. She was there to pick up this Cachini, maybe after he met with the man on the ground. We have reason to believe that the man's of foreign birth—his dental work suggests he was European." The general seemed to be choosing his words carefully. "What if there was going to be some kind of deal and something went wrong?"

"A deal?" Perspiration beaded across Hap's hairline.

"You know better than I what was in that cockpit. Prototype electronics that we won't even have ready in much under a year—you think that wouldn't give someone an advantage? What was on that plane shows the world exactly where we're headed—tosses our strengths and weaknesses right in the enemies' lap." The general turned back. "This could be one of the biggest breaches of security we've had for awhile."

"You think the man on the ground was there to meet the plane? Along with this Begay woman?"

"Why not? Makes sense to me. The three of them dismantle the display screen in the cockpit, load it in a vehicle, then Cachini and the woman kill the man and blow up the plane to cover their tracks."

"But how did they leave? Her truck was left with the keys in it."

"Who's to say there wasn't a second car? Something driven in by the dead man—but driven out by the pilot and his girlfriend. The old truck wouldn't have gotten them very far; so, they left it as a decoy. They both knew the area, could get in and out easier than any of us. In fact, landing on the reservation was a smart idea, gave them the advantage."

"That's true." Hap thought of his dealings with Ernie Old Talker which weren't going smoothly. This would be a hell of a story for the old man to swallow.

"You must know what they could get for the electronics on the international black market. A couple million, maybe? Enough to make this caper more than well worth it."

"Probably."

"We've brought in Intelligence on this one. Just to be on the safe side. There's a real chance that we're talking espionage. At any rate, my guess is that the pilot and this woman are long gone. Still there will be interviews—no stone unturned. You know the drill. I'll expect you to give them a hand."

"Jesus." Hap slumped back in his chair. What a mess. "What will you tell the Cachini family?"

"Feds are going out this afternoon. We can't keep this quiet for long. I'd say our evidence is fairly solid. I imagine the Feds will be all over them; the interview won't be pretty. I don't know what I'd do if a son of mine turned traitor. These are proud people. That woman's family, the Begays, won't be pleased either, but evidence sure points to the daughter being up to her eyeballs in a criminal act."

Tommy took the highway into Gallup. From there he'd drive the forty miles to the reservation on Route #602. He'd driven past the Hawikuh Tribal Police station at the edge of the reservation before he braked, cut a U and headed into the parking lot. It would be politic to say "hello", let everyone know he was on the Rez and would be interviewing the Cachinis.

The slump-block building felt coolish as he pushed through the door. He could see his old boss on the phone behind a plate glass partition in an office to the right of the reception area. The girl at the front desk was new and doubled as a dispatcher judging from her interaction over a radio. She was busy trying to get two cars to respond to cattle roaming across the highway one mile east of El Malpais.

"Hey, there's someone here from alien-land."

Manard, his old boss, was trying to be funny, and after a moment's hesitation, Tommy laughed. There had been a time when his decision to move into Crownpoint had been met with hostility. Leaving the Rez could cause hard feelings. Younger person trying to better himself, take advantage of a chance to succeed in a larger puddle.

"I take it you're a non-believer?" Tommy said.

"I don't rule out anything. I cover all my bases. Someone says they see little green men, I'm all for it. Why not?" He grinned widely showing off a gold cap on the left incisor. His uniform looked mussed with sweat creases across the back. Tommy wasn't sure why but he found it irritating that everyone called them "little green men". They looked almost human—but wasn't he starting to sound like a believer?

"What brings you this way? Not enough to do in the big city?"

Tommy ignored him. "I'm going to be talking with the Cachini family. I'm trying to figure out how Brenda Begay ties into all this. Ronnie Cachini was her fiancé."

"Yeah. I know Brenda. What's funny is that you're the second person in the last ten minutes wanting to talk to the Cachini's. Had a couple Federal Agents through here needing directions to Ronnie's folk's place. Wouldn't admit it but my guess is they'd gotten lost. Said it was real important that they talk with Ronnie's family."

"Federal Agents?"

"Uh huh. Grim looking sort, all business, everything's a crime against your country until proven otherwise. I was just on my way out to the Cachini's. There's been a little too much Ruby Ridge rhetoric lately. Ronnie's got a hothead of a younger brother."

"Let's go." Tommy hadn't planned on company but if there was a crowd, it might be better.

The Cachini's lived at the far end of the village in a stone and adobe house attached to three others that sprawled between two dirt streets filled with identical adobe and stone houses. Tommy saw the white government-issue car parked in front and two men standing at the door talking with someone through the screen. Tommy thought of Mormons without bicycles but knew that these men were all business; he could tell from their posture—intent, stiff, ramrod correct.

Tommy pulled up in a cloud of dust and didn't wait for his old boss before he walked briskly up the flagstone walk.

"Thought maybe I could help."

One of the two men, perspiring under the weight of his black suit coat turned slightly as Tommy approached. That's not a happy camper, Tommy decided. The set of his jaw said he was disappointed with his welcome—or lack thereof. It was obvious that he and his pal hadn't been invited in, and might not be.

"Is the family fluent in English?" the man asked Tommy in an undertone.

"Last time I checked. You're still on U.S. soil here."

Now it was Tommy's turn to sound a little flip. This wasn't going well.

"I'm Tommy Spottedhorse." He held out his hand but

thought the agent blanched and would have probably uttered an expletive if he hadn't been surrounded.

"Word travels fast. I don't think we need any help."

"Might be better if you have some from the look of things."

The agent chose to ignore him, turned toward the screen and held up his credentials.

"Ma'am, we need to talk with you. It's important that you give us a few minutes." The agent started to say something else, hesitated and then closed his mouth. He seemed stymied.

"Tommy, is that you?" The screen door opened and a round Indian woman leaned out. "I thought it was you. Do you know these men?"

"They need to ask you some questions, Mrs. Cachini, that's all. They won't stay long." Tommy almost crossed his fingers to stave off a lie.

"Well, if you say it's okay."

The woman pushed the screen open and the two agents pressed close, the tangy scent of Aqua Velva floating up and away. Mrs. Cachini stepped back from the threshold and motioned for Tommy, Manard and the two agents to enter. She didn't look happy, just accommodating.

"We can sit in here."

The four followed her into the living room and found seats. Tommy chose one of the plump, gold, crushed velvet sofas, the agents sat on straight-backed chairs brought in from the dining room. Ronnie's mother sat down heavily in a rocker. No one was at ease and there was an awkward pause of shuffling feet and adjusting ties, before one agent asked, "Is Mr. Cachini home?"

The woman looked at the floor, and Tommy jumped in

to say that Ronnie's father had passed away about three years ago. The agent made a note on a small pad that fit into his shirt pocket.

"I apologize for what I'm about to say. Let me preface it by saying I do not believe that you, personally, are involved."

Tommy leaned forward. This woman lost her son, for god's sake, what was all this swearing to innocence?

"Mrs. Cachini, I have the duty to tell you that your son did not die in the crash of the F-117A aircraft as previously reported."

He paused but no one uttered a word; the room itself seemed struck dumb—then everyone spoke at once.

"What do you mean?" Tommy was half out of his chair.

"Didn't die? Ronnie didn't die?" His mother rose from the rocker and Tommy moved to steady her. "I don't know what you are telling me. What's he saying?" She turned to Tommy who shook his head.

"Simply that the body presumed to be the pilot's—that of your son—wasn't his. We have not identified the body that was found, but we have proved conclusively, through dental records and x-rays on file, that it is not your son."

"Ronnie's alive!" The statement was a wail. The woman took a step forward, teetered and sank against Tommy who helped her sit back down. "But where is he? Do you have him?"

"Uh, no, we'd like to know where he is as much as you would." The agent cleared his throat. "Ma'am, this isn't easy, but I know you want to know the truth. We suspect that your son was involved in a covert operation to steal and possibly sell national secrets to those hoping to gain from advanced knowledge of our fighter's electronic configuration." The agent took a breath and went on. "We are looking for your son to question him. At this time your son has not been charged. But the longer he eludes us, the rougher it's going to be for him."

They think Ronnie's a traitor. Tommy was stunned. He glanced at Ronnie's mother but didn't think the impact of what the agent said had sunk in.

"Have you or any member of your family been contacted by Ronnie or his girlfriend, Brenda Begay?" the second agent asked.

"Brenda?" Tommy hadn't meant to say anything but it slipped out. Were they thinking Brenda was involved? Somehow supporting Ronnie? Of course, he could see it on their faces.

"There is reason to believe that Miss Begay is an accomplice."

"How can you say that?" Tommy took a step and leaned down so that he was in the agent's face. "A woman struggling to graduate from college so that she can provide for her daughter and her mother. And is this far away from doing just that." Tommy held his index finger and thumb about a half inch apart.

"Officer, step back. You're out of line here."

"I'm out of line?" Tommy didn't hold his anger back nor did he step back. He was convinced that Brenda was innocent; he just couldn't prove it. Brenda had accepted an invitation for coffee that night. With him. She did not have espionage on her mind. He'd stake his life on it. "You can't come into a person's house making accusations, ruining the names of innocent people. Telling a mother her son's alive and then saying he's a traitor."

"There's substantial evidence to—"

"Believe me, Brenda Begay has done nothing wrong."

"We think otherwise, Mr. Spottedhorse. Let me remind

you that any information that you might have concerning Miss Begay must be reported—"

"This is ridiculous!" Tommy was barely under control.

"Easy, Tommy." Manard clasped his arm.

"I know Ronnie Cachini! He's a patriot! How many times has he been decorated?" Tommy looked around wildly but no one seemed to know the answer. "I can't think of anyone more . . . devoted to his country," Tommy finished lamely.

No one said anything. The sound of quiet sobbing permeated the room.

"Mrs. Cachini, I'm sorry. I can't believe what they're saying. I know Brenda and Mariah and Ronnie. Brenda wouldn't do something like this. And we know Ronnie's record. There's been some mistake." Tommy knelt before the woman, his anger dissipating.

"I wouldn't count on that," the agent said. "There's been a citing of a couple matching their description in California."

How could someone go from dead to America's most wanted in 60 seconds—and which was worse? From the looks on the faces of the agents, death would be preferable, Tommy thought. But if Ronnie was alive—and he knew that Brenda had been there that night . . . he had to admit it looked bleak for the couple. If they weren't involved in something criminal, why hadn't they come forward?

Tommy walked out the front door and then leaned against the chipped rock side of the house warmed now by the sun. His thoughts were a jumble. Ronnie Cachini alive. And didn't that make a pretty good case for Ronnie Cachini being the mysterious Ian? Abruptly, Tommy turned back.

"Mrs. Cachini? Did Ronnie have a tatoo?"

"Don't you remember? He got one the same time your younger brother got that cat on his shoulder. Only Ronnie's was a Thunderbird."

Tommy thanked her and promised to stay in touch. He recalled Edwina's diary. A man in fatigues comes into the Center, loads up on junk food, uses the phone to call his mother . . . that was the first lie. Tommy was certain of it. If the man at the Information Center was Ronnie, he didn't call his mother. But who did he call?

Tommy closed the screen door behind him. "What a mess." He didn't say it to anyone in particular. There's no way that Ronnie's a traitor. And no way that Brenda's involved. He kept repeating the phrases under his breath. But Pansy Manygoats saw an alien pickup an Indian girl and run from the scene of the crash. An alien? No, more like a man in a flightsuit or the test gear of a pilot. But why was he holding her hostage? Or was he? . . . Head over heels in love. . . . What wouldn't you do if you were head over heels in love? You'd team up with your partner—that's one thing he knew. Had going for coffee been a smoke-screen? Would she have begged off, hopped out of the Bronco anyway even if he hadn't been called to work?

"Shit."

Had he been taken? Betrayed by someone he really cared for? Wouldn't be the first time. Had he been set up to give Brenda an alibi? He felt the churning of anger. Because there was nothing he could do now—not to change anything, anyway. A pickup turned the corner. Tommy watched until it was out of sight. He couldn't seem to move into action. If a couple was spotted in California meeting their description, Brenda was long gone. He might not ever have a chance to hear her side of what happened. Did he feel better knowing that Brenda was probably alive? He didn't know. His anger was doing a good job of burying any feelings.

"Hello, Mariah." Ben recognized the child peeking around the office door. The secretary had said that she'd scheduled a crisis patient, but Mariah? He picked up the chart from the wire basket. Sure enough. Mariah Begay was his four o'clock. No wonder the secretary had put him in the child psychiatrist's office. Yet, as he watched, the bouncy three year old seemed in excellent spirits—anything but a crisis.

Sam Begay stood and shook hands. "Hi, Doc. Thanks for seeing us on such short notice." His palm was moist and he seemed a little embarrassed to be there.

"This is a treat." Ben eased a red enameled chair with stenciled yellow flowers across the back out from the play table in the corner and folded his six foot plus frame into it. "Now, what can I do for you?"

Mariah was already stacking blocks on the table's Formica top.

"I think Mariah has something to tell you," Sam gently prodded.

"I saw my mommy." The child offered the information matter of factly as she fitted a green "A" block on top of a blue "B".

"Where was this, Mariah?" Ben glanced up at the uncle and saw the deep concern etched across his face.

"In my bedroom."

She seemed on the verge of saying more, but the C, D, and E blocks had to be strategically placed first, though not in alphabetical order it seemed.

"It was dark. But I wasn't scared."

Sam whispered, "Last night".

"Your mommy came to see you last night?"

Mariah nodded her head until her braid flopped up and down.

"Did she talk to you?"

"Uh huh." Mariah dumped a box of plastic figures next to the blocks. Thank God the child psychiatrist was on vacation. It would have been difficult to meet in the office usually assigned to him.

"Doc, we're worried that this isn't normal. She could be getting sick in the head from all this." The uncle tapped his temple.

"I see." And Ben did see. It wouldn't be unusual for the child to fabricate, if not actually believe that the missing loved one was still a part of her life. There was certainly reason for Mariah to have slipped into her imagination and now confused it with reality.

"My mommy said she was coming back, an' I had to be a good girl."

"When is your mommy coming back?"

Mariah shrugged. The blocks had just toppled and were demanding all her attention in order to be righted again. "Before the snow."

Interesting answer. Would a three and a half year old— even a precocious one come up with that on her own? Or had someone coached her?

"My mommy lives with my daddy."

This sounds more like imagination, Ben thought.

"Where's that?"

"In a house in a hill, in a big round hole with a little hole for a door. Mommy climbs up and mommy climbs down."

This last was accompanied by Mariah "walking" her two fingers back and forth across the table.

This definitely sounds like fabrication, Ben thought. It was possible she was beginning to make up her world the way she wanted it to be.

"I think Brenda reads to her too much," Sam offered, "In English. These ideas aren't good. She takes her to the movies, too." This last seemed to seal Brenda's suspect parenting skills, at least according to her brother.

Living in a hole smacked of Alice in Wonderland, but Ben doubted that Brenda would introduce Alice quite yet. . . .

"I can't go with mommy now but maybe tomorrow."

Sam looked at Ben nervously, "Do you think she'd try to run away? Go find Brenda on her own?"

"I don't know. Isn't your mother with her most of the time?"

"I'm not sure she's able to watch her every minute. She's getting old."

"Mariah, I want you to listen to me." Ben waited until she turned toward him. "You can't try to find your mommy. You have to stay with your grandmother—wait for mommy to come back. If you go away, mommy might not find you."

"I know." She turned back to the table and stacked the G and then the H block on top of the E and F. The tower was good size now. "I have to be a good girl. Do you know my Daddy?"

"No, I don't."

"My daddy drives airplanes up in the sky."

At least he did, Ben thought to himself and couldn't shake the sadness that settled over him. Mariah would never know her father.

"I don't think she'll try to leave." Ben stood and walked

behind the desk leaving Mariah to her blocks. "I'm guessing that her imagination is going to be active for awhile and then with time . . . let's just see if there are any changes—that's about all we can do. To be on the safe side, bring her back in a week."

Ben walked them to the door of the office and said good-bye, reassuring Sam once again that he felt Mariah would be fine. He watched the two of them pass the receptionist's desk, the man taking small, half-steps so the toddler could walk beside him. Mariah turned once to smile back at him. The child was beautiful. To think that her mother might not—

"Could I have ten minutes of your time?"

Ben started. He hadn't seen the man sitting in a chair blocked by the open door to his office.

"Colonel Anderson?" Ben's first impulse was to lie. But he did have a few minutes before his next patient. "Come in. I don't have anyone scheduled until the half-hour."

"Good. I apologize for not calling first, but I had some business at the Tribal Office. As long as I was out this way, I thought I'd drop by."

Ben indicated a chair next to the lone window in his office and moved to sit behind his desk. He waited for the colonel to speak first.

"I'll come right to the point. We have reason to believe that Ronnie Cachini and Brenda Begay are involved in espionage." The colonel hastened to fill Ben in on their discovery of the pilot's identity or rather, lack of.

"I can't believe that Brenda is guilty of anything like that."

"I appreciate your sticking up for one of your students, but I think you're being a little naive. There's some big money to be had in the sale of this country's secrets. But that's not the reason for my visit."

Ben waited. The colonel seemed to be weighing his words, reluctant even to say why he was there.

"I guess it's best if I just put it on the table. I wouldn't be here if I wasn't concerned."

"Concerned about what?" Ben was beginning to feel irritated. There was too much staging in the colonel's delivery. Ben wished he'd just say whatever it was and get it over with.

"Word's gotten back that your friend, this Mr. Spottedhorse, didn't make a very good impression on a couple of Federal Agents. I might add that this investigation has enlarged somewhat in scope—thanks to some recent developments. Your friend is tampering with something the United States Government has a pretty big stake in."

"How is Tommy tampering?"

"Let's just say by not keeping us informed when he finds something out. I'm over at the Information Center at Chaco a little earlier and one of the rangers lets drop that this Edwina woman kept a diary. Seems the man who lured her to her death wore fatigues. One of the rangers even saw him leaving the Center. Now, that sounds like a military man to me, what do you think?"

Ben knew he wasn't expected to answer.

"It could be that Ronnie Cachini and Brenda Begay never left this part of the country. And that puts a whole new spin on things. So I call the dead girl's mother and lo and behold she's given this diary to your friend." The colonel leaned forward. "I need to see that diary. It could have a direct bearing on our case here. Do I make myself clear?"

"Why are you telling me all this? Why not just talk to Tommy's superiors?"

"I don't necessarily want to get him into trouble . . . yet.

And you may have some influence. But due to the fact that you're a government worker and all . . . might just behoove you to be cooperative. We're all together in this under one flag. Do I presume correctly?"

Ben chose not to answer.

"I suppose you've seen the diary?"

"As a matter of fact, I have." Ben had nothing to hide and he didn't hide his irritation. In all truthfulness, he wished he could tell the colonel that Tommy had turned the diary in, given it to someone who had the authority to do something with it. But it bugged him that Tommy assumed that he could simply keep it, use it for his own investigation. This was the reservation but in a case like this, they weren't in a vacuum. "I really didn't think there was anything of importance. Just a lot of babbling by a love struck woman in her forties."

"I guess I need to be the judge of that. Where's the diary now?"

"You'll have to ask Tommy."

Ben rose to see him to the door.

"You're positive there weren't any clues to her murderer?"

"Not exactly. She'd met some guy who was camping at the park. The guy made a call from the Information Center. He said he was calling his mother, but the records might prove differently. It's not clear if this man could have been involved with her murder." Ben immediately wished he could take the words back when he saw the set of the colonel's jaw and a flash of anger in his eyes. He braced for another tirade on the obstruction of justice, but none came. The colonel just turned, started down the hall and continued out the front door.

THIRTEEN

The vultures ate the goat. And what wasn't eaten was sun-dried, flesh scorched to bone, knobby front legs spraddled across the sand floor of the corral. The head looked like an awful painting, one he'd seen in Santa Fe as a young man. The price tag had been $100,000. One hundred thousand dollars. Amos had never forgotten it. Someone painted pictures of skulls of animals and made a fortune. Anglos could be a puzzle.

But the disappearance of his goat's flesh uncovered something interesting—something that hadn't been there before the goat was murdered. Amos was certain of that. That old goat would have eaten it. As the haunches melted from bone and sank into the earth, a bump appeared. Amos waited for the vultures to eat it. They didn't. In fact, it didn't seem edible. Now, Amos was curious and he prodded and poked and worked the strange thing from under the carcass.

Even when he held it in his hand, he wasn't sure what it was. It was round and black, a little bigger than a fifty cent piece but its edges curved up and the letters N-I-K-O-N were printed across its center. Puzzling, but a clue. Amos was pretty certain that its owner had already gone blind, but he tucked it into his pocket anyway. Maybe he'd show the young doc this afternoon, the head doctor, that Ben Pecos.

Amos was waiting for his daughter. They were going to visit Pansy. His wife had been admitted to the hospital at Crownpoint. For observation, they'd said. But Amos knew it was to keep her safe.

She had been getting better, then a strange dog wandered up to the hogan. It sat patiently by the door every morning until Pansy came out. When it saw her it would thump its thin, hairless tail up and down on the hard ground and scramble to its feet to follow her. Amos tried to warn Pansy. Everyone knew that when a strange dog appeared that way, it was probably a *skinwalker*.

It was a *baahagii*, a terrible misdeed, to feed that dog, and encourage an evil spirit, but Pansy gave it scraps. She seemed lately to have no sense of taboos, no sense of proper behavior in dangerous times. Amos wasn't a Christian even though his daughter had gotten him to attend the white man's church. He believed that sins were accounted for in the Navajo way—in the here and now—not in some afterlife where threats of fire had no meaning.

A taboo was a sin against nature, the natural balance of things and must be righted immediately. Punishment was always sudden and unavoidable. But the Ancient Ones expected you to take precautions. To know better. All his life he'd collected his fingernail and toenail clippings. Amos kept them in a big blue-tinted mason jar so no one could steal them and use them to witch him. A while back he'd buried that jar so that Pansy couldn't find it.

He didn't know what to do. He was afraid of his own wife. But when Pansy fell down yesterday and couldn't get up, Amos had gone for help. There was no phone. It was his legs that carried him some twenty miles seeking a doctor. When his daughter found out, she renewed her insistence that they move to town. He hated to think of riding to Crownpoint with her later. He'd be cornered and unable to get away from her pleading.

"My father wants to know if you're free to talk a minute?"

Ben looked up from his desk. He was still thinking about what the colonel had said. His next patient was a no-show, and he'd welcomed the opportunity to catch up on his paperwork, but he recognized Mary Manygoats and motioned her in. He stood up as Mary ushered her father to a chair nearest his desk, then took one against the wall for herself.

"My father has found important evidence in the killing of his goat."

There was no hint of trying to keep a straight face. Apparently, Mary was privy to this evidence and took it seriously. She and Ben both watched as Amos, with great ceremony, dug something from his shirt pocket and held it out for Ben to take.

Ben turned it over in his hand. "It's a lens cap."

Before he could add anything else, Mary was explaining to Amos, then she turned back. "This is something off of a camera? Are you certain?"

"Yes."

More conferring, then Amos uttered a single word and sat back smugly.

"What did he say?"

"Shadow catcher. In the old days, that's what people called photographers."

"Where did he find this?"

"Under the goat."

"And it isn't yours?" Ben asked.

"I do best with an aim and fire, you know, those disposable ones."

Amos tugged on Mary's sleeve and said something to her.

"My father says it's fitting that a shadow catcher loses his eyes. Without sight he can no longer take pictures of the soul."

Ben wasn't sure what to say. He simply nodded. Who could have been taking pictures of the skinned goat? Who would have wanted to? And this loss of sight was an eery thing. If anyone would have had problems with his sight, it should have been Amos. He was knocked out almost on top of the burning pile of rubble that night. Had his eyes been open, he might have suffered severe chemical abrasions to the cornea. Amos had been lucky.

"Someone said you had opened a hogan & breakfast." Ben had overhead talk in the cafeteria—not very positive talk either—but the idea intrigued him.

"Yes, a college project that has been popular. I'm thinking of closing it now with my mother's illness."

"Did you have problems booking guests?"

"None. I advertised nationally in B&B guides. We usually had 5 to 8 guests every weekend."

"Did you have guests the night the Stealth crashed?"

"Last weekend? Yes. Let's see. I left after dinner. We had four guests that evening—two men traveling across the U.S. and a man and his teenage son from Albuquerque."

"Do you remember any names?"

"The man with the fifteen-year-old was a Harold Anderson. The boy's name was Jerome. The other two were from Iraq or Iran—one was a professor, I don't know about the other. And I can't remember their names."

"Tell me about the Andersons."

"I felt sorry for the kid. His father gave orders, chose all the activities. Said his wife wanted him to spend some positive time with the boy. He had picked the research topic for his kid's history class paper—Structures of the Southwest. It was the father's bright idea to start by spending an overnight in a hogan. The father was getting ready to retire and he had some parenting to catch up on. Or so he said."

"Did they seem close?"

"Not exactly. The boy did everything his father suggested but wasn't very enthusiastic."

"Probably just the age. At fifteen it's not too cool to like what your parents like."

"Jerome was enthused about his dad's car—I remember that. He went out after dinner and just sat in it."

"What kind of car?"

"I have no idea. I'd never seen one before. It was shaped like a bullet and the driver and passenger rode in the open. According to my mother, no one stayed the night."

"Why not?"

"I don't know. But no one was at the hogan when my mother brought the flock back."

"Odd."

"I thought so but I've been too busy to give it much thought."

"What time did she get back?"

"Probably around eleven—maybe a little earlier."

"Seems unusual that the guests would pay and then not stay for breakfast."

Mary shrugged. "People do strange things. One woman

left when she found out we didn't wash the sheepskin rugs every day. Can you imagine?"

Amos tugged on Ben's sleeve then pointed at the lens cap. He seemed to want Ben to take it.

"He thinks you'll know what to do with it," Mary interpreted.

Give it to Tommy, Ben thought. And he had more to share with Tommy—could this Mr. Anderson be Colonel Anderson? Hap could be a diminutive of Harold. And if he could place him at a hogan a scant mile from the site on the night of the crash, was it just a high school research paper that brought him there? That would make for an awfully big coincidence.

"Don't you see? It was Ronnie Cachini that Edwina met at the Center. The tattoo nails it."

"Maybe."

"Don't be such a skeptic. Ben, I think Mariah did see her mother last night."

"Tommy—"

"No, listen to me. We now know that Ronnie wasn't killed. Why couldn't Ronnie and Brenda have stayed in the area? They could hide on the reservation. No one would find them and they'd know their way around. It's the perfect cover."

"The question is still why. Why would a man who apparently faked his death not take off? Put as much distance between himself and this place as he could?" Ben looked at his watch. It was almost seven, and they were still arguing the case long after the pizza had disappeared.

"I don't know." Tommy leaned back on the couch. "I can't get over how upset Mrs. Cachini was. The shock of losing a son, then getting him back only he's not exactly here. It's criminal the way she's being emotionally jerked around. And the Begay family . . . I'm assuming the same two agents called on them?"

"Sam didn't say anything this afternoon. They may not know yet."

"They won't accept it easily . . . the part about Brenda being an accomplice. Brenda's grandfather was a code-talker during World War II. Damn. I still feel I'm not putting the right things together somehow."

"Like what?"

"Hell, if I knew that—" Tommy abruptly stopped, took a deep breath. "Tell me again exactly what Mariah said."

"I can do one better. I have a copy of my notes." Ben brought his briefcase to the couch.

"Let's see. Supposedly, her mother told her to be good . . . that she'd be back before the snow came. When do you have the first snow around here?"

"It can be any time. Usually after Halloween but sometimes not until after Thanksgiving. Then again, I've known good weather to hold until almost Christmas. But it would give them a month to go elsewhere and come back."

"Are you now saying you're not so certain that they're still around?"

"Maybe. It's possible they really were sighted in California."

"Oh, here's a good part. Mariah thinks they live in the ground."

"Who?"

"Her mother and father, I suppose. She asked me if I

knew her father. She knows that he 'drove' airplanes."

"But what about where they live?" Tommy leaned forward.

"Mariah thinks they live . . . ," Ben looked on the back of one of the pages torn from a yellow legal pad. "Here it is. She said that they live in a hole in a hill with a little hole for a door."

"A little hole for a door? Ben, that's it. I knew it was right there. Brenda and Ronnie are living in a cave. In Chaco. It's got to be. For whatever reason, they stayed around. Couple this with the stuff in Edwina's diary and I think we've got proof."

"Maybe, yes—maybe, no. Edwina never mentioned a woman. In fact, had there been another woman, there might not have been sandwiches."

"So, Brenda stayed hidden. They decided it was better for him to forage for food on his own." Tommy paused. "Maybe Brenda's injured. What if she couldn't go with Ronnie to get food? What if she had to stay in the cave? Remember Amos Manygoat's wife said she saw someone carrying a woman away from the wreckage."

"She indicated that one of them was an alien. I'm not sure we can rely on her observation."

"So, she's a little excitable and her eyesight isn't very good."

"Tommy, do you know what you're saying? Brenda and Ronnie could have caused Edwina's death—lured her to their hideout. And if they did that, who's to say that they didn't kill that man who burned with the plane? All this does is point a finger at those two being involved in two deaths. A lot of money could be made by the sale of the electronic equipment on that plane. How can you be so certain that Brenda wasn't in on it from the beginning?"

"Because Brenda wasn't planning on being out there

that night. She had other plans—we had other plans and then I got called for backup. I know, she could have been setting me up—I've thought about it a thousand times. But I can't believe that. I don't have any good reason that places her at that crash site, but I believe there's an explanation. She hasn't done anything wrong."

"Then why is she hiding? Why are they hiding?" Ben asked. "You need to be investigating with an open mind."

"Who says I'm not? I don't have an explanation. I'm just making damn sure I don't condemn the innocent. That's more than I can say for some people."

Ben wasn't sure if he fit in that category but he didn't want to ask. "Tommy, where's the diary?"

"Safe."

"But you still have it?"

"I didn't have time to do any copying, but I will in the morning."

"The colonel asked for it."

"How does he know I have it?"

"The guys at the Information Center. Then he called Edwina's mother. Tommy, you're not making any points with the military on this one. I'm beginning to agree with the colonel. It comes real close to obstruction of justice to keep evidence."

"Is that your opinion or the colonel's?"

"Both, I guess. I'm more concerned as to what Colonel Anderson might do. He's not a man who likes to be crossed. And somehow you've managed to get crosswise with him."

"What'd you do? Kiss ass? Yes, Colonel; No, Colonel; whatever you say Colonel—it's obvious Mr. Spottedhorse isn't playing ball, Colonel."

Ben had never seen Tommy this angry.

"You know better than that. You're being unreasonable. I don't like the colonel any more than you. But he has a point. I think you've gone into this investigation determined to save Brenda at whatever cost—make her the good guy even if it means covering up evidence or just delaying its getting to authorities. You have no right to tamper with, or hide anything you find out. You've stopped investigating with an open mind."

Tommy stood up, dug his billfold out of his back pocket and put five dollars on the coffee table for his half of the pizza, then walked out the door.

He was mad. But was Ben telling the truth? A good friend just trying to be helpful? Was Tommy's own perspective that colored that he wasn't being rational? Maybe. But he was tired of talking, second-guessing those who couldn't defend themselves and he had a hunch. And to prove that he was right, he had to visit the cave where Edwina was killed. And what better time to do it than when he wouldn't be seen by the rangers? It was almost straight up seven; it would be pitch black in an hour.

If he was right, there was every possibility that he'd find Brenda. Hadn't Mariah seen her mother just last night? He couldn't explain why Brenda would visit her child and then leave again, go back to the caves. She could have slipped away from her captors but was afraid of what they might do if they found her gone. But shouldn't he be making that singular—captor? Ronnie Cachini and no one else? But that didn't make sense. What reason would Ronnie have to threaten Brenda?

He rolled down the driver's side window of the Bronco. The night had a distinct feel of fall but the cool air felt good on his face and neck.

Tommy couldn't stand admitting that he might be wrong about Brenda. He was never wrong when it came to people . . . well, almost never. Someone could threaten harm to Mariah, and Tommy knew that Brenda would do anything to protect her.

The night was overcast. Maybe that was best for what he wanted to do. He gunned the Bronco up 5th Street and turned left onto Highway 371.

Ben saw the headlights of the Bronco flash on and watched the SUV back out of the driveway and turn north. Had he expected an apology? Not really. Not right away. Tommy had to do some soul-searching first. Ben just wondered if he'd been too hard on him. But if Ben couldn't speak frankly, who could? Tommy needed to be looking at all the possibilities and not let his thinking be swayed. Given time Ben thought Tommy would react like the good lawman that he was—at least Ben hoped that he would.

Suddenly the apartment seemed cramped. Ben flipped on the TV set but saw it barely flicker to life before he snapped it off. Television wasn't his thing and certainly not tonight. He felt like doing something, not staying caged up. This might be a good time to drive over to Gallup and finish up the last two week's paperwork. Seeing patients one night a week didn't seem like much of a workload but last month he'd seen twenty-seven individuals and three families. He needed to add his notes to the charts of eight.

✛ ✛ ✛ ✛ ✛

"So, where are we going? When I agreed to drive I didn't think we'd be going cross-country."

"Listen, tonight's perfect—I say we take a little scouting trip. Maybe even leave our mark." The passenger was turned away staring at the landscape as it rushed by.

"It's been three days. You don't think it would be a little suspect to have duplicate mutilations so soon after the first ones?"

"Something a month from now or six months won't make a difference. We need to capitalize on the alien hysteria now."

"I think we're asking for trouble," the driver said.

"I think you're losing your nerve." The passenger had turned back to lean across the console.

"Maybe I am."

"Then let's just do a circle."

"Where?" The driver's agitation had turned to testiness.

"I think the site's been chosen for us."

"Chaco? No way."

"As close to where that ranger died as we can get. Pull over a minute, I want you to look at these sketches. I was thinking of something like the maze of life."

The car bumped to a stop and the driver turned to look at his passenger. "Just how long do you think we'll have?"

"Hey, do I hear a little sarcasm?"

"Damn right. You tell me how we're going to get in and out of there and do a maze in anything under three to four hours. And where are we going to find the grass—"

"Dirt."

"We're doing an intricate maze in the dirt? You're crazy."

"I've checked it out. It's doable."

"I've got a bad leg and you've barely got vision out of one eye and we're going to produce a fucking work of art in ground hard enough to crack walnuts—"

"I'm going. You're either in this or you're not."

The driver turned to squarely face the passenger. "Look at me. You know what you should do."

The second man was silent.

"Are you paying attention to me?" The driver leaned closer.

A nod.

"You should report what you saw—what you took pictures of."

"And do time—watch a career go down the tubes—never to be resurrected?"

"I'd think your government might be lenient. You're giving them evidence of a serious crime—murder, even—if we think of the pilot."

"It's my life." The passenger paused, slipped off a pair of polarized sunglasses and pressed a tissue to his right eye.

"My God. That eye is terrible. You're not going to testify to anything if you don't see a doctor. Chuck the circle idea and let me drive you to an emergency room."

"I'm fine." The passenger twisted his head away.

"Oh yeah, one eye swollen shut, the other running with pus. That's my idea of fine."

"There's too much at stake."

"Like your sight."

"It's just allergies." The man was pressing wadded tissue to his eyes with the fingers of both hands.

"Then get the right meds and treat the condition. Come on, we're halfway to Gallup. We could be there in under an hour."

Funny, the parking lot was half full. Ben parked close to the street and hiked back to the hospital's front door. He checked his watch, eight thirty on the dot.

"Hey, you're in time to help," the night nurse greeted him from the desk.

"What's going on?" He leaned against the counter and surveyed a room with thirty or so people. Some obviously just trying to sleep it off out of the cool night air but others were in need of medical attention.

"Power failure next door." She nodded toward the east indicating the county hospital. "They need to save their generators. It was easier to just close down emergency and send folks here. It'd be a big help if you could check people in. I'll finish up with the front two rows, you start with the man on the end of row three."

The two hospitals were less than a block apart. On more than one occasion, Indian Health Service had stepped in to help out.

There were two men on the end of the third row of folding chairs that had been set up to accommodate the crowd. Could be a couple, Ben thought, as he took in the solicitous gesture of the older man as he pressed fresh tissue into the younger's hand. The tissues were quickly wadded into a ball and not once did the younger man even acknowledge his companion. The set of his jaw seemed to indicate he was in a great deal of pain.

An accident? Ben couldn't tell but he supposed it was his duty to find out. He picked up a clipboard and form from the counter and scooted a chair up beside the two.

"I've been volunteered to try and make this process go

faster. I need to get some information and then you'll be ready to see a physician. I'm the painless part, I hope." He smiled.

The man barely nodded and didn't take his hand from his eyes.

The older man turned to him. "Let me help with the particulars. His name's Bruce Bartholemew. I'm Nate Stevens. A friend."

Ben nodded and shook the extended hand.

"Here's his medical card. The address is current."

New England Financial, One Health Plan. Ben wasn't familiar with the coverage. But he'd copy the card and put it with the chart. Indian Health Service was only helping in an emergency. Who paid what would be sorted out later. Nate offered an address and phone number and place of business, then rattled off a litany of previous eye problems. He seemed well-versed on the other man's medical history, Ben thought.

"Will it be long?"

Ben and Nate both turned to Bruce who had removed his hands from his eyes and was smoothing the tissue across his knee. He looked up directly at Ben.

Ben checked an intake of breath and put on his best "there's nothing out of the ordinary look" when he really wanted to grab the man by the arm and head for the near-est doctor.

Bruce's right eye was swollen closed—eyelashes pulled into puffy blue-veined flesh. The left eye was an angry beet-red and encrusted with a yellowy ooze. Ben looked away.

"How long have your eyes been this way?" He feigned checking something on the chart.

"Three days," answered Nate. "No, maybe this is the

fourth." He waited for Bruce to correct him then added in an undertone, "Is he in danger?"

"I'm not a physician, but I'm glad you came in this evening."

"Are you trying to say I could go blind?" The tremor made Bruce's voice barely audible.

"I'm a clinical psychologist here part time. Ophthalmology, obviously, is not my specialty but it appears that you could have an infection in both eyes. Your physician will want to reduce the swelling, of course, and get you on a course of treatment right away. This might be a case of episclereosis. If left unattended, it could leave you with permanent damage." Then thinking of Amos Manygoats, Ben added jokingly, "You won't go blind unless you mutilated that piebald goat on the reservation a few nights ago. At least, that's what its owner believes."

Bruce's reaction was immediate—first a piercing wounded animal wail then a leap toward Ben, both hands on Ben's shoulders shoving him and chair over backwards— then stumbling over a drunk stretched out on the floor to land spread-eagle himself on the cold linoleum. Ben was stunned but scrambled to his feet. Nate was bending over Bruce saying ". . . if you don't tell him, I will" when Bruce burst into tears, struggled to a sitting position and clasping his sides, he began to keen.

The nurse-receptionist was immediately at Ben's side.

"Dr. Pecos, your office is available. Let's take your patient in there."

Clearly willing to forego help to get a disturbance out of her area and instantly making aberrant behavior his domain, she actually "tsked" as she watched Bruce weaving back and forth.

"Do you need help? I could page security." She leaned in close to whisper but never once took her eyes off of Bruce.

"No, we'll be fine." Ben met Nate's glance and was reassured by a nod. "I usually use the office three doors down on the right. Let's get him in there."

They navigated the short distance of hall with Bruce slumped heavily between them.

"Put him down on the couch." Ben always felt that he should apologize for having what was thought to be standard equipment for a shrink. This one in cracked tan leather would be put back in the lounge once that area was painted. But for the time being, it was coming in handy.

Bruce seemed catatonic leaning over the couch's arm, head in hands. When it didn't seem like Bruce was going to volunteer anything, Nate spoke.

"Do you believe what you said about going blind? If you were the one who mutilated that goat?"

"The goat's owner is a Navajo man. He believes that way."

"But you. Are you Navajo? Do you believe it's possible?"

"I'm Pueblo." Ben paused, "In my training I've read documented cases—maybe nothing more than the power of suggestion—but nonetheless, recorded instances of individuals who have fallen prey to . . ." Ben struggled for a word other than death or blindness, "some malady that seems to be the direct result of simply believing it will happen."

"I think someone has something to tell you." Nate nudged Bruce, not getting a response, he turned back to Ben. "What I'm about to say will ruin two people, but it has to be said—"

"I did it. I mutilated the goat." It was said so quietly that, at first, Ben thought he hadn't heard Bruce correctly.

"Why?"

"Career move." Bruce shifted his weight to sit upright and dig his wallet out of a back pocket. He handed Ben a business card and a well-folded square of newspaper print. "Read this."

Bruce Barthalomew, Newscaster, Weatherman, Channel 7. Ben didn't watch enough television for the name to be familiar. He smoothed the worn article and adjusted the lamp on the desk for better illumination. A quick scan showed Bruce to be an expert on UFOs, mutilations, and crop circles.

"Are you saying that you do these things, then report them supporting . . ." Ben glanced back at the article, "the theory that it's all the work of aliens?"

"Yes."

Ben wanted to lecture about deceit and criminal acts and punishment but knew he needed to find out just what Bruce knew about that goat and more importantly, perhaps, the crash of the Stealth Fighter.

"Are you saying that you were close to the crash of the F-117A?"

An affirmative nod.

"Did you see the crash?"

A deep sigh. "Not the crash itself, but shortly after."

"He has pictures."

Ben turned to Nate. "Are you serious? Why didn't the two of you come forward with this information? People have died—maybe because of your self-grandizing, criminal acts—" Ben didn't try to keep his voice down. Bruce deserved to hear how he felt. He was thinking of the pilot and Brenda and the Park Ranger. How much heartache could have been prevented if this career-minded asshole had been able to put aside self-interests? "You know, I think I have something of yours—something you lost while photographing that poor goat." Ben fished the lens cap from his pocket and held it out. "Tell me, how did you kill him? Or for that matter, any of your victims."

"I kill livestock for God's sake. The four-legged stuff that people kill and eat anyway. Not dogs or cats—some little old lady's Muffin or Mitsy or Poochie . . ." Bruce was yelling. And Ben didn't care that he looked prime for a coronary.

"That calf was valued at $100,000. Tell the rancher that it didn't make a difference. Tell Amos Manygoats that his goat didn't deserve to live—"

"The only thing I'm sorry for is that old man who got in the way."

"What old man?" Ben sat forward.

"Some old guy out looking for his livestock. Scared the b-jesus out of me. Wandering around making these clucking noises. I struck him out of self-defense."

"And didn't stick around to see if you'd killed him? Or if he was still alive? Did it dawn on you to drag him to safety? Away from the fumes?" Ben was livid. "You're an irresponsible piece of shit—"

"Doctor, is there some problem? Is everyone all right?" The desk nurse paused in the doorway.

"I'm sorry. We'll keep it down." Ben sat back in his chair. He closed his eyes. His head hurt. He wanted to punch this man sitting in front of him—great bedside manner for a shrink, but he was human. Of all the things confided in him, cruelty was the thing he understood the least—against man or animal. And Amos could have died.

"I'm ruined." Bruce's voice was hushed as if someone had let the air out.

Ben took a deep breath and stood up. "There may be criminal charges. I'm going to admit you to the hospital, under guard. What I know now doesn't negate the fact that you have a very serious eye condition. I'm going to let law enforcement decide whether to hold both of you. You mentioned pictures, ones you took that night. What exactly did you see?"

"A bunch of men dragging a body toward the Stealth. And then this Indian woman runs over after they leave and tries to revive the guy but is picked up and carried away by another guy in a flight suit."

Ben forced himself to breath evenly and not look at Bruce. Evidence that exonerated Brenda and gave credence to Tommy's hypotheses about abduction—and made Pansy a pretty good observer. Ben felt the rise of anger but steadied himself. Would it have made a difference if this had been known before? Certainly to Tommy.

"I'm sure the Air Force will be interested in what you've seen. I know I don't have to suggest that you cooperate—which starts by staying here while I set things up."

Ben walked out to the front desk, paged one of the physicians on call and dialed the number of the Gallup police station.

FOURTEEN

It was all the coyote's fault—or the animal's careful planning, depending on how a person looked at things. Had she been at the right place, at the right time? Or just the opposite? Brenda sighed. Pale, gray light disappeared from the crevices between the boulders crowded overhead. The sun had set and now darkness enveloped the cramped space they called home. For the fourth day in a row she'd go to sleep longing for Mariah, aching to hold the child, bring her into her bed. She'd never been away this long before.

She'd risked everything last night to see her daughter. When her mother had stirred and called out, Mariah had reassured her without being prompted and didn't cry when Brenda left. So old for her age. It was like she understood. And the promise to be with her by the first snow. Where would Brenda be at that time? A chill shinnied up her spine. If she didn't do what she was told, she might not see her baby again. Hadn't Ronnie told her that he'd been ordered to keep her with him? That she knew too much to be released? If she didn't do what she was told, Mariah was in danger? She'd had to see her daughter last night—make sure nothing had happened to her already.

A shudder and the man beside her turned on his side. She waited until his breathing was even, then pushed to a sitting position. She had to think, make a decision that would be the right one. But what was right? Take a chance? Leave again, take Mariah and . . . do what? Go to the police? Live in terror for her life and Mariah's? If she did that, Ronnie would be killed.

They were coming under the cover of darkness. She could smell Ronnie's fear. The meeting was set for midnight. But one wrong move, one word out of place . . . how could she be safer staying? Wouldn't they kill her anyway? They'd already threatened her child. Could Ronnie save her? Would he save her?

Stupid. Of course he would. He was Mariah's father. But somewhere deep inside, she wasn't so certain. And she couldn't die. Not now. Not for a long time. There was her mother to take care of. And Mariah. She wanted to see Mariah grow to womanhood.

The closeness of the rock was intimidating. Even her breath seemed to bounce back at her. She felt trapped by the tight space, by her decision . . . damned if you don't, damned if you do. Whatever Ronnie had done, it had been his decision, not hers. She had to safeguard her family as best she could. She truly knew nothing about Ronnie's involvement but she needed to tell someone about what she had seen the night of the crash. She breathed deeply and felt calmer.

One time as a child she'd slipped away to come here to the canyon. Her parents were angry until the medicine man said that she'd heard a calling. That she'd had to come. And maybe that was the truth. All her adult life she remembered that day. She'd roamed over the ruins, play-talked with Ancient Ones—even now she could call upon that feeling of peace, of euphoric isolation.

She glanced again at the man snoring softly now, chin tucked against chest, his head cradled by bended elbow. And once again she felt her resolve fade. No one should ever have to choose between a child and its father. No one. But if she didn't leave now, she might not have another chance. She slipped to her feet and stood a moment thinking of her plan. He'd relaxed finally, fought sleep for two days only dozing long enough to keep going. Now, exhaustion had set in. Last night and tonight, he'd slept. If she were careful, he wouldn't know she'd gone until she was miles away.

But it was so difficult to go. For most of her life she'd been in love with Ronnie Cachini. There hadn't been any other boyfriends. And she'd always thought they would marry, maybe even live on the reservation. But it was Ronnie who had to leave, see the world. He wanted to make his mark. And now, this mess. Could he have wanted money so badly that he sold out? Became a traitor?

His family would be devastated. And he wouldn't answer her questions. She begged him to talk to her. She'd seen the men in the truck. She'd watched them dismantle the plane. Hadn't she tried to revive the man she thought was the pilot? But no, he'd say nothing. Only that her not knowing would save her. That she had to remain ignorant of certain facts to stay alive. And him? She'd implored him to save his own life. Let her go to Mariah and save himself.

He was meeting someone. It was the end of the deal, as he put it. One last item, the pilot's helmet, and he'd be free. Those were his words and that was all she knew—that and the fact that Ronnie had a gun, felt he needed one. And he was angry. An anger that ate at him. Something she'd never seen in him before. Anger and a restlessness. But it had been four years since they were close. Could she have misjudged him even then?

Missed the traits that could make him turn against his country?

He hadn't tied her up last night or tonight. Was he beginning to trust her? What had happened to the man she would have sworn she knew so well? Last night they'd made love in the narrow, cramped space between the boulders and she'd cried out that she loved him, and he'd held her and rocked gently, and she felt his tears stain her cheek. But there was no proclamation of love from him. And finally, her tears mingled with his as an immense sadness enveloped her at what could never be. Everything she had ever wanted in life was once and for all a shattered dream. She'd crept away in the darkness when he fell asleep, heart heavy but driven to see her child.

She was small enough to wiggle through a crack overhead and be well away from the ruins before midnight. She knew she had to be careful. Someone might be watching. But who was the someone? It was all a puzzle, but she felt that Ronnie was wrong. Very wrong in what he'd done and that made her physically sick. She lifted on tiptoe and pulled her body upward, holding her breath as a scattering of pebbles bounced over the face of the granite boulder. She waited but Ronnie didn't move. Then she reached up, found a handhold, and another, then a foothold, and another as she worked her way upward into the cloudy night.

The night air was calming. Tommy rolled the passenger window down and let the cross breeze cool his face and neck. He had some thinking to do. And he was headed toward the stables almost before he realized it. Harley never let him down. Maybe he was a little quiet for a sounding board but he never passed judgement and he would stand there as long as needed, just listening.

The horse knew the sound of the Bronco and trotted to the front of his corral. His greeting was always the same, a low reverberating nicker that sounded like someone had just cleared his throat.

"Hey, big guy." Tommy held out a half of an apple, brown from being under the seat since yesterday's lunch but none the less tasty, if he could judge from Harley's enthusiastic munching.

The thirty gallon half-barrel water container was almost empty, and Tommy dragged a hose from a coil by the tack room, fastened an end to a faucet and then primed the pump. The water that gushed out was well-cold and he scrubbed the sides of the barrel with his hands, dumped it, rinsed it and then left the nozzle in the bottom to fill. It was mindless work but seemed to help him get his thoughts in order. Harley stood quietly after he'd nuzzled the front of Tommy's shirt searching for more apple.

"You think I'm being stupid about Brenda?" Then Tommy laughed. This to a stallion that had taken out two panels of pipe fencing last month because a cute little quarter horse mare had cycled. "Something tells me you'd agree with what I'm about to do."

After a couple more minutes of scratching behind a big, black ear, Tommy turned off the water and recoiled the hose.

It took him forty-five minutes before he hit the washboard entrance to Chaco.

"Damn."

Quickly, he grabbed the steering wheel with both hands and cursed the Bronco's lack of suspension. The road was beating him to death. He was fighting to hold the car on course. Abruptly he pulled to the side, got out and looked down at the left front tire. A flat. What else could go wrong?

The fact that the spare bounced on the ground made him feel a little better. But should he continue on the spare? How long had it been since maintenance had checked any of the tires? Of all the rotten things to happen. He hated having to worry about the roadworthiness of a vehicle. But grousing wasn't getting the tire changed.

He dragged out the jack, propped a flashlight to shine squarely on the wheel, seated the jack, cranked up the left front and reached for the tire iron. The moon was well up now. He should be glad that the clouds had thinned. What he tried not to think about was the time that would be wasted. He pried off the hubcap, and leaned in to twist a lug nut—

"Tommy?"

Tommy jumped backwards staggering to stand. He couldn't see the figure blocking the light, yet the voice. . . . He knew that voice.

"Brenda?"

He rushed to put his arms around her, but she pulled back.

"I didn't mean to scare you," was all she said. Tommy felt awkward his arms dangling by his sides. He stepped back. Abruptly, he leaned over to pick up the flashlight.

"I've . . . we've all been worried. Are you all right?" He tried to keep the emotion out of his voice. He wanted to grab her and hold her not let her push him away. But instead he just stood there.

"Yes—more or less. I think I need to talk to someone."

Understatement, Tommy thought. "I can offer an ear, with or without the badge."

"Um, unofficial. Maybe, you could just take me home?"

He didn't say anything, didn't question her wanting to go home. He simply finished putting the spare on and then held the passenger-side door open. Was he doing the right thing? He didn't even want to know.

They drove a back way, yet another dry arroyo-road that approached Brenda's trailer from the west and kept the car hidden most of the time by steep, canyon-like sides. The going was slow. Tommy didn't want to challenge the spare which so far seemed to be holding up. But they wouldn't gain anything by pushing it and breaking down again. They rode in silence. He respected her silence. She'd talk when she was ready.

He wanted to tell her it would be all right. But maybe it wouldn't be. Maybe that's why she kept him from touching her. At this moment he was a police officer taking a suspect to her house, not to jail. Did she realize what he was willing to do for her? He'd never jeopardized his career before—so, why was he doing it now? But he knew before he glanced sideways at the figure huddled against the passenger's door. There was no spark in this vivacious women who used to joke and poke fun at him.

At first Brenda stared out the window. Tommy watched as she closed her eyes and pressed her cheek against the cool glass. But it was the tears that spilled over swollen eyelids and simply slid without a sound down her cheek that made his heart ache. He slowed the Bronco, then stopped, turned it off and pulled the emergency brake.

She roused herself to look at him, fright registering in her eyes. "Why are we stopping?"

"Brenda, you know you may be arrested when we get to the house. I can't guarantee that someone isn't watching, waiting for your return." There, he had said it. At whatever cost, he had to know the extent of her involvement.

"Arrested? Me? For what?" Brenda's voice trembled.

"For being an accomplice in the downing of a very expensive aircraft, the death of an unknown man, the theft of fifty million in prototype electronics, aiding and abetting one Ronnie Cachini—"

"No. It wasn't like that. I had no idea people would—"

"What did you expect them to think? Someone signaled that plane to crash-land. It's on tape. Ronnie Cachini was the pilot. You were at the site to meet him. The authorities believe another man was with you. A man who lost his life, became expendable and was blown up with the plane."

"That's not so. The man was already dead. He was brought there by others." She grabbed the door handle. "I can't do this—I can't report Ronnie, talk to the law. Talk to you." Fresh tears.

"Brenda, I'm a friend. A friend who's realized how much you mean to him. I don't want my badge to get in the way. I want to listen as a friend and help you."

She searched his face, started to say something but simply said, "Thank you." But she took her hand off the door handle.

He leaned over, put two hands on her shoulders and gently eased her to face him. She didn't pull away.

"Let's start at the beginning. Please? I want to listen." He spoke softly. "I want to know exactly what happened. I won't make judgements. Who knows, maybe I can help." Tommy snapped off the headlights and squared his body to face her. Night sounds pushed into his consciousness, the chirps and rustle of insects and small animals. A light breeze skipped across his neck. The air was cooler now but smelled richly of piñon and sage. He'd let Brenda take her time. And, yes, he felt exhilaration. She was with him. She was safe. He took a deep breath and waited.

Brenda began slowly and recounted first how the coyote forced her to drive out of her way, how she saw the plane land, then be dismantled by a truckload of men speaking a language she didn't recognize. She recounted how their leader sprayed the ground with bullets while she hid. But she was emphatic that these strange men, all six feet or taller, dressed in black, left the body, that she didn't see Ronnie until he pulled her from the fire and carried her to safety.

"Why have the two of you been hiding?" He just came out with it. But he had to know.

"Ronnie . . . he insisted. He's . . . " More tears. Tommy pulled a box of tissues from the glove box. "I'm so afraid he's done something he shouldn't have. I think he was involved in deliberately landing the plane so that it could be ransacked. He's in on some deal to sell secrets."

"To whom?"

Brenda shook her head. "I know Ronnie's been in touch with someone. He's had to wait until a deal was completed. There's a meeting tonight. Ronnie kept one item that these people have to have. As soon as he turns it over, he'll get paid. And as he says, it'll all be over."

Tommy thought of the call Ronnie'd supposedly made to his mother using Edwina's phone. He'd been right. More likely it was to his accomplice. "You're certain about this?"

"Fairly. He didn't tell me much, but I don't think he lied."

"Was Edwina killed because she found out where you were hiding?"

"Edwina?" Brenda looked blank.

"The Park Ranger."

"We didn't see any rangers."

"Well, this one knew Ronnie, probably followed him back to the caves. Didn't you wonder where he'd gotten the ham sandwiches and chips?"

"At the Information Center. He bought them at a snack bar."

"No. A ranger provided them. Then this same ranger fell to her death—after her murderer crushed every bone in her hand."

Brenda sat forward so suddenly she grazed her head on the visor. "People think we, I, had something to do with the death of a Park Ranger?" She was incredulous. "That's terrible. How could people believe—"

"Because the facts point to the two of you." Tommy swallowed. No matter how uncomfortable she might be, he needed to know what happened. "Think. Did Ronnie say anything about meeting someone at the Information Center? Or did he meet her at the caves? I guess I just want to know how someone convinced her she was being attacked by an alien."

"You're not making sense." Brenda twisted away and again reached for the door handle.

"Wait. If you're innocent, you need to know the mess you're in."

Brenda slumped back against the seat, her eyes closed.

"Let me tell you what I know." Tommy skipped the gory details but used the word murder again and finished with Edwina's portrait in blood of her assailant. "Like this." Tracing his index finger through the dust on the dash, Tommy drew the infamous alien head.

Brenda gasped. "Oh no, oh my God they've found it. They'll kill him. They don't need him any longer. They already have what they want."

"Who has what they want?" Tommy grabbed Brenda by the arms. "Look at me. Why is Ronnie in danger?"

Suddenly, Brenda began to sob. Tommy waited, then tried again. "Please, let me help you."

Finally, Brenda nodded, the sobs subsiding to occasional gulps for air. "Ronnie kept one piece of equipment. Maybe to safeguard his life in the first place, maybe to ensure payment . . . anyway, the electronics in the cockpit weren't complete, not really workable without the pilot's helmet. He took that with him." She paused and put a hand to her forehead. "When he picked me up? Dragged me away from the exploding plane? I thought he was an alien. That drawing looks enough like the headgear, the slanted visor, the oblong roundness . . . but if this ranger was pushed off the edge of a cliff, then it means she surprised someone who'd found Ronnie's helmet and flight suit."

"I think you're right." Tommy almost smiled. Such a simple explanation to all the alien hysteria. The true believers would be disappointed.

"This is so terrible. Ronnie and I hid the stuff in one of the caves. It was too heavy and cumbersome to drag around. He's going back for it tonight, meeting someone there. . . but that person already has what he wants. Oh Tommy, he'll be killed."

Tommy sat back. He knew Brenda was telling the truth. The hose that they'd found in the back cave proved that. Wasn't that the very thing he was going to search for himself tonight? But who had killed Edwina? Obviously the same one who would confront Ronnie later that evening.

"I'm going back." Brenda opened the door.

"No. Wait. You have to think of Mariah."

"I have to warn Ronnie." She stepped out but hesitated. Tommy came around to stand beside her.

She turned to face him, "What would you do if you were me?"

What would he do? "It's a tough decision."

"I still want to believe that there's an explanation for what Ronnie's done. Even if he did this thing, crash-land to sell electronics, he deserves to know the helmet's been found and that someone may try to kill him. I owe him that. I can't just let him be killed."

"I'm going with you." The words seemed to hang in the air. Tommy almost wished he could take them back. But he knew he couldn't let her go alone. And he knew he wasn't going to detain her even if that's what a code of ethics might call for—arresting her, taking her into Crown Point for further questioning. And he wasn't going to call for help. Not now, anyway. He would go with her as her friend. He wasn't trying to be a hero but he'd try to protect her. If they had any chance of being together, what he was doing was the only way—support her in something she had to do. If time was on their side, they could warn Ronnie before the meeting. But what would he do then? He honestly didn't know.

"We can't take the car. The shortest way is cross-country and it's a couple miles, at least. Are you up to a little hike?"

"You don't have to do this. I know what this could cost you." Brenda stepped close and took his hands. "I wish things could be different. I'm so mixed-up. But when this is all over—"

He stopped her from finishing the sentence by kissing her. He hadn't planned on it. But she put her arms around his neck and kissed him back and it felt good. She relaxed a moment nestled against his chest. Then she pulled away and said, "A little payment for being so nice."

And he had the presence of mind to quip, "On an installment plan, I hope. But I could get to be expensive." And she had laughed and nothing made him feel better than to hear the sound of bells.

Tommy didn't think he had ever been that thirsty. They were pushing it now. Trotting a quarter mile, slowing to a jog, then fast walking—trying not to stumble over cactus and scrub brush. But the going was smooth and fast on the more or less level flatland in comparison to what the terrain would be like in another fifteen minutes when they would begin to climb. They didn't talk. He tried not to think about what they would find. He wondered if they would be in time to warn Ronnie. But even more, he wondered if he would arrest him.

The moon was obscured by clouds, but Tommy used the flashlight sparingly. He stripped to a tee-shirt and left his stiff poplin shirt draped over a cholla cactus. Sweat glistened on his forearms and prickled across his neck. He'd tucked a snub-nose .38 in his pants pocket and left his revolver in its holster draping the cumbersome leather belt over his shoulder. The key to being on the winning side would be surprise. That he knew.

Brenda was part mountain goat when it came to covering ground. If she was fatigued, she didn't show it. Once or twice she'd reached out to steady herself by touching his arm, then grabbed his hand while scrambling over a clump of granite. And each time she smiled, shyly but with a warmth he hoped wasn't his imagination. He watched the curve of her back and hip as she climbed ahead of him and entertained thoughts of evenings in his apartment. But would he get that chance?

Finally, he signaled for them to stop and he pulled Brenda back under an overhang of rock. They were at the base of the cliff that they would have to climb in order to get to the caves. To the right about a quarter mile was the Information Center. But straight up, protected by darkness was the quickest way to Ronnie.

"I don't think we should use the flashlight beyond this point. Even a pinpoint of light will carry a hundred yards."

Brenda nodded. She leaned over and rubbed a calf muscle.

"We need a plan," Tommy said.

"What kind of plan?" He heard her sharp intake of breath.

"Help. Backup, I guess. I'd personally feel a lot better if there was some muscle covering our flank. Guys spraying the ground with machine-gun fire don't sound too pleasant to me. I think Ronnie could be outnumbered. We all could. I guess I wasn't thinking straight when I let us just take off like this."

"But who would you call?"

"With what you've told me, don't you think the Air Force should know that Ronnie is alive but being threatened?"

"Do you know someone?"

"Colonel Hap Anderson. I'm not his biggest fan but he's been in charge of the investigation along with another colonel. He'd be the logical one to call. And I guess I probably owe him."

"Would he arrest Ronnie?"

"If he's guilty. But aren't we faced with a tough choice here? Ronnie has to be alive to explain himself." He stood silently and let her think. She needed to consider Mariah, too. There needed to be an end to all this. Finally, Brenda nodded.

There was a pay phone outside the Center. Had the rangers said that it had been fixed? Tommy could only hope. Cell phones weren't dependable in this remote part of the state. He chose not to carry one.

"Stay here out of sight. Give me twenty minutes to reach the Center, make the call and come back."

"I want to come."

"Too risky. Two of us would be spotted easier than one."

Tommy stripped off his white tee-shirt. "I'm not giving anyone a target if I don't have to." His dark skin would blend with the night. He wiped the sweat from his face and neck, then tucked the shirt in his belt.

"I'm afraid for you to leave me."

"Stay here against the rock, under the overhang. You'll be safe. Here. Take the revolver." He took it out of the holster.

"No, I couldn't."

"Please. It would make me feel better about leaving."

"I'll put it here." She placed it at the base of a large rock.

"It won't do much good unless you can get to it quickly."

"Tommy, I'll be fine." Her smile didn't look very encouraging. "What if you don't come back?"

"I'll be back." It was his best "Terminator" imitation and brought the low chuckle he wanted. And with that he took off at a trot for the Information Center.

Tommy always had quarters. The pop machine at the station only took exact change. He dug out the colonel's card and dialed his cell.

"You've done right by coming forward, son." The colonel had listened patiently while Tommy told him what he knew. "I want you to be careful. I know you believe this Begay woman is innocent but don't let a skirt cloud your thinking. And I want the two of you to stay put until I can get some troops in there. I don't want the two of you to get mixed up in what's going to take place, you hear me? You wait for me at the Center."

Tommy was reluctant to agree. Ronnie still needed their help. . . .

"I appreciate your concern." Tommy stopped short of saying "Sir" and he stopped way short of agreeing to stay put.

"I'm taking that to mean you'll stay out of things. I'm out your way as it is—a meeting at the tribal office ran late. Won't take me long to swing over to the Information Center. Let's say I meet you there in under an hour."

Tommy didn't doubt he was on the road somewhere, the throaty growl of something without a muffler almost overpowered their conversation.

The colonel was abrupt when he hung up. Tommy looked back to where Brenda was waiting. Under an hour put the colonel somewhere close by. Should they try to find Ronnie or wait for help?

The moon peeked briefly from its cloud-cover and sparkled across the sand but showed nothing moving. Tommy had loosened the bulb in the Center's back light.

Had the sudden darkness that enveloped the phone been noticed? He had no way of knowing. But he stood there anyway, watching. Maybe he should call Ben. He owed him an apology and strangely Tommy had a feeling that he needed to let someone else know what was happening. He could call his boss but he wasn't about to tell Leonard Tom about Brenda. Not yet, anyway. Leonard would have to wait.

Tommy dropped another quarter in the slot and was surprised when Ben's answering machine came on. Where could he be? Tommy hadn't been gone much over an hour. But he launched into a message anyway.

"Ben, I've got Brenda. She's innocent and we hope Ronnie is, but he's in trouble. I called Colonel Anderson—that'll make you happy—and he's on his way. There's a meeting tonight, midnight in the first row of cliff houses. Looks like the—"

The machine cut him off and he dropped another quarter, waited for the message and then continued.

"Looks like the crash was prearranged. We just don't know the extent of Ronnie's involvement. We're supposed to meet the colonel by the Information Center in forty-five minutes or so. I haven't decided whether to warn Ronnie first. I suppose we better. I owe you an apology for earlier. I was out of line. It's about a quarter past nine—"

This time when a beep announced the end of the recording, he just hung up.

At first Brenda paced. Tommy said he'd be gone twenty minutes. She felt uneasy, fear prickled across her shoulders and made her shiver. She started to whistle then almost bit her tongue. What was she thinking of? To whistle at night attracted ghosts. Did she want more trouble than she was already in? She was aware of the wind that gusted around her. It sprang from nowhere to ruffle her hair then skip away. She couldn't stop herself from thinking it brought evil. Why had she consented to staying behind? She glanced at the gun then turned away.

"Brenda?"

She didn't know what kept her from screaming. The man pulled himself up and over the ledge to stand upright in the shadows. She didn't know him. He was older, military bearing, short haircut. . . .

"Who are you?"

"A friend of Ronnie's. We watched you and Mr. Spottedhorse come into the canyon and I offered to escort you back to the caves."

There was something wrong. Ronnie would have come himself.

"I need to wait for Mr. Spottedhorse."

"No need. I've spoken with him and he's waiting at the Information Center for all of us. We'll join Ronnie and then go on down."

"I prefer to wait here. Send Ronnie to—"

"You don't have a choice." He pulled a gun from the back of his jeans. "And don't think of screaming. Your boyfriend isn't doing very well. I'd hate to jeopardize his health. Just walk ahead of me nice and easy."

The gun—could she reach it? It hadn't been detected. But would he shoot her? More importantly, could she shoot him? If she got to the gun first; if she could grab the gun, roll to one side before he realized—no, there was no way that she would get away with it. But no guts, no glory . . . .

She threw herself forward scrambling across rocks that cut her hands, but he was quick and grabbed her ankles pulling her back.

"Now let's see what's so interesting over here." He jerked her upright by the shoulder in a wrenching movement that made her dizzy. His gun now pressed against her neck.

"Well, look what we have here. A little protection, I'd imagine—only you were too stupid to keep it with you. And there are those who recommend women for combat." The laugh was derisive. "Sorry the heroics didn't work, sweetheart. Let's get moving." He roughly pushed her ahead of him.

FIFTEEN

Ben was exhausted by the time he got back to his apartment. He was glad he'd forgotten to give Tommy the lens cap. Now it was in the hands of the police—where it belonged. He was sorry that he'd neglected to tell him his suspicions about the colonel possibly being close to the crash site that night. He'd just plain forgotten to give him the lens cap but he wasn't sure he hadn't purposefully withheld info on Hap and son. Tommy didn't need anything else to fuel his hatred of the man. And he wasn't positive it had been the colonel. But now he had to share the information about Bruce and Nate.

Ben grabbed the phone but the incessant beeping indicated he had a message. Maybe Julie called—Ben excitedly punched in his code.

"This message is for Dr. Pecos. This is Ed over at the Chaco tourist center. I'm really looking for that cop friend of yours—Spottedhorse. Somebody at police headquarters saw you guys with a pizza and I thought I might catch him. Hopefully, you can get a message to him. This phone call that he had me check . . . the one made from Edweener's phone? Well, it was long distance all right. Placed to Albuquerque and it's not to our headquarters. I can't believe she'd go and let someone do that. Against all regulations, you know. But then the pay phone was out. I don't want to second guess the dead. And this guy could have told her it was an emergency."

It took a minute for Ben to figure out the players. Of course, the call to dear ol' mom by the mysterious stranger. The one Edwina mentioned in her diary.

"There was only one call—not that that excuses it, it don't. Guess it was the morning they met. Nothing unusual on the records after that. Well, anyway, looks like the guy called Kirtland. Here's the number. 821-5907. Maybe ol' Edweener had herself a flyboy. That guy I saw sure had a military bearing. But I would have guessed Marine. Might be worth following up on, though. I think Mr. Spottedhorse might find it interesting. Sorry I didn't call earlier—I nearly forgot altogether."

Ben had no idea how anyone could tell a difference in the services by watching a guy from behind at fifty yards, but he did find the information interesting. Then he surprised himself. He dialed the number the ranger had given him. It was close to ten. If it was the base he wouldn't find anyone there, but he might get a recording and he was helping Tommy. Or should he just admit to having more than a little curiosity himself?

"You have reached the office of Colonel Harold (Hap) Anderson. Colonel Anderson will be out of town until Friday. Please leave a message at the sound of the tone."

Ben hung up, then dialed again and listened to the message. Again, the chirpy sweet voice of some female junior airman assured him whose office it was. Hap Anderson, actually Harold Anderson. But what did it mean? Why would someone on the run stop long enough to call the base? Call a particular person on the base, that is. He felt a blip of excitement and maybe a little foreboding. Ronnie Cachini had called Colonel Anderson. So why was the good old colonel playing dumb? Only one reason came to mind—somehow Colonel Hap Anderson was in on it—whatever the "it" was. Ben wasn't sure of what. But there was duplicity. Of that he was certain. And he knew for a fact that Harold Anderson and Colonel Hap Anderson were one and the same. Hap for all his posturing was out there that night. But Ben still kept coming back to Ronnie. Why was Ronnie checking in? That didn't sound like a man on the lam.

There was one more message. Ben listened to Tommy's recounting of having Brenda with him and then he almost stopped breathing—Tommy had called Hap Anderson. Would he have called if Ben hadn't been so hard on him about withholding evidence? Now, with the colonel on his way, Tommy and Brenda both might be in trouble—trouble they were totally unprepared for. The term "sitting ducks" popped to mind.

He had to find Tommy. He could get to the Information Center in forty-five minutes. He grabbed a jacket and didn't take time to lock up.

Tommy was huffing more than he wanted to admit by the time he reached the overhang. But it took less than a nanosecond to see that Brenda was gone.

"Shit."

He rarely cursed but this warranted it. He should have taken her with him. But he'd thought she'd stay, wait on him. She was fairly traditional and to walk alone at night invited evil spirits to do harm. But she'd braved those spirits already once this evening. Was she so afraid that he'd arrest Ronnie that she took off to warn him about Tommy, too? He'd given his word as a friend. But calling for backup probably didn't instill confidence. She must have had second thoughts. So, now what? Did he wait for Colonel Anderson or take off and try to find Brenda? There was only one decision. She had a twenty-five minute lead but he should be able to make up some of that time. This time he cursed the promises to go back to the gym. And the chili-fries and Navajo tacos. He knelt and tightened his shoe laces.

Then, he stood a moment listening. The night was quiet. A coyote sang out from a ridge above him and another to his right and another answered along the top of the mesa behind him. So what was he going to do? He needed a plan. If all went well he could find Brenda maybe with Ronnie and get back to the Center before the colonel. But, it was an awfully big "if". And wasn't he assuming that the two of them would just skip right back down to the Center and meet with the colonel? Naivete. But what else could he do? Would Ronnie, at least, tell him the truth? Exonerate Brenda?

He'd follow the ridge and stay out of sight until he reached the base of the cliff dwellings. He figured he could get there in forty-five minutes. The moon drifted out from hiding illuminating the sandy ledge. He needed to figure out which way she'd gone. He squatted and looked at the loosely packed dirt near the base of the granite outcropping where Brenda had stood. Then he saw them—the extra set of prints. A man's boot—heavy heel, rounded toe, smacked of military. So, Ronnie had come for her. He slammed a fist against the rock outcropping.

Why hadn't they waited on him? But that was easy to

answer—he was the law. He represented the one thing Ronnie couldn't risk getting involved with—if he was guilty. And didn't this seal his fate? Tommy was disgusted. He'd been stupid. It served him right. Had Ronnie forced Brenda to go with him? Probably. He honestly didn't think she'd just take off again. She said she was mixed up, that she wasn't sure. . . . After all this, did she still love Ronnie? She suspected he was involved in wrongdoing but would that squelch her feelings for him? The next thought caught him like a blow to the solar-plexus—had they made love? They had been together for three days. Had Ronnie held her, caressed her, maybe asking her to give in, maybe demanding. . . .

"Shit."

What should he do? It was obvious that three made a crowd. He wasn't wanted. Should he just abandon the chase now? Give them the time they needed to get away? Could he live with his conscience if he let them go? Could he live with his conscience if he tracked them down?

Anger was beginning to keep him from thinking clearly. Anger that started with thoughts of maybe they had used him, made fun of him. But no, she was the one who left first, tried to go home and only went back when he'd told her about Edwina and the alien look-a-like headgear. He needed to believe her intentions were honorable. Of course, she would feel she should warn the father of her child. But for him the chase was over. It was up to Brenda to do the right thing. If she left with Ronnie, didn't convince him to turn himself in—then, the consequences were clear. She knew that. He had to trust her—trust that she'd do the right thing. But no matter what, she was an adult. She would have to face the consequences of her actions.

Maybe he would meet Colonel Anderson at the Center after all. He pulled on his tee-shirt. The gun. He'd forgotten to check. Had she taken it? A quick look along the base of the cliff revealed the revolver was gone. How could he keep getting in deeper and deeper? Now, there was a charge of stolen government property—a firearm he'd gladly handed over to someone who, to outsiders at least, was still a suspect in a murder case.

The Jaguar ate the miles—one hundred, one ten, one twenty. He watched the needle flicker, then bobble before squarely resting on the next highest number. Abruptly he eased off the gas. Wouldn't do to get there too early. He touched the butt of the 9-mil in his belt. Comforting. If he had to use it, that is. Could be that everything would be taken care of without his intervention. Then again . . .

He only hoped that Indian cop would have the sense to follow directions. But what red blooded male, red skinned or not, didn't think with his dick? He'd be out chasing that Begay woman. And that could mean he'd get in the way. Unless there was a decoy and he took the bait. It was something to think about.

But so was his career. This should put him over the top. A last hurrah. Younger men might think he was over the hill but they should see him now. He was a hard-ass. He acknowledged that, enjoyed his image. Hadn't he earned it? And now this. Who could have done it better? Orchestrated all the players? No, tonight was his night. As he always said, "It's not the arrow; it's the Indian." He didn't care what firepower they might have, he'd outwitted them. Revenge was sweet.

The military had been a good life. But soon he'd just be a citizen, average Joe on the street. But he'd have his memories. And he'd have gone out in a blaze of glory.

The roar of the engine drowned the ping from the high-powered rifle but the right front and rear tires exploded in an unraveling of tread as metal rims hit the pavement before the Jag tumbled sideways then rolled twice into the median to rest upside down. One headlight thrust a beam steadfastly through the swirling dust of debris then flickered and abruptly went out. There was no sound.

The man dressed in black, a rifle slung over his shoulder, trotted across the highway and stood looking at what was left of the Jag. Dropping to one knee, he prodded the arm that stretched out from the mangled cockpit and attempted to find a pulse. Satisfied there was none, he retraced his steps and disappeared toward the mesa.

Tommy returned to the Center but stayed well back from the building itself. Sparse grass skirted the parking lot. Cover meant lying flat beneath a piñon some thirty yards to the north. The area was deserted. Eerie. The wind had died to an occasional rustle of dry leaves and the moon, no longer playing hide and seek with errant clouds, stretched the shadows of posts and accentuated the white striping of the parking spaces. He felt utterly alone.

Surveillance. One of those things that drove him nuts. He never liked that duty at the academy. But maybe this once sit and wait would be the best approach. He'd see the colonel first. Probably hear him first.

Tommy flattened his body to fit a natural indentation

between two tufts of three foot high buffalo grass that sprouted beside the small evergreen. He'd be tough to see and he had the advantage of having a 180 degree view. No one could get past him or come up from the south without his seeing them. He relaxed and stretched his body full length but not before he'd eased the snub nose .38 from his pocket and placed it beside him. Luckily, he wouldn't have to wait for the colonel long. Maybe another fifteen minutes.

The night sky displayed a dizzying array of bright twinkling lights among wisps of the once thick clouds. The Ancient Ones enjoyed a sky like this. He wondered what they thought—how they explained their universe, why they disappeared without a trace. Did he believe the recent research that branded them cannibals? It didn't upset him like it did some. And their name instead of Anasazi, which means "ancient enemy" in Navajo, was now Puebloan. That seemed fitting. Both the Navajo and the Hopi considered these Ancient Ones their ancestors. But their disappearance—that was the mystery. Around the year 1300 whole villages just picked up and moved 250 miles away. Was there village-on-village violence? Somehow, he wanted to believe in a peaceful, happy people tending their fields, building the homes that were left for him to marvel at.

Then he felt the nudge of the gun at his elbow as he shifted position—a grim reminder that people weren't very peace-loving today. Why did he expect more out of the Ancient Ones? His favorite ruin was Pueblo Bonito, a towering maze of rooms probably used for religious or political functions. On a night like tonight the moonlight would make the hollowed windows seem like a hundred eyes.

He knew all the structures by heart. He had wanted to

be an anthropologist—being a cop was practical. But it was a dream not quite dead, just one that eating, and feeding Harley made impossible.

Yet, even being this close to the ancient houses was exciting. He remembered that the rounded outer wall of Pueblo Bonito hid a giant kiva, a circular room used for ceremonial purposes. What kinds of things went on in there a thousand years ago? Was it true that human sacrifices were made? Marrowless bones were turning up with signs of being gnawed by two-footed animals. Humans were predators. And times hadn't changed that much. Nothing made the Ancient Ones any different from men today—except, perhaps, their taste for human flesh.

Tommy shivered and tried to superimpose some happy thoughts. But he couldn't seem to come up with any.

Brenda didn't look at him. She simply knew that the gun was still pointed at her back and Tommy's gun was tucked in his belt. They climbed in silence. Once, he had reached out to steady her when she'd lost her footing, left leg skittering out from the wall. He'd let her get her breath before motioning her on. When they reached the first stretch of level land, they kept to the rocks and skirted the first two dwellings.

Who was he? He'd remained in the shadows and she couldn't see clearly. She thought he was an older man. Older than she anyway. It was difficult to tell. He was dressed all in black—some kind of jumpsuit. And he seemed to be a walking arsenal. The butt of the rifle slung over his shoulder bounced against the rocks dislodging a sprinkling of pebbles when he'd leaned over to steady her. There was no trying to get away.

She knew Tommy was out there. But what had he thought when he found her gone? Would he suspect wrongdoing? She didn't think so. He'd see the second set of tracks and believe that Ronnie had found her. And he would find the gun gone. That would be the clincher—he'd think she'd abandoned him, taken the gun for protection, or maybe that Ronnie had taken it. She knew Tommy. He'd let her go—wouldn't follow. He'd step aside to let her be with Ronnie, but his heart would be broken.

Tommy had kissed her earlier. And she'd responded. She hadn't consciously compared him to Ronnie but it had been there—the man she'd made love to last night, the man she was kissing now. She had thought once she had warned Ronnie, she could just walk away. Start over. Begin a new dream.

"This way."

It was the first time the man had spoken in twenty minutes and roughly grabbing her elbow, he steered her away from the rock overhang.

"Are we almost there?" She had no idea where "there" was but it seemed important to ask. She half-turned before the barrel of the gun pressed behind her right ear. There was no turning around to get a good look at him.

"Maybe." This time he grabbed her hand and pulled her to the right where they left the path and slipping down a short incline stumbled onto a wash, a narrow arroyo that twisted around several large boulders before disappearing into the distance. Where was he taking her? They'd be above the ruins in another fifteen minutes.

"In here."

The pistol was frigid on her neck raising goosebumps down her arms, but Brenda didn't complain to its owner. They had reached the first of several plateaus that slanted to her left. The man motioned for her to climb down the steps of a small kiva. This one had been restored to show the latillas, the rounded wooden sticks that laced the roof. The air that rushed up was dank and almost sour. This was a room below ground that never saw sunlight. She stumbled on the last step and a hand roughly jerked her upright.

"Sit here."

Brenda sat on the ground that sloped slightly to meet the wall. The wall was one stone thick and covered with generous applications of mud mortar. It was old construction. They were in an area that dated back to before 1100 AD—before they had raised their walls using thick inner cores of rubble and relatively thin veneers of facing stone.

She shuddered. Was Ronnie dead? Had this man killed him? If so, why hadn't he just killed her? No. She couldn't think that way. Ronnie was alive.

The dimness of the cave shrouded her vision, but there was someone leaning against the far wall.

"Colonel?" The shadow stepped into view.

"Ronnie?"

She called out before she thought then slumped against the wall as a hand clipped the side of her head.

"Now, bitch, you want to try that again?"

She shook her head. Roughly her captor grabbed her hair and wrenching her head forward tied a rag over her eyes. Then trussed her wrists with rope after jerking her arms behind her. Where was Ronnie? He'd never let anyone treat her this way. Her cheek stung. The rope chafed her skin. She didn't dare wiggle the blindfold, but she sensed movement more than she heard it. The man was moving away from her. And there seemed to be others.

Ben parked in the front lot of the Information Center. He didn't know where else to go. He'd come rushing out to the ruins without really thinking things through—not knowing where Tommy might be or how to find him. There was a phone in back. He could call the dispatcher and get a message to Tommy's boss. Give him a brief account of what was happening, maybe get some help. That idea had merit.

The Center was darker than usual, he thought. When he found the pay phone in back, he realized that not one of the back lights was on. Well, he could remedy that. The lights, some four in number, were just within reach. Surely, there was a switch close by. He ran his hands along the wall on both sides of the phone booth. Nothing. Then on a whim, he reached up and twisted a bulb. Light. He twisted the remaining three and then stood back in the halo of pale light. The bulbs must be no more than 40 Watts apiece. But it was something.

He couldn't imagine the rangers unscrewing these bulbs every night. And this was a pretty out of the way place for kids . . . Suddenly, Ben wasn't sure what he had done was the right thing. The light around the phone booth might be dim but it could be seen for miles—of that he was certain. Before "easy target" had time to fully register on his brain, he quickly stepped into the shadows.

But what now? For the first time since he came chasing out here, his idea of finding Tommy seemed stupid. He didn't even think he'd have nerve enough to step out into the light to use the phone. Could he find his way to the caves? Tommy thought Mariah had given them a clue—was that where he had gone? Ben had to do something. He couldn't just stand around now that he was here.

Ben worked his way around the south side of the building.

"What the—" A figure stepped from the shadows.

"Ben? What are you doing out here?"

"Thought I'd help. I mean, I don't know exactly how but thought you ought to know about Colonel Anderson and the guy who killed Amos Manygoat's goat—hey, where's Brenda? I thought you said that she was with you."

"She was. I came here to make the call to the colonel and she took off. I should say she and Ronnie took off."

"Did you talk to him?"

"Didn't get a chance."

"Why didn't you go after them?"

"Guess I thought I'd give them the opportunity to get away."

"What are you saying?"

"If she wants to be with him, they deserve a chance."

"And if he's guilty? If she's taken off with a felon?"

"I don't believe Ronnie killed Edwina." Tommy filled Ben in on what Brenda had told him. "Nor did he kill that pilot. Brenda was there. She saw the men who dismantled the plane drag the body out of the truck and leave it beside the wreckage."

"And I have proof that Colonel Anderson was at the hogan bed and breakfast the night of the crash. I also know that he was the one Ronnie called from Edwina's office. In addition, there are pictures of the crash—"

"Pictures?"

"Pictures that support Brenda's story."

Ben told Tommy about Nate and Bruce, finishing with their being held in Gallup. The results of Bruce's night photography locked up in his office in Farmington was soon to be federal property.

"I talked to both of those guys. Who would have thought? I feel badly for the 'believers'."

"I wouldn't worry. There will be something else to get everyone excited."

"What's your make on the colonel?"

Ben thought a moment. "Truthfully, I don't know. If we think on the positive side, he could have set a trap to catch the real crooks and Ronnie was a part of the plan. There could have been a totally legitimate reason for him to be at the B&B and to have been in touch with Ronnie. There would be no reason for the Air Force to share any of this with us. Then Brenda got in the way, and Amos, not to mention Bruce and things got sticky."

"Maybe we'll get a chance to ask him. He's supposed to meet me here, at the Center."

"What time was that?"

"He should have been here by now. Said he was only an hour away. And he's already almost an hour late."

"Already heading in this direction? What was it you said about Ronnie meeting someone to hand over the last piece of equipment? It's beginning to sound like that contact might have been good ol' Colonel Hap. I'm not sure he planned on talking with you first."

"Shit. It'd be a good way to keep me out of the way. Make me promise to stay at the Center."

"It's your call, Tommy. What do you want to do?"

"Check the caves."

Ben fell silent. Tommy had put his job on the line to help Brenda. Not a smart thing to do, but something a person in love would do, he thought. But still there were only two of them—they needed to be thinking about that.

"How about a deal?"

"Such as?"

"Let's make sure we have backup—that we can trust. Get a hold of your boss. Tell him where we are."

Tommy hesitated.

"I didn't say you had to tell Leonard about Brenda. But it might be a good thing."

"Back-up makes sense." Tommy dug in his pocket for a quarter. "But so does total darkness." He reached up and twisted a bulb, then another and another before moving into the shadows next to the phone.

"I don't know who's dispatcher tonight but guess I'll find out."

Whoever the dispatcher was, he or she was chatty. Tommy was obviously being treated to some long-winded account of something. Ben wasn't listening closely until he heard the word, "rollover" just before Tommy hung up.

"What was that all about?"

"Single car accident on 371." Tommy seemed lost in thought. "Driver's dead. Looks like it was a forced accident. Couple tires shot out. Ben, Hap Anderson was the driver."

"I didn't like the guy, but I find it hard to believe that he's dead. But, if he was involved—if he was the person in a position to set up the crash landing, coerce Ronnie, cover up his tracks . . . there's only one person who stands to gain now. This is just a hypothetical question . . . ok? Was Ronnie any kind of a marksman that you knew of?"

"Try Indian All American two years in a row. I came in second."

"Could Ronnie have hiked down to the highway, caused the rollover, hiked back up here, picked up Brenda and took off?"

"Anything is possible. For a man in good condition, maybe even probable. I just find it impossible to believe that Brenda would become an accomplice—take off with him. Ben, she didn't know anything about the death of Edwina. She made a good case for someone threatening Ronnie, someone who wanted the headgear. But she's an adult. It's her life to live. Or throw away."

Ben could hear the misery in Tommy's voice.

"It's probably safe to assume that Brenda's out of danger. If they decide to run and not come forward, that's another story. I don't think it should be up to you to track them down. Let the Feds get involved."

Tommy just nodded.

"I don't know about you, but a cup of coffee sounds good."

"I don't want to leave. I mean since we're out here anyway, what harm is there in just taking a look around? Just make sure that—"

"Brenda's really gone?"

Tommy shrugged, "Maybe. Something like that, I guess."

"You might want some backup." Colonel Bertrand stepped out of the shadows. "Ronnie Cachini is one mean SOB. Hey, sorry, I didn't mean to startle you."

"Colonel—" Tommy started.

"At ease gentlemen, you're just the two I've been looking for. "

"Uh, we heard that Colonel Anderson—"

"Yes. That's why I'm here. He left a message with his wife that he was meeting you here."

"Do you know what happened?" Ben asked.

"Won't be a secret now. Guess I can share. Hap was a short timer, would have retired in a matter of months—not necessarily his idea but the Air Force has a way of thinning its ranks. That was hard for Hap to take—go out without a star." He paused and seemed to be considering what he should say. "You want my opinion? I think I can trust you boys. Hap just snapped, developed a 'get even' mentality. I watched it happen. When the opportunity came along to screw over the Service, he took it—masterminded a plot to become very, very rich. Pity. But he was in over his head. We've been onto him ever since the Stealth took a dive. I was assigned to double-team him from the start on this one. We've been monitoring his activities. We just needed to be there when the money exchanged hands." The colonel paused. "I have to say no one saw the Cachini thing coming. We all thought he was in Hap's hip pocket. He's a bit of a maverick but to kill Hap, well, what is it they say? No honor among thieves? I'm sure the two of you find it shocking to work closely with someone in authority and then find out he was on the other side."

"Everything was pointing in that direction," Ben offered. "We know that Colonel Anderson was at the crash site that night and that Ronnie called him two days later. I still find it difficult to believe that a retiring officer who'd had a great career would risk everything—"

"Greed. As I said, once in a lifetime opportunity. I've known Hap for years—always on the ragged edge of right vs. wrong. There was a time when his kind of bravado was revered—men would follow him into a snake pit and up the other side."

"So, forced retirement made him snap?" Ben was curious—clinical curiosity actually. The retaliating worker going postal. It wasn't out of the question. There seemed to be a case a month.

"He should have realized that he'd outstayed his usefulness. The Air Force has changed. The Services are all big businesses today. The Pattons don't have a place. It's no longer an act first, think later kind of organization. Engineers and MBAs are the new breed. Yahoos are a thing of the past."

Ben wasn't too sure about that.

"It'll be tough on his widow and son—late in life baby. He's only about fifteen now. But Hap should have thought about that. Another good example of his M.O."

"Is there proof? I mean do you know for a fact that Colonel Anderson was the mastermind?"

"Oh yes, an Iranian professor from back East came forward. Seems he valued his U.S. citizenship enough to give up a terrorist group who had planned the whole thing—with help, of course. Well documented help that puts everything in Hap's lap."

"Do you think Colonel Anderson had any idea that you were onto him?"

"I've wondered about that. Could have. Might have shared that with Cachini. That would explain the need to narrow the playing field. Look, I'm sorry about the girl. But let's give her the benefit of the doubt for now. Let's just say she's standing by her man. We'll know more once we get them down here."

"You believe they're still out there?" Tommy asked.

"No way out or we'd have seen them."

Ben wasn't sure who the 'we' were, but sounded like the colonel had company.

"I'm going with you. You in?" Tommy turned to Ben.

"Sorry, I appreciate the support but this is a federal case now. I can't be responsible for civilians—even local law enforcement. I mean it men—this is an order, stay out of the way."

Tommy just nodded. Ben had been afraid of that. It was going to be all Air Force, big Government from now on.

"I've got the number of your supervisor. I'll let him know exactly what happens. And, hey, I appreciate your help." With that Colonel Bertrand turned abruptly and trotted briskly away from the Center. The rifle case slung over his shoulder barely jiggled as his black jumpsuit melded with the shadows.

"If he thinks I'm staying here, he's got another thing coming. You with me?"

Ben grinned. "Now why did I know that was what you were going to say?"

"We're a little undermanned when it comes to fire-power—unless you're packing?"

"Oh yeah, first order of clinical requirements—stay armed at all times."

Tommy grinned. "I didn't think so. But that's all right. I've got a little support."

Tommy held out the automatic with two extra maga-zines. "I can't risk Brenda getting in the way—accidentally getting killed just trying to do the right thing. I've got to be there. You'd do the same for Julie."

Ben thought of saying that things were a little different with Julie, they were engaged. But maybe things weren't that different.

"Do you know where we're going?"

"I still think they've been holed up near the large

house—Pueblo Bonita. I know a path that will keep us out of sight. We'll come in over the top not too far behind them if we hustle."

Ben took a deep breath. This wasn't going to be easy.

The going was smooth to start with just up and around the empty gray-black monuments that had been dwellings. The moon, now not necessarily on their side, boomed out from wispy clouds, fully illuminating their path.

"That's something we can do without. Too much light."

"Maybe it'll help us see them quicker."

"Works both ways if Bertrand is keeping an eye out for us."

Tommy didn't slow until they entered a small clearing. A meeting place for women to grind corn? Probably. But the mix of footprints said it had served the purpose of a meeting place rather recently, too.

Tommy squatted. "I think I'm glad we missed the crowd. Looks like the colonel has some backup."

"How many?"

"Oh, four, at least. Pretty good coverage."

"It looks like they all left together heading up and over the top of that rise."

"What do we do now?"

"Follow."

Tommy didn't say anything but thought Ben knew that the tracks were leading to the caves—the way that Brenda surely must have come.

They fell silent again as Tommy led the way then stopped every fifty feet or so to look at the ground.

"They've separated."

"Are you sure?"

"Yeah, three went to the right, that leaves two continuing forward."

Tommy scanned the horizon. He hated being unprotected, out in the open, following someone who might know they were back there all the time—but he hated worse the thought of someone circling, coming up from behind, not seen or heard until it was too late.

Tommy wished he had all the facts. But he had very little, really. He had the colonel's explanation but mostly, there were still a lot of questions. Was Ronnie a pawn working with others or had he acted by himself? Had he killed Hap to claim all of the prize for himself? What were his intentions when it came to Brenda? If he was a murderer, he'd be out of the picture for a long time—maybe permanently. Would Brenda continue to support a killer?

He motioned for Ben to follow him closer. He had to know, and he had to get his gun back. He hadn't shared that part with Ben. It had been a really stupid thing to do and thanks to his old nemesis, hindsight, he wouldn't do it again.

"I think if we cut through here we'll be above them—at least the two that seem headed to the caves."

At a trot, Tommy cut across a rugged strip of rocky soil that banked the crumbling stone wall that ran for a hundred yards and posed the last defense between the people of the rock houses and unknown foes from the south. The yellow fractured cliffs of sandstone rose straight up as backdrop to these stone and mortar homes that once extended some twenty miles along the floor of a narrow rift, cut by the once life-giving waterway.

Tommy and Ben were parallel with the Chaco Wash, now only a trickle but history proved it had been a good sized river some fifteen hundred years earlier. The footing was more secure along its sandy edges. Saltbrush and Shrub grass clumped to periodically slow their progress, but they were making good time.

The helicopter was a surprise. They saw it resting on the flat mesa above where the ranger had died.

"What do you think?" Tommy slowed, then stopped.

"Makes sense. The colonel would have that kind of clout, be able to order transportation. And I think it tells us that my hunch was right. They're in this area big time. Tommy, according to the colonel, they're tracking a murderer. They're going to have the manpower and the equipment."

"Wonder how long it's been up here. We would have heard it if they brought it in tonight."

"I was just thinking that. Maybe Hap brought it in— had planned some sort of getaway."

"Could be. I just hope it's not being guarded."

Tommy and Ben approached from the rear but saw no one.

"All by itself. Lucky for us."

"We should be just a couple hundred yards from where the opening is. The trick will be finding it."

"What are we looking for?"

"Hole in the ground with steps leading into an underground kiva."

"Be careful. I'll use the flashlight, but only if I have to."

SIXTEEN

"Let her go. You and me can go get the headgear and finish this deal."

Ronnie's voice. Brenda leaned forward to listen.

"Sorry, my man, no can do. The helmet is already safely tucked away. I did some snooping in the caves the other day while I had the two of you under surveillance. Just happened to find what should have been left in the cockpit of the Stealth in the first place."

"With all due respect, Sir, I wasn't sure your support group wouldn't have killed me—if I'd stuck around and just handed everything over."

"Airman, you made one god-awful mess out of things. You know that? I had to take an innocent life to get that gear. Some idiot ranger came tracking me."

"Ranger?"

"Good tits, great ass and a face that'd stop a clock."

"Edwina."

"Ed . . . what?"

"Did you have to kill her? She was looking for me. She didn't do anything wrong."

"Blood's on your head. None of this would have happened if you hadn't tried to set me up. Are you really going to tell me you wanted more money?"

"Sir?"

"Don't play dumb with me. Our deal was the electron-ics. That included the headgear. At the time of the crash-landing."

"I suppose your goons would have just loaded up and driven away? Shaken my hand?"

"Something like that."

"You know what? I think my body was supposed to have been left—not the cadaver like I was told. The prom-ise of a new life was never going to happen, was it? I never was supposed to have the payoff for making the plane avail-able. You know, Sir, you're one double-crossing son-of-a-bitch."

"Probably so. But now it's time for the fat lady."

"I have backup on the way. You won't get away with this."

"You mean Hap?" Loud laughter. "I think you're going to be disappointed."

"What happened to Colonel Anderson?" Ronnie's voice was so quiet, Brenda strained to hear.

"Had a little mishap. He told me to give you his regards." Maniacal laughter.

"What did you do to him?" Anger. Brenda shuddered. She'd never heard Ronnie like this.

"Let's say he was just recently retired—permanently retired."

Ronnie must have lunged because Brenda heard a scuf-fle and a sound of gasping—had he been kicked? There was another scraping sound, a thud, then quiet.

"I know how disappointing this must be. So close but no cigar. You know I'm going to have to kill you. If you'd just done like you were told—"

"I'd be dead sooner."

"I know what it seemed. I know the boys got a little overzealous the other night. But there was never any reason for you to go running off." Silence and then, "Son, believe me, I was all for saving you until you called Hap. Thank God for me if you had to suddenly find a conscience, you sought out someone who was stupid enough to handle it by himself. The last hurrah. That was Hap. This would have been his chance at redemption."

"How do you know Hap wasn't in on it from the beginning—after you first approached me at Holloman?"

"Because I'm a good judge of character. You weren't some random roll of the dice; I knew your habits, your gambling debt, the obligations. You didn't want to come home to the dirt huts and poverty out here. You're no sheepherder, son. As they say, how you gonna keep 'em down on the farm after they've seen Paris. You were going places—you just needed a bankroll." The colonel paused, then the sound of his moving away. "You and I are a lot alike. We like the good times—the things big money can buy. Cars, women— they're expensive. I knew a lot about you. It was easy money. Money you needed. Crash land, the electronics would have been suspected as the culprit. A story of sabotage would have been circulated. You would have taken a blow on the head and gotten paid. But you had to do things your way and look at the trouble it's caused."

Brenda felt the panic make her knees wobble. Would they kill her also? Of course. She was truly the expendable one. If she could only see. The blindfold was big but not that tight. Pretending to scratch her cheek on her shoulder, she inched the right side up. Damn. There was simply no way to slide it up far enough to have a clear view of her surroundings. She felt something sticky on her fingers and thought maybe she had cut her palms scrambling across the rocks to get the gun—the gun that was tucked into the belt of the man Ronnie called colonel. She had no feeling in her hands. Her shoulders ached from her arms being pulled behind her. But all this was secondary to the awful realization that she and Ronnie were going to die.

"She wasn't part of the deal." Ronnie sounded adamant. "Leave her here."

"I'd say her being here makes her a part."

"She doesn't know anything. It was a fluke that she was even near the crash site."

"If she's been paying attention, she knows more than is good for her. No, I have a plan for our little lady here. In fact, you may have done me a favor. Gave me the perfect setup to get rid of Hap and you. Of course, you know no one's going to question the fact that you killed Colonel Anderson. I'm not sure what story I want to circulate—he was coming to your rescue after you'd phoned for help; then you had second thoughts. Or maybe documents should be found implicating Hap from the beginning, the master-mind who relied on his protégé but didn't realize your greediness."

"Bastard."

"Name-calling won't win you points."

"Don't kill Brenda."

"Oh, I won't. That's the good part. She'll kill herself—right after she kills you. She is so appalled by what you've done and how you've treated her, she takes the only way out."

"No!" Ronnie screamed.

"Enough of this. Let's get going. Bring the girl here."

Someone grabbed Brenda's arms and pulled her up. She felt the backside of the knife blade as it sliced through the ropes at her wrists. Instantly her hands began to tingle.

"Jesus. She's bleeding. How'd she cut her hands? Pretty difficult to prove she wasn't held against her wishes. Doesn't look good for you, Ronnie baby. Take the blindfold off, but gag her."

Brenda blinked her eyes as the man behind her pulled the cloth roughly to one side, then stepping in front of her rolled it to a penny-thick cord and forced it between her teeth. Both men then grabbed her upper arms and held her between them. The kiva was shrouded in darkness broken only by the occasional beam of a flashlight. There were only four in all besides Ronnie. Was that everyone? Hadn't she heard movement above the kiva just a moment ago?

Brenda could see Ronnie by the entrance. His hands were tied behind him and he was being forced to kneel. As her eyes focused, she could see a man with a gun on either side, one was holding him up by the shoulder. Both men were dressed in military garb—baggy camouflage pants tucked into black lace-up boots.

"You have what you want. Get it over with. But don't make the mistake of taking innocent blood. She has a child for God's sake."

"Mistake? I don't make mistakes." The colonel's voice was steely. "In fact, just how we're going to do this is absolutely brilliant." The colonel brought a pair of gloves out of a pocket of his jumpsuit and slipped them on. "See this?" He pulled Tommy's gun from his belt. "Your girlfriend here is even going to shoot you with the lawman's gun. That should take him out of commission for awhile once they find out he plays loose with government firearms." More laughter. "Wonder if people will just think it's a lover's spat? You wouldn't take her with you and she couldn't face the disappointment and shame that your families would go through—there could be a thousand reasons. But don't tell me the plan isn't brilliant."

Suddenly he whirled on Brenda.

"Hold her. Brace her arms out in front."

Brenda tried to kick the man to her left but it only got her a knee in the thigh. Sharp pain traveled up through her hip. She twisted, then suddenly slumped down going completely limp throwing both men holding her forward and down with her.

"For God's sake. Hold her upright and still."

Both men scrambled up. Both her arms were jerked forward as a third man grabbed her from behind and putting his arms around her body held her immobile and upright—this time there was no moving.

"Now sweetheart you'll hold the gun just like this." The colonel grasped her hands; she balled her fists; he brought the butt of the pistol down hard on her wrist; she jerked in pain but the men forcing her arms forward locked them in position. The colonel forced her right hand around the barrel. Then suddenly with his finger over hers he swung their hands outward as he stepped to the side. She fought to unlock her elbows, squirming, screaming without coherent sound but another man braced her arms. She was sobbing. The gag, wet with saliva, cut into her cheeks. They were going to kill Ronnie—make her kill him.

In rapid succession three shots filled the cave with reverberating noise. She saw Ronnie jerk forward to sprawl on the cave floor just as the colonel doubled her arms back. She heard rather than felt the crack of her forearm. Gathering all her strength, she lifted her legs upward and knees to her chest struck outward connecting with the colonel's groin.

"Bitch."

The colonel fell toward her carrying her weight and his into the cave's wall. The gun went off. Blackness rolled over her as she slipped to the ground. She felt the colonel push her body away and saw him stagger upright. Blood gushed from her left temple running into her eye. She tried to reach up to push it away but her arm didn't move. The colonel turned away.

"Get those ropes off Cachini. And don't touch the revolver." He leaned against the kiva's wall his breath coming in short spurts.

"We'll need pictures. There's a camera in the bird." He slowly peeled the leather gloves off. "No one, I repeat, no one touch anything." He translated in Farsi just to make certain there was no misunderstanding. "Get the camera. Take pictures from every angle. Don't move the bodies." Again a translation before the men around him began to move and Brenda slipped into silence.

"Shots." Ben couldn't tell the direction exactly but there had been three muffled staccato bursts of sound more or less in front of him.

"Over here".

Tommy was already running, gun drawn, crouched. Then a fourth shot split the air. Louder, this time a bit to the right. Ben wished he had a gun. Galloping across the top of a mesa toward the sound of gunfire empty-handed seemed ludicrous.

Suddenly, Tommy stopped.

"It's here. It's got to be here. I know we're on top of it."

"Use the light."

Tommy swung the flashlight in a large circle.

"There." Ben pointed to a blackened circle thirty feet in front of them as one man and then another appeared to rise out of the ground.

"Let's go. Stay behind me."

As the head then torso of the second man cleared the top of the opening, Tommy dropped to one knee and shouted, "Halt."

The man seemed to be unarmed but he dropped back down the hole. The first man turned to face them.

"Mr. Spottedhorse?" Colonel Bertrand stood in front of the kiva entrance. "I thought I suggested that you stay out of this. But as long as you're here, come with me."

Tommy and Ben followed him down the wooden ladder.

"We've had a little mishap here. We got here just in time to see Miss Begay shoot her boyfriend then turn the gun on herself. God knows, I tried to deflect—I was just too late."

Tommy had already pushed forward, kneeling beside Brenda's body, fingers frantically searching for a pulse. "This is my fault. I left her alone where he could find her. Brenda, talk to me. Don't leave me."

Ben had rushed to examine Ronnie but the fine red mist that covered the floor and wall and the three exit holes gaping in his back pronounced him dead before Ben's search for a sign of life proved futile.

"She's alive!" Tommy yelled. "I need help over here."

"What? My God . . . We've got to get her to a hospital." Colonel Bertrand bent over Tommy.

"Gallup's closest. Get the chopper. Ben use the helicopter's radio to call ahead." Tommy was in charge.

"Of course. Rev it up." The colonel shouted to the men around him. Two hurried up the ladder and disappeared.

"Give me your shirt." Tommy held his hand out.

Ben quickly stripped off the cotton collar-less shirt that Julie had given him and ripped it into strips saving the two sleeves to fold as pads to be pressed against Brenda's forehead.

"Pulse is weak."

"I didn't even find one," the colonel said.

"She's lost a lot of blood. Head wounds are the worst." Tommy seemed to be talking to himself. He pressed the folded sleeves to the wound, held the makeshift pad a moment and then bound it in place.

"Sounds like the chopper. Are we going to do more harm lifting her? I mean, shouldn't we just bring a doc out here?" Tommy acted like the colonel hadn't even spoken.

"I'll need two more men. Ben take her feet. The ladder's going to be a bitch. We need to keep her head elevated but in line with her spine."

Tommy cradled Brenda's head then supporting her shoulders with Ben picking up her legs they started for the ladder—six feet almost straight up. Brenda's right arm slipped to the side and dangled—the odd angle of the forearm a dead giveaway.

"Shit. Her right arm's broken. For now, we can tie it against her body."

"Oh God, I must have done that. I tackled her pretty hard trying to get the gun." The colonel hovered over them.

They lowered her to the ground.

"We could use a shirt here." The colonel gestured for one of the airmen to take off his shirt. Carefully, while Ben slightly raised her, Tommy bound the arm across her body.

"That'll stay. But we have to hurry." Tommy was talking to himself. The sweat beaded on his forehead.

Turned backwards, Tommy supported Brenda's head against his body, pressed against the ladder and inched his way upward. At the top he gently laid her on the ground and yelled above the copter noise for a cushion or board or something and the colonel responded with cushions and directing his men helped Tommy slip her onto the floor of the copter behind the first row of seats.

"How long will it take to reach Gallup Indian Hospital?"

"Thirty minutes. I'll call ahead," the colonel offered.

He seemed as shocked by what had happened as they were. Ben looked at Tommy steadying Brenda. Would they be in time? It didn't look good. Her breathing was shallow and her ashen gray pallor indicated shock from the loss of blood. As if reading his thoughts, the colonel reached across Ben and handed Tommy two wool blankets. Tommy barely acknowledged his helpfulness.

They rode in near silence. Ben's call to the hospital seemed to push in on the gloom. At one point the colonel had tried to discuss what had probably taken place, all conjecture, but possible scenarios. Tommy had waved him off. Lovers quarrel wasn't his choice of conversation topic. Not now. He wanted to hear the story from Brenda and a part of him knew he might not have that chance.

The pilot circled the hospital and then brought the chopper in over the heli-pad behind the main entrance. Ben looked down on the blue circle with a white "H" and saw two attendants waiting with a gurney. When they had landed, the two paramedics were quick but careful in getting Brenda strapped down and on her way inside.

Ben, Tommy and the colonel followed.

A doctor stopped them at the entrance.

"Going to have to make you three stay out here. I'll let you know the minute we can determine her condition. My best bet is we'll go into surgery after the scan. This could take awhile. I probably won't have news for a couple hours at the very least."

"Doc, is there any way . . . I mean can you tell . . ."

"The extent of her injuries or the severity? Let's just say I don't want to get your hopes up. But I'll keep you posted."

With that the doc turned to jog back to the emergency area.

"Want to use the phone in my office to check in?" Ben had already started down the hall.

Tommy nodded. His adrenaline seemed spent and he looked half-dead.

"Colonel? Is there anything that I can get you?"

"No, thanks. I need to get the chopper out of here and tend to the body of Mr. Cachini. I'll be back later." Then he paused in the doorway. "Good work, men. If there's any chance that woman can be saved, you've given it to her. I'm leaving an officer here, of course. We'll need to talk to her if she pulls through." With that he was gone.

Ben checked his watch. A little after two in the morning. What a night. Ben insisted that Tommy stretch out on the couch in his office—damn thing was coming in handy—while he got a blanket. He'd try to catch a couple winks at his desk.

"Do you think she could kill Ronnie?"

"I guess tests will have to determine that. Where did she get a gun?"

"I gave it to her. It's my service revolver. I thought she'd feel better having some protection when I left her to make a call. I thought there was a bigger chance of two people being seen. Two people would have provided a bigger target. In hindsight, I was stupid not to take her with me. But I was only going to be gone twenty minutes. I wanted her to feel safe."

"The gun is yours?" Ben really hoped he hadn't heard right. Tommy nodded.

Ben thought of a couple things to say but nothing would match what Tommy had probably already thought about—and under the circumstances beaten himself up over.

"Do you think Brenda would be capable of taking a life? Especially Ronnie's?" Tommy asked. "She was trying to protect him; she wanted to believe in his innocence; she wasn't angry, disappointed would better describe it."

"If she found out that he was a killer or if he threatened her—tried to kill her—then it's not unreasonable to think that Brenda would defend herself," Ben said.

"She might not have known it was Ronnie—there might have been some mistake."

Ben hoped Tommy wouldn't ask him to speculate on whether she could take her own life. "I guess we have to hope she can explain. In the meantime, we need to rest."

The doctor knocked on the door about four thirty. Ben and Tommy were both awake instantly.

"Not good news, but not the worst. The bullet took some scalp with it and left an ugly wound but that's not the problem. Apparently, she struck her head—didn't Colonel Bertrand tell me he had tried to get the gun? Anyway, she took a powerful blow to the back of the head that's resulted in a severe concussion with a fair amount of edema. She's not responding to stimulus—"

"She's in a coma?" Tommy was standing now.

"To put it bluntly, yes. As you both probably know, head wounds are unpredictable and given the trauma of the situation, I don't even want to venture a guess as to when she might come out of it—an hour from now, a day—"

"Never?"

"That isn't what I believe."

"But possible? She might never regain consciousness?"

The doctor sighed, "Possible."

"Where is she now?"

"Still in recovery, but I'm moving her to a private room."

"I want to stay with her."

"I don't have any problem with that. I'll have a cot moved into the room."

Ben stepped into the hall with the doctor.

"What are the chances that we'll lose her?"

"Always a chance. Frankly, I'm worried about the coma. She's really not responding at all but, otherwise, vital signs are good. She's been through a lot of trauma—the palms of her hands are badly cut, there's a massive bruise to her left hip, another knot and bruise on the right side of her head not to mention the broken arm. My guess is that she's been beaten."

"Beaten?" This was the last thing he expected to hear. By whom? Ronnie? But she willingly went back to him. Which he reminded himself fit the profile of a battered woman. "I guess waiting is the only choice we have."

"Unfortunately, yes. There's no way to hurry this. The healing has to take place first, then we'll see." The doctor excused himself and hurried off down the hall.

Tommy had tucked his tee-shirt into his jeans and stood in the office doorway. "I'm going to go down to her room. Are you coming?"

"I thought I'd go home and get some clothes. You and I could use a shirt."

Tommy was quiet, then, "It's tough to live with the fact that the gun was mine. I mean if she dies, I might have just as well been her killer . . ."

"Tommy, you were only trying to protect her. You had no way of knowing that Ronnie would intercept. That there would be a fight or whatever happened." Ben hesitated to tell him about the extent of the bruising. "Maybe Ronnie picked it up when he hiked down to get her—or had followed her—maybe, she tried to leave it for you. No use beating yourself up until you have some answers."

"Yeah. You know something, though, if I can't imagine what could have made her want to kill him, I have a harder time imagining her turning the gun on herself. She would always put Mariah first."

There it was—finally. Ben knew Tommy would question that. And it did seem out of character. Still, under the circumstances . . .

"Emotions can cause people to do crazy things." Ben took a deep breath. "You know about the broken arm which the colonel thought had happened when he tried to get the gun, but there was other bruising—"

"What are you trying to say?"

"She could have been a victim of battering." He just spit

it out and watched as Tommy's jaw muscles worked just below his right ear.

"Ronnie beat her up? It's hard to believe but sometimes we just don't know people. Maybe under the circumstances . . ."

"We won't know what happened until Brenda wakes up—so let's not try to second guess. Go stay with her and I'll see you for breakfast. Did you get the dispatcher?"

"Yeah. Left a message. If I know Leonard, he'll be here in the morning."

"That should be it for tonight, or morning I should say. It'll be breakfast before you know it." Ben smiled but there wasn't any feeling in it.

Ben walked down the hall with Tommy in time to see the orderlies push Brenda into Room 123. She looked small and ashen against the white sheets. She was dwarfed by the bandage across her forehead and the soft cast on her arm looked like a swollen blue and white club. A young airman stood outside the door to her room. Tall, deeply tanned, the uniform hugged a muscular body. He nodded as Ben approached. Ben thought he had been the pilot of the chopper. How was that for double-duty? The name tag on his pocket read Captain Quintana. Maybe he was New Mexican.

A cot was already in place on the far side of the bed and Tommy sat on the edge. The room was crowded with machines and monitors. Ben was struck at how sterile and surreal it was.

"I'm going to call Brenda's brother. I want him to be prepared. I'm going to suggest that they don't bring Mariah to see her quite yet."

"I agree." Tommy glanced at the bed and the monitors.

"Mariah wouldn't understand."

"Try not to worry. It won't help. We have to give this thing time."

Tommy nodded then swung his feet up and laid back. "Just the same I really appreciate your being there. It means a lot to me."

Ben reminded Tommy about what friends were for, hoped he didn't sound too trite, and closed the door. He acknowledged the guard and went to the receptionist's desk to sign out a hospital car. His was hopefully safe at the Center. He'd try to remember to call the rangers to fill them in. They would have to send a team to the kiva, make a report. He was sure the Air Force would be collecting Ronnie's body as soon as they could.

Armed with a clean shirt for Tommy, Ben returned to the hospital at seven thirty. Nothing seemed to have changed. Captain Quintana was still outside the door and a very groggy Tommy answered the third tap.

"Any change?" Ben whispered.

Tommy just shook his head.

"I'll wait here if you want to go change. The restrooms are around the corner."

"Thanks. Not a bad idea." Tommy took the denim shirt and walked down the hall.

"Captain Quintana? Can I get you coffee or something from the cafeteria?" No response. The man didn't even turn his head. How could that be? Ben was just a few feet away, surely the man had heard him. "Captain Quintana?"

"Oh, sorry, I not hear good. What you want?"

"How about coffee? I'm going to the cafeteria in a few minutes and could bring you a cup—or something else?"

"Nothing, no thank you."

Odd. Heavy accent. Not Hispanic. Probably not a local. Funny, Ben couldn't remember hearing any of the airmen at the cave even speak before. That was certainly odd, come to think of it. He'd have to get their background from the colonel. Probably some specially trained international group.

Ben walked into the room and checked on Brenda. It hadn't taken much persuasion to deter Brenda's brother from bringing Mariah to the hospital. She looked so ill; it would have been a shock for the child.

"Great shirt. I might forget to give this one back." Tommy whispered, then grinned. First time Ben had seen a hint of his old self in a couple days. Now, if Brenda would just recover.

"Hey, that didn't take long. You need a break. Go down to the cafeteria, I'll stay here." Ben kept his voice low.

"I'm afraid to be away. Brenda could wake at any minute and it will mean a lot if I'm here."

"I'm afraid that won't be possible." Leonard Tom looked like he'd rather be any place on earth but where he was pushing through the door, chin dragging the ground as Ben's grandmother used to say.

"Leonard. . . ." Tommy greeted his boss but didn't look happy to see him. Ben thought he knew what was coming.

"Let's step out here." Leonard held the door open and both men followed him into the hall. "The charge is aiding and abetting . . . but then you know that. I have to take you in for questioning. I'm sorry as I can be about this, but it's been called to my attention that a service revolver was used in the murder of Mr. Cachini and the wounding of Miss Begay." Leonard stuttered, then, "A revolver given to Miss Begay against all restrictions—"

"How did you come by this information?" Ben interrupted. Who knew? He hadn't told anyone.

"Colonel Bertrand thought I better handle things—outside his jurisdiction. Tommy, you know I hate to do this, but we need to get going. I need to have you turn over any other fire-power that you might be carrying."

His boss knew about the automatic; everyone carried backup—something in addition to his service revolver. He handed over the gun and the two extra magazines.

"That it?"

"Yes."

"OK. Let's move."

Tommy turned to Ben. "Stay with Brenda?"

"Sure." What else could he say? Ben knew what this meant to Tommy. "Don't worry, I'll be right here. But I am going to get a cup of coffee—I'll be gone ten minutes, no more."

"No problem. Call me if there's any change?"

Ben nodded. Would Tommy be in jail? Probably. He walked with Tommy to the front entrance. The cafeteria was past the main double glass doors at the back of the first floor. Ben watched Tommy and Leonard continue out into the parking lot. Something was bothering him. Something not quite right, and it was probably right in front of him.

For starters, he couldn't figure the accent of Captain Quintana standing guard. Spanish name but more than likely a Middle Eastern accent . . . and for that matter, the man didn't even answer to his name—acted like it wasn't his. Ben slowed, then stopped. What was it Brenda had told

Tommy? She had overheard a language she didn't recognize as the group of men dragged a body toward the plane. And the men were tall. Two of the four men he'd seen were taller than he at six one—the other two were his height. This was probably overreacting and he had no proof. But what if Hap's killer wasn't Ronnie? The description of the airmen with Colonel Bertrand fit Brenda's description of the hijackers. Flimsy. But if even a part of his suspicion was true, Brenda was in danger at this very moment.

He didn't realize that he had turned around, was walking faster, now jogging toward the room and Brenda. And Colonel Bertrand knew the gun was Tommy's—because he had found it? Watched Tommy give it to her? Ben could be wrong, really wrong. But what if Ronnie Cachini wasn't the one who had killed Hap? What if Colonel Bertrand had killed Hap? And then had to kill Ronnie? By now, he was running. It was the perfect setup. If Brenda didn't regain consciousness, no one would know what had happened. No one. Even Bruce's tapes wouldn't completely exonerate Ronnie.

He'd left Captain Quintana alone with Brenda. Alone with Brenda—the words pounded in his brain. He turned the corner. The airman wasn't on guard. He was gone—but Ben knew better . . . he was in Brenda's room.

Ben hit the door and without losing momentum grabbed the airman as he turned toward the sound—the palms of both hands wrapped with the ends of a two foot strand of wire stretched taut between. Knocked off balance, both landed hard on the floor. Staggering upright, Ben grabbed the man's shoulder as he twisted to the side. Ben ducked the first blow, and landed one hard to the kidneys reaching up for the gun that the man had pulled from a pocket. Ben leveraged all his 180 pounds to keep the man off balance then he grabbed the gun forcing the man backwards, off balance, before the two of them crashed to the floor again.

"What the hell is going on? Break it up." Leonard might look short and squat and sound out of breath, but he had the strength of a bull. He neatly kicked the gun out of the airman's hand that Ben had pinned to the floor, sent it skittering across the room and with both hands on his own revolver ordered the man to stand.

"You can explain this?"

Ben nodded. He'd caught the airman in the act. One second later and Brenda would have been dead.

"Ben, what happened? We saw you run back . . . Is Brenda . . . ?" Tommy stood in the doorway.

"Get a doctor." She was breathing but it seemed too shallow—had the airman been successful? Had he harmed her?

"Tommy?"

It was a second before Ben realized that Brenda had spoken.

"He's gone to get the doctor. Try not to speak. You've been injured and you're in a hospital." Then he added, "You're safe, Brenda. It's over." He watched as she closed her eyes.

The doctor pushed through the door. "Clear the room. I need to examine Brenda without an audience."

"She spoke. She asked for Tommy."

Ben watched the tears well up in Tommy's eyes.

Suddenly, the airman lunged for the bed. This time he was screaming something in his language. He was quick but the doctor was in the way. He struck the doctor swinging clasped hands as a club, stumbled as the man struck the floor under his feet and couldn't duck Tommy. Tommy jerked him backwards, got his arm around his neck, spun him around and delivered a deciding blow to his chin.

"He'll be out for awhile, but these will come in handy." Tommy cuffed him, arms behind his back. "Now, explain. How'd you figure out—"

"Explain in the waiting room." The doctor, badly shaken, had lost all patience.

"OK by you?" Tommy turned to Leonard.

"I'll know where to find you." Leonard bent over the silent cuffed suspect. "You and me are gonna take a little trip."

"Let me help." Tommy hauled the still unconscious airman to a sitting position. "Going to be tough to carry this guy very far. Where's the van? I'll move it up to the front door. No use making this too difficult."

"Back row near the street. On your left when you leave the building. Catch." Tommy's boss tossed him the keys. The van was really a cage on wheels great for transporting drunks and holding one foreign airman, or whatever he was. It was going to come in handy.

"Be back in a minute. Don't guess you think I'm going to run out on you." Tommy grinned.

"Probably couldn't get too far."

Tommy walked out through the automatic glass doors and squinted against an overly bright sun. His sunglasses were somewhere—maybe in the Bronco, which was still on the Rez—somewhere between Brenda's house and the Information Center. With no spare, he reminded himself. He sighed. He was beat. Little sleep, too much spent adrenaline, worry . . . at this rate he'd be old before his time.

And there was still a lot to do. Brenda . . . he didn't even want to think about what might lie ahead. But she had spoken . . . called out his name. That had to be a good sign. He wondered how long he'd be detained. Would they take his badge? Somehow, he doubted it. A wrist-slapping, maybe a few days off without pay. Maybe Leonard would see fit to not write it up. He saw the van and cut across the packed lot to the last row.

He unlocked the driver's side door and climbed behind the wheel. He had more than one memory of driving this thing around. He swung the wide-chassis Chevy through the semi-circle drive and then backed up to the front door. He opened up the back double-door entry before heading back into the hospital.

"Hey, I'll get him." Tommy moved to intercede for his boss. The man was 200 pounds at least and at this point dead weight.

Leonard stepped aside. "I'll be out in a minute. I need to phone ahead—get someone looking for the rest of these folks." Leonard looked relieved that he didn't have to wrestle the airman into the van. Tommy had helped him save face or so Tommy wanted to think. Brownie points now wouldn't be a bad thing.

"I'll watch him. Take your time." So much for being under arrest, or almost. But he knew his boss trusted him— probably thought he could do some really dumb things— but meant well.

Heaving the solid 200 plus pounds of the airman over his shoulder, Tommy walked back out to the van and dumped the inert weight on the floor in the back. Hardly broke a sweat. Maybe going back to the gym wasn't going to be so hard after all.

A partition and steel mesh divider separated the prisoner

from the two rows of seats behind the driver. Another mesh divider separated the airman from the door itself—a cage within a cage, a space-eater but effective when you picked up a mean drunk. Tommy could remember being thankful for this arrangement on many occasions. He bolted the divider and stepped back to watch the man. Still out. He'd be easier to handle if he'd just stay that way for awhile.

He went around to the driver's side and got in. He'd park in a handicapped slot but first, he needed to clear the emergency entrance.

"Keep driving. Don't turn around. Leave the parking lot and go east, take a right onto #40." The voice was directly behind him.

"Shit. I thought you'd be long gone, Colonel, the minute you saw one of your men in trouble. The one that you left to finish off Brenda." If the colonel heard the anger in his voice, he didn't let on.

"Loose ends. Just a couple of threads out of place. I like a tidy package. How about you?"

"I have no idea what you're talking about."

The gun was pressed into the back of the seat. "I'm not one to leave my pals. Little did I know that you'd deliver my friend here and provide transportation. How can I thank you?" He laughed derisively.

Think. Think. Tommy willed his brain past exhaustion. He had no gun. No weapon of any sort.

"Shit." A stop sign. He'd almost run a stop sign. The lurch of the van brought a response from his passenger.

"Don't get smart. Be a good cop and follow the rules. Can't have you pulled over now, can we?"

Tommy didn't answer. How long would it be before Ben and Leonard would realize that he'd been gone too long—

maybe wasn't coming back? Too long, he figured. Maybe they'd think he'd gone to the john or to get coffee or . . . he was driving himself crazy. He needed a plan. But first he needed to know where they were going.

His hands sweated into the steering wheel cover, some god-awful fake suede and from the feel of it, his sweat wasn't the first. He wiped one hand across a thigh, then the other.

"Both hands on the wheel." The colonel was sitting upright now in the seat behind the driver's. "I'll need the keys to those cuffs."

"Didn't bring them."

"That's bullshit. What's that?"

"Where?"

"Key ring. Stupid place to carry a key but you guys out here aren't known for smarts."

What did that mean? Tommy didn't have time to waste wondering. And, yes, a cuff key was in plain sight dangling among other keys on the ring that held the key to the ignition. Truly stupid. Keys were almost interchangeable—unless you had some pretty expensive cuffs—which he didn't. But how many times did they use this van for something other than the transport of drunks? Never. He didn't feel any better. Somehow one time was going to be enough.

"I'll release my friend here but don't worry, I'll need you for awhile longer. He's in no shape to drive. So, nice and easy, slip that ring off the ignition key and pass it back."

Tommy could hear the beating of his own heart, a thudding that seemed to stop up his ears. Was he going to have a stroke? Oldtimers said that no matter how old you were, how many years you'd been on the force, it was always like this in situations where you knew you were going to die. And that was it. He knew he was going to die.

The colonel moved to the back of the van. "God damn it. Does this partition only open from one side?"

"Yes." Tommy had forgotten. They'd have to stop in order for the colonel to undo the cuffs and free the airman. So, it was still going to be one-to-one. At least, for awhile. But a gun upped the numbers for the opposition a little. Made his chances a little lopsided. But wasn't this what he had trained for? The terror of the moment? Raw emotions riding up and up to end in a giddy rush of adrenaline? Wasn't he supposed to get off on this?

"Where are we going?"

"No need for you to know." The colonel returned to the seat behind him. "Just get on the freeway. Head toward Grants."

SEVENTEEN

Leonard seemed in no hurry to join Tommy and the airman in the van. He questioned Ben on the case's particulars and seemed especially interested in the explanation of Amos Manygoat's skinned animal. Ben watched Leonard's face register incredulity as he related how the mutilations were done precisely and then the pictures and story released along with accusations of alien intervention. Listening to the story, Ben found it hard to believe it himself—just one more aspect of Anglo society that might be difficult to swallow.

Leonard took him up on the offer to use the phone in his office. Ben could use the phone in the lunch room. He needed to call the Federal Agents holding Bruce. Leonard could hold the airman until the Feds came—probably at the Gallup jail. Ben had a feeling that the man wouldn't give up the colonel and by now with the electronic equipment in hand, the colonel was probably long gone. It was obvious that the airman was supposed to kill Brenda and then just disappear himself. He came so close. Ben tried not to think what might have happened.

Leonard emerged some fifteen minutes later looking like a man satisfied with his morning.

"Got those guys coming over to the jail pronto. Could be a big break."

Ben could understand why he was so pleased that local law enforcement had made the collar. Kudos didn't come easy out here—but criticism was ever present.

"Any idea what might happen to Tommy?"

"Can't say. I got some thinking to do. Tommy's a good man. Heart is right here." Leonard thumped his chest.

Ben thought he meant to say Tommy's heart was in the right place. Whatever. The meaning was clear.

"Better go take my prisoners in." Leonard laughed. To include Tommy as a prisoner was a joke.

Ben had appointments in Crownpoint that afternoon so the quicker he could finish up the paperwork, the better. He had seen Brenda's brother coming down the hall. He'd be able to sit with her, but Ben would check in before he left.

He stacked three folders near his briefcase—those he'd take with him. There were a couple books he'd brought over from his own collection—he walked to the bookcase but didn't see them right away. He looked up at the light knock.

"Leonard?"

The man was leaning against the door jamb—not in a cavalier way but more for support looking dazed and disoriented.

"He's gone."

"Who's gone? The prisoner? What did he do to Tommy?" His mind raced to Tommy being overpowered, maybe killed; he wasn't prepared for what came next.

"The van, Tommy and the prisoner. They're nowhere."

"Tommy would never have left on his own. Either he was overpowered by the prisoner or . . ." Ben couldn't come up with another possibility. "He's in trouble. I mean something's wrong. He wouldn't leave." Ben grabbed his jacket.

"Come on. I'll get a car."

"Big tan Chevy's easy to spot. Go by the station first."

Ben tried not to break any speed limits, but he covered the 5 miles in record time. Tommy needed help. Ben knew it. What would have made him take off? When they reached the jail, Leonard was out of the car and taking the steps two at a time before Ben had the car in park.

A young man jumped up and came out of an office to the right of the reception area when they came through the front door. "Hey, been trying to raise you on the radio. Your van's heading off toward Grants. Something going on over there?" Then it looked like it had just dawned on him— "Hey, if you're here, who's in the van?"

"Good question." Leonard was noncommittal.

"Look at this. There you go right down the highway." The man was pointing to a monitor in his office

"Global Positioning Satellite—GPS? Right?" Ben was excited. This meant pinpointing the exact position of the van. There was a receiver probably in the hub of a wheel that transmitted every move.

"Yeah, we got it to trace Leonard here. We know every time he visits his girlfriend or gets a cheeseburger at Sadie's." The young man was the only one laughing.

"Get someone out there. Now!" Leonard barked orders, grabbed keys off a peg board and headed for the door. "I want backup."

"That's me." The kid looked at Ben. "Any idea what's going on?"

"Man might be in trouble. Disappeared with a prisoner."

"Wow. I better get going. They got a forty minute lead. I'll follow Leonard and radio Grants for help."

Rollover. The minute the concept flashed across his brain, Tommy knew the idea had merit. As long as they were on the Interstate, he was probably safe but the colonel was looking for a side road. Tommy figured that the chopper and the remaining airmen were waiting for their boss, and then they'd take off.

He'd be killed. Simply no longer needed and discarded—like the colonel had gotten rid of Hap and Ronnie and Edwina and almost Brenda. There was no doubt that they might find Brenda's prints on his revolver but she never pulled the trigger—not without strong-arm help. And the battering? Another no-brainer. The colonel or one of his support group. Anger threatened to wipe out all rational thought. He had to be careful. But he'd made up his mind. He was not about to die somewhere outside Grants, NM and let one of the most heinous murderers in recent state history just walk away.

"Watch your speed. Don't let your badge blind you. You're not exempt. This stretch is heavily patrolled. I don't think you'd want to endanger the lives of others." The colonel leaned against the seat behind him. "We're looking for a side road but we'll see the copter first. Should be coming in from the east."

Shit. The rest of the men. Now what? He'd have to dump this thing close to civilization—anything to discourage the copter from landing. Hopefully, innocent bystanders wouldn't get in the way.

The van was top heavy, tall and long—a pig when it came to soft dirt or sand. If he dropped the right side tires off the pavement going up or down an incline, the thing would, at least, go onto its side. Would it buy him enough leverage to get the gun? The assumption was that he wouldn't be injured and would be able to get to the colonel who was behind him before he chose to shoot. Long shot. But what else did he have?

In the cage behind them, the airman began to groan. He might be in the safest spot—small area, no threat of getting thrown from the vehicle.

He'd need surprise on his side and an unpopulated exit—one that he could accelerate on approach to at least seventy-five. He wouldn't be able to put on his seatbelt without warning the colonel. Damn. If he lived through this thing, then right after swearing off chili-fries, he'd promise to always wear his belt.

"That clock right?" The colonel motioned toward the dash.

"Far as I know." In the rearview the colonel slipped off his watch and made adjustments. "Any minute now." The colonel leaned against the glass and scanned the sky.

It was said more to himself but struck resolve in Tommy. It was now or never. The exit ramp on his right banked sharply about halfway up and curved to the left. And there were no cars in sight. The nearest car behind him was a good mile back. If he kicked up the speed about now. . . .

"What do you think you're doing?" The colonel lunged over the seat.

But Tommy had already entered the ramp. Wrenching the steering wheel back and forth, he rocked the van knocking the colonel off balance and giving the van sideways momentum as he drove off the edge of the pavement.

The right-side tires dug into the soft embankment but there was no stopping. The speed and rocking pushed the van to teeter and balance while still going forward, leaving the left tires a foot in the air before the van toppled—once, twice, down and over, finally coming to a rest on its roof.

The screams of the caged man surrounded him. At least, the airman was still alive. The colonel had been thrown through the windshield on the second roll. Tommy had braced himself between the console and the front passenger-side seat and now feet-first punched out the rest of the windshield and wiggled forward, out from under the collapsed roof onto the ground. He pushed back against the van. There was a sharp pain in his side, a cracked rib, maybe, but nothing else. Tomorrow might uncover some bruises but he was better off than he thought he would be and had a chance to be alive tomorrow.

Did the colonel have the gun? Was he alive? Where was he? Tommy pushed to his feet. The airman continued his screaming, tearing the air around him and making it impossible to hear. Then he saw it. The gun lying about six feet in front of him. Tommy lunged, grabbed the gun and squatting quickly scanned the slope. Nothing. Then movement caught his eye. The colonel was running down the frontage road, running and waving his arms above his head.

The helicopter was still two miles to the east, a dot above the horizon but closing fast. He wasn't going to get away. Tommy started after him, the gun tucked in his belt until he could get a shot off. A trucker had pulled his rig off to the side of the ramp above him; two other cars were slowing down. Tommy didn't look back. His target was fifty yards in front of him, but he was gaining.

The colonel's frantic waving was slowing him down, but still an impressive sprint for a man in his fifties. An oncoming car had already pulled over; two others had slowed. No one seemed to be doing anything heroic. So far, so good.

Just stay out of the way. He wanted a clear shot, no one jeopardized.

Suddenly the colonel veered to the side, down the drainage ditch and up onto the bank. Tommy followed suit, the second he saw a break in the fence. Was he close enough to get a shot off? And have it mean something? He kept going, faster, the soft dirt of the ditch top cushioned his feet. Hardly slowing, he pulled the gun from his belt. The first shot went wide but the second found the colonel's upper thigh. Just grazed him but Tommy could see the blood. The man kept running.

The copter was almost on top of them. Another shot. The colonel grabbed his left shoulder. Sirens broke through his concentration, and Tommy made a decision. Let the copter land, and shoot out the gas tanks. Ground it with back up coming—but he'd need the ammo and he didn't know what was left in the magazine. There was one in the chamber and maybe a couple more. He wasn't going to take the time to look.

The machine-gun fire took him by surprise. He rolled down the ditch embankment and dove for a culvert. At least this time of year there wasn't any water. Then as the copter hovered overhead, he got off a shot, and another, and another before he heard the impotent click and knew he was out of ammunition. He ducked back under the cement bunker-style protection just as a ball of fire erupted above him.

As Tommy leaned forward to watch, the fiery mass came down hard shearing the tops of a stand of cottonwood and hit the ground disintegrating upon impact. He had no idea whether the colonel had made it aboard. There was a part of him that hoped so. He pulled himself upright and walked up the ditch bank.

The area was swarming with law enforcement—agents, Grant's police, Leonard and the computer-whiz kid. Two firetrucks and three ambulances roared up. It looked like no one had escaped. Then he saw him. Cuffed, bleeding from Tommy's hits, the colonel was slumped between two agents who were leading him toward a patrol car. He should be dead. How could this man have survived? He didn't deserve to live.

"Wait." Tommy yelled. He stumbled down the steep side of the ditch the empty gun still in his hand. He rushed the threesome and wadded the front of the colonel's shirt at the neck jerking him forward until they were nose to nose.

"You sorry son of a bitch, you should be dead." Tommy drew back his arm—

"Officer, put down your weapon."

The yell startled Tommy—jolted him. My God, what had he been about to do? He dropped the gun to the ground and stepped back. He was shaking and didn't trust himself to speak.

"Take it easy, pal. You the one these guys held captive?"

Tommy nodded.

The cop gave a low whistle. "You're lucky. Can't say I'd blame you if you knocked this one around a little. But he'll get his. Don't need no help from you."

The other officer had scooped up Tommy's gun, ejected the magazine and checked the chamber.

"Why don't you just put this back in your pocket?"

Tommy took the gun and stepped aside. The colonel never looked at him, just stared at the ground. Tommy watched as the two cops pushed him into the back seat of the patrol car. Then the colonel turned to look at him through the rear window. No emotion, just a cold stare. He turned back to face forward only when the car bumped up a short incline to the highway.

Tommy couldn't stop the shiver that started somewhere at the base of his spine. Hatred. Anger. It could eat him alive if he let it. Wasn't this the very reason that anger management was part of the Police Academy's curriculum? He'd come close. Too close to throwing his career away right then. Maybe he'd talk to Ben. That brought a smile, Tommy Spottedhorse seeing a shrink. But he thought it was a good idea. He stood for a moment then tucked the gun back into his belt and walked toward Leonard. Tommy was exhausted, and he knew he'd be questioned for hours. He might as well get started.

Ben sat talking to Brenda. The morning sun pushed into the corners giving a false warmth to the otherwise starkness of the hospital room. The doctors had asked him to answer her questions—not volunteer anything but not to leave anything out if he thought it was an appropriate time for her to know. He assumed Tommy had been detained in Albuquerque. The Ten O'clock News had featured his story. Tommy the TV star. Ben smiled. His friend had been through a lot. But the colonel was behind bars and two of his supporters dead. Three more were wanted for questioning by the State Department.

He looked at the woman in front of him. She had pieced almost everything together. There would be no visible scars but killing Ronnie was something, even though forced, that they would have to work on. It wouldn't be easy.

"Hey." Tommy stood in the doorway.

"Should I ask for an autograph?" The hint of a smile dimpled the corners of her mouth.

"Not today." He slumped into a chair by the foot of the bed. Ben thought he looked exhausted. He'd probably just gotten out of questioning—but he was out, not being held in jail because of the revolver. Hopefully, that meant Leonard had been lenient.

"Ben's told me that you saved my life—never gave up; believed in me. Followed the colonel to the kiva—if it hadn't been for you getting me to a hospital . . . thank you. "

Tommy shrugged. Clearly embarrassed, Ben thought.

"You see, it's about this cake-walk at a fall festival I was invited to. Sorta promised an angel food cake with orange icing—now that'll get a man to do just about anything. You think that invitation still stands?"

"Maybe."

"The last time you said that, a coyote put a crimp in my style."

Brenda just laughed that tinkling sound of bells.